WHAT PEOPLE ARE SAYING '

I, HU

In John Nelson's futuristic and aptly ⌐py thriller, *I, Human*, he explores the boundaries of what it means to be human. Set at the end of the 21st century, when humanity has split into two groups, the techno elite with implanted neural brain processors that vastly increase intelligence, but which suppress emotion and intuition, and those called 'Bornies,' who have refused the artificial enhancement. Intelligence analyst Alan Reynard is sent on a mission to secretly infiltrate a Bornie spiritual community whose leader, Maria Fria, seems to be able to heal people and enhance emotion in ways beyond what the brain processors can do. But those who have sent him have not revealed the real purpose of his mission and Reynard and an outcast former operative, Emma, will find themselves on a dangerous exploration into the truth of self, consciousness and who we are and can be. An intriguing and superb futuristic spy thriller.
Andrew Kaplan, author of the *Scorpion* and *Homeland* spy novels.

In the late 1970s, I gathered together with a group of doctors to found Physicians for Social Responsibility and the International Physicians for the Prevention of Nuclear War to prevent what we called the final epidemic of the human race. If we do not annihilate ourselves in an atomic war, John Nelson, in *I, Human*, imaginatively gives another apocalyptic scenario about the dark sides of pharmacogenomics and neural implants. He tackles a ticklish question. What exactly is a human being, and is there an invisible line inside that splits the human biocomputer into part man and part machine? And how will governments of the future manipulate it?
Henry David Abraham, M.D., author, and cofounder of PSR and IPPNW, recipient of the 1985 Nobel Peace Prize

I, Human

I, Human

John Nelson

COSMIC
EGG
BOOKS

Winchester, UK
Washington, USA

First published by Cosmic Egg Books, 2016
Cosmic Egg Books is an imprint of John Hunt Publishing Ltd., Laurel House, Station Approach, Alresford, Hants, SO24 9JH, UK
office1@jhpbooks.net
www.johnhuntpublishing.com
www.cosmicegg-books.com

For distributor details and how to order please visit the 'Ordering' section on our website.

Text copyright: John Nelson 2015

ISBN: 978 1 78535 330 7
Library of Congress Control Number: 2015953282

A CIP catalogue record for this book is available from the British Library.

Design: Stuart Davies

Printed and bound by CPI Group (UK) Ltd, Croydon, CR0 4YY, UK

We operate a distinctive and ethical publishing philosophy in all areas of our business, from our global network of authors to production and worldwide distribution.

For Susanne,
Who could've taught me something about living and loving,
if I would have only listened.
I'm listening now, sweet sister.

By John Nelson

Starborn
Transformations
Matrix of the Gods
The Magic Mirror

Author's Note

My three full-length novels: *Transformations* (1988, 1997), *Matrix of the Gods* (1994), and *I, Human* (2016), chart the course of main characters who are "eating their shadows," as Carl Jung would say, or the dark sides of themselves, individually and collectively. The collective aspect of this process was superbly elucidated by Maria-Louise von Franz in *Shadow and Evil in Fairy Tales*. Thus, their journeys start out dark and haunting, but I ask the reader to bear with this exploration for there are insights and rewards to be gleaned as they transcend their limitations.

"The central problem of an intelligent species is the problem of sanity."
– Freeman Dyson, physicist and author

Acknowledgments

Six years ago, I was asked by a visitor to Hawaii if I could arrange a meeting with a kahuna for them. The only one I knew of was the daughter of a woman I had met in Charlottesville, VA a few years earlier. I contacted Laurie Grant, now known as Maa Uri, and while this facilitation didn't come about, I took her to dinner for the inconvenience of it all.

I was not prepared for this woman's presence and the impact of her energy. This started a journey for me into energy medicine, and the results of that exploration infused my thinking and inspired the writing of this novel. Thanks, Uri. You've been a blessing to me and many others.

I would like to thank my agent, Susan Crawford, who loved my earlier novel, *Transformations*, and took on the somewhat thankless task of trying to get *I, Human* published. In the meantime she kept me afloat by sending me fledging novelists in need of editorial assistance. Susan, without your help, I could never have sustained the effort to write this novel.

And finally I would like to thank John Hunt and his wonderful staff. Speculative fiction is a hard genre to accommodate in today's publishing market. I can only hope that this book will beat the odds and find its audience and justify their support of this effort.

Chapter One

1.

I don't know when I first crossed the boundary between human and what 20th-century Neo-Luddites would call transhuman, but I do remember, while in college, running over a cat in my new cruiser and wondering if I got any blood on my fender, with only mild concern about the animal whose life I had so abruptly ended. This was revealing, given my childhood affection for my Siamese cat, Slink, even given the usual callousness of youth. Of course those feelings—my school psychologist said I was feeling oriented—arose before puberty, after which my first neural processor was implanted. They do repress feelings but the trade off in computational functioning is amazing. Later, when we were preparing to move to a techno-housing complex that didn't accept animals, my mother fed Slink rat poison and had animal control dispose of the remains. I was upset, even cried about it, but soon recovered—there were so many enticing distractions for a teenage boy with heightened technical proficiency in the new complex.

Today's scientists would gauge the transhuman threshold by the number of terabits per second my neural processor can process, as compared to the average borny brain—that's what we call unenhanced Homo sapiens: a borny, given that they mostly accept the limitations they were born with. However, my employment test for K Industries, the private sector think tank for all levels of law enforcement, was telling. There was the standard IQ test—I scored more than 200—but the result for emotional empathy was high or at least for them. But, I was accepted and placed on the fast-track for surveillance work, where empathy could prove useful when dealing with the "borny problem," since it's one of their chief characteristics.

"Hey, Alan. Whatta got there?" Sherry asked, passing through the living room from the kitchen, wearing a see-through robe over her pink nightie and clutching her morning pep shake. "Is that a newspaper?" It was Sunday morning and I was reading it on the sofa, since we had nothing else planned, or nothing outside the apartment complex. This was a modern high-rise on the upper West Side of Manhattan, with a good view of Central Park through a wall-size tinted window, with all of its now lovely artificial trees gleaming, and the thirty-foot dike surrounding the island peaking through the buildings.

"Yeah. The *Times* Sunday edition. Checked it out of the library archives."

"Whatever for?" She shook her head, her short, red shag-cut hairdo shimmering as I readied my feeble explanation. "Don't bother," she added. "You're so fucking retro sometimes I can't believe it." She went back to her bedroom and closed the door. I could hear her cranking up the stereo to drown out an autoerotic session with one of her virtual playmates. I checked once and found that most of the programs were with women. I guess I should have felt reassured; truth is, it really didn't bother me. But, that's another story.

I checked out the newspaper and a few paper books, because it was safer to record this journal in a subprogram of my neural processor, without detection, if I had this split 3D focus at the same time. Performing multiple simultaneous processes is what we're geared to do. But a non-computer interface, such as reading a book or writing on a pad, makes the monitoring of my mental activities via brain-wave scanners harder. I know that sounds paranoid, but welcome to the new post-techno world. Of course, according to the Techno Privacy Laws of 2050, no computer brain scans are allowed without permission. But K Industries, like other military contractors, often operates above the law, and I was fairly certain they monitored employees off the farm. Another precaution was that I downloaded my sessions and stored them on a remote device, wiping my processor clean each time. Of course, needless to say, I have to hide this kind of activity from my wife. We don't exactly live in a *1984* Big Brother world, but spousal loyalty is only as good your marital contract due date—ours only has three years remaining on it.

So, why would somebody like me, as part of the techno elite of the so-called New World Order—talk about a retro term—with all the privileges of my class, risk such a dangerous venture? It's hard to explain in a purely rational way, but I can share an experience I had last year that seemed to propel me along this track. As part of my job in surveillance, I had to infiltrate one of the borny villages in the Midwest Sector and write a status report. I went in with a cover wife—Sherry doesn't work for KI, given her contentious streak, not that she'd be interested. Emma was a new recruit who also had mediocre EE test scores. She did need conditioning in order to act as my wife and sleep with me, but we hit it off and it wasn't a problem after the first week.

The major challenge at first was acting as slow as the bornies—I should say, by our post-techno standards, since our average IQs are twice theirs—and putting up with all of the retro hassles like computers in which you could actually count the microseconds before a response, or we could. But, what really flustered me was the high-feeling expression of their society: I mean, people hugging and kissing each other in public, helping strangers rebuild their house or an old lady with her groceries and the Shakespeare plays in the park. The first time a casual woman acquaintance tried to hug me, I kept her at arms' length. So the woman blew me a kiss. Now I differentiate feelings from emotions, since, according to my psychologist, feelings are a natural function of the psyche, whereas emotions have some kind of mental component. I'm used to emotional outbursts in my world on a daily basis, but not all of this touchy-feely stuff.

Something else that really bothered me was their church service, with all the singing and praising the Lord. We had chosen a born-again revivalist church over the Buddhist one, where you were expected to mediate for an hour. I mean, close down all my neural nets and don't think about anything for an hour. Impossible, I thought back then. Well, either way, this aspect of their society really confused me. The word God was never brought up in my family, and only as a primitive cultural fixation in my education. My public withholding of affection was suspect, and the only way Emma could open me up was with a marathon sexual session, which was almost as threatening, especially without stimulants. I couldn't wait to leave the place. (I later heard that Emma had dropped out, and at the time no one in our group had heard from her, so I thought maybe she was on a deep-cover assignment.)

But, it did provoke me into thinking that there was some lack in my life and in our society as a whole, and I began to wonder if we hadn't lost some essential quality as a species in our rush toward technological progress. We're not cyborgs; our neural processors are made from human brain cells—the idea of sentient robots has long been discarded, a sci-fi fantasy, as well as electronic mental devices—our transhuman advances a mere conditioning of living matter. But they do repress the feelings. So I felt compelled to pursue some kind of personal exploration and hopefully adjust my expectations. I was beginning to notice kinks in my behavior, and if I could detect them, other more discerning eyes could also spot them.

Well, the company was impressed with my previous borny village report and wanted to send me on another recognizance mission, but I got a doctor's pass due to my ongoing psychotherapy treatment. Of course they know that and were just testing my progress, or my assessment of it, since they've probably reviewed the sessions themselves, despite doctor/patient privileges and the laws upholding it. It was all too threatening, or I wasn't sure what more exposure would bring— some kind of psychotic break I feared. But, I did need to address this issue and …

"Alan, get the fuck in here."

I looked up from my newspaper and turned to find Sherry standing in her doorway, the nightie pulled down to her waist, her lovely breasts glistening with sweat.

"My damn virtual broke down. Take a Bluie and get in here pronto … and fuck me."

She stepped back into her room, and I could hear her throw the device against the wall. I hurried in before another outburst was picked up by the monitors, and she got called up for more ECT—emotional conditioning training. That would've made my life a living hell again. Oh well, it was part of our contract, but I decided to modify that language if I renewed.

2.

Work was a real drag that week. I helped arrest somebody and that made me feel rather guilty. While the local cops and the sector police handle most crimes, from murder to financial scams and the FBI focuses on global problems like tech pirating and antigovernment activity, we are a privatized think tank for all levels of law enforcement, with outreach monitoring functions as well. That is, when the criminals are too creative or erratic, and they slip by computer watchdog surveillance and the kind of thinking employed by the public sector, they call us in. For instance, it just doesn't compute for them that criminal activity could be anything but goal—or agenda—oriented. With all the genetic engineering to weed out "bad" or "antisocial" traits from the population base, and the behavioral drugs mandated for anybody with such leanings, they just can't figure out "irrationals," as my boss would call them, or they can only "see themselves and their own motivations."

The case we worked on that week, which had been referred to us by a government regulatory agency, was a pharmaceutical company, where somebody had tampered with the formula for one of their top mood-enhancement drugs. The effect was to give the user a kind of old-fashioned psychedelic trip, the opposite of its maintenance function. The company had figured it was plant spore contamination, but when that was ruled out and it became obvious that one of their scientists had tampered with the formula and completely covered their tracks, the government had gone looking for subversive agents with political agendas, since profit didn't seem to be a motive. After thorough background checks, psych evaluations on all fifty of their scientists with access, they still had not found their suspect. So they sent us the video of their interviews and months of lab footage of the scientists at work, which we quickly scanned.

To understand our methodology, we are definitely the creative types in the law enforcement area, not that any of us are artistically creative, just a little out there with our thinking. Our offices in mid-Manhattan are also unique with their large open work areas—no cubicle mentality for us—but with a fairly understated décor. However, our investigative sessions could be a little unnerving for outsiders, like government suits. On Monday we began examining the footage on the main vid screen with its 180° curvature. After thirty minutes I pointed out one of the white-coated scientists.

Gene, the department head, a cuddly sort—or so the women say—in his early forties, freeze-framed his image as the man turned away from the camera.

"He's smirking. I mean, that's a smirk, isn't it?" I asked.

"He's smirking while he works, better than whistling," Beatrice added. She is an ex-political analyst, older and savvy, with a cutting wit.

"Let's isolate this guy, all the footage," Gene insisted. So we used facial recognition to pull up all his coverage, about three hours of it over a six-week period, which we processed in minutes. He wasn't smirking as if he had a condescending attitude, but had an odd or superior smile at times.

"Let's look at his blood work and physical exams." The blood work was normal, but his eye examine showed slightly dilated pupils. "He's high or something, but it's not organic."

"Maybe, it's interior, some kind of natural high or mystical state," I offered. Everybody scrutinized me as if I were the suspect.

"What have you been smoking, Alan?" Jeffrey asked. If there was a real outlaw druggy amongst us, it would've been Jeff.

Gene gave this possibility serious consideration, while the others continued to mock me. "Alan's right. The superior attitude, dilated pupils, no drug trail. It's got to be interior."

Bart, the new guy, shook his head. "How do we go to the Feds with that? It's flimsy as hell." He was pudgy and smarmy and nobody liked him.

"We do a full profile on him, from childhood if necessary. Bring in the scientists. Given this guy's specialty and access and the drug tampering, they can figure out how he could have done it."

"Based on a guy with a smirk or suspicious smile?" Bart asked incredulously.

By Wednesday the guys in sci-fi, as we call them, came back with an assessment as to how Dr. Leonard Quirk could have changed the formula without detection. But again, that wasn't proof. They had scanned his neural processor, but he had been flushing it daily—definitely suspect behavior. Fortunately, or not, given your civil rights position, Quirk was brought in by the Feds for "drug" interrogation. They have truth serums today that make Sodium Pentothal look like aspirin, and together with brain-wave scanners, they got him to confess. When asked why, he said, "I wanted others to see God."

"Boy that's fucked up," Bart said.

"So, Gene, what's going to happen to him," I asked.

"Well, normally, when nobody's hurt, they would use behavioral modification and drugs to recondition the perp, but this kind of thing scares them."

"Yeah, when there's something inside your head they can't quantify," Beatrice offered.

"I figure ten years, and he's a vegetable when he comes out," Gene said. "And they'll circulate his gene genome here and to police agencies abroad, to catch this tendency before it spreads."

I looked around at the others, and we all were thinking the same thing: as if this was strictly genetic or chemistry-based, but nobody was willing to air that opinion in public, since we were also being monitored.

Gene turned to me. "I told the guys upstairs that you nailed him. You should get a bonus out of it."

"Wow, that's great," I said, smiling at the hidden camera in the ceiling.

On the way down in the elevator after work, Bart asked Beatrice and me if we wanted to get a cup of coffee. Since neither of us drank much of the stuff and he knew it, we figured Bart had something else on his mind. Since the genetic basis for alcohol and drug addiction had been somewhat weeded out of the genome, the most popular stimulant of the day was still coffee and its derivatives. *Maxi's* was a new chain, with a retro Art Deco style of furniture and posters that appealed to the post-modern artist types or the pseudo intellectuals. But it also offered a smooth coffee blend for those winding down from their day, instead of revving up, or taking a break. It was also chatty and loud and thus harder for others to monitor conversations.

"You know, the whole thing with this Dr. Quirk is really fucked up," Bart finally said after the waitress had served us and walked away.

"Yeah, kind of thought-police stuff," Beatrice added, sipping her cappuccino.

"Bart, I thought you said his motive was fucked up," I added.

"Well, it was, but squeeze-drying his brain isn't the answer."

"No, I agree. But, if you remember our contract, we agreed to carry out operations and not question the results." When I don't know or trust somebody, I usually give them the company line.

Bart glared at me as if I had changed my leopard spots.

"So, we don't take responsibility for our actions? Is that it, Alan?" he asked.

"We can always leave and take our conscience with us."

My attitude seemed to upset him. "You sound like one of the politicals. Bucking for a promotion, are we?"

"No. This was a bad one, but mostly we're a force for good and the results are justified," I said.

"And we're not supposed to question them otherwise?"

"As I said, we can always leave."

Bart stood up, electronically paid his bill, and walked out on us.

Finally Beatrice turned to me. "Let's go." We paid and headed out of the coffee shop and strolled down the street. It was winter but at this latitude still in the 50-degree range in the early evening, so we were dressed fairly lightly.

As always, the street lights passing through the green, overhead, UV environ screens cast an eerie glow. "I figured this was safer," she said.

I nodded my head.

She glanced over at me. "So, you think he was profiling you?"

"I trust Bart about as far as I can throw his fat ass," I told her.

"Aren't we paranoid?" Beatrice laughed, squeezed my hand and said with a smirk, "Say hello to Sherry for me."

I watched her walk down to the underground; she lived downtown, and I headed home for another fun-filled weekend with my rather deranged wife. Since we couldn't afford to fix her virtual computer yet, and she seemed to like our last "session," my romantic services were in high demand. Lucky me.

3.

Apparently Bart was working undercover for Internal Affairs because Monday he was transferred to another unit in our division, for more of the same I assumed, and I was scheduled for an appointment with Dr. Klaus. Of course, that isn't his real name—none of the higher-ups use given names in intelligence. Since he's the company psychologist and the government's security compliance officer, he had probably picked a name out of an old Nazi film to make him more menacing. He needed it because at five-foot-five, with his baldpate and retro eyeglasses, Gerald Klaus wasn't physically intimidating. Of course, that was for effect as well. My session was set for the end of the week, but on Wednesday there was an opening and I was notified after lunch to see him at two o'clock. A typical mind game ploy to throw you off-balance.

I took the elevator up to the 18th floor and walked down to his office. While sitting in his rather pleasant waiting room, with impressionist paintings on the walls and classical music piped in, I tried to clear my emotions, figuring the room was wired to check one's anxiety level. After fifteen minutes, the holographic receptionist told me that he would see me now.

"You have a lovely glow, dear," I said, opening the door to the inner sanctum.

"As if I haven't heard that before," she replied, rolling her eyes and flirtatiously twitching her nose at the same time. I almost did a double take.

Unlike the waiting room, Klaus' office was all chrome and glass, with simulated black leather chairs and dark abstract paintings on the walls. The whole set-up was so yin-yang that I had to suppress a smile.

Dr. Klaus pointed to a padded chair with head and armrests across from his glass-top desk. He was wearing a brown suit with a dark shirt and tie—very post-Nazi. I could almost feel the monitors clicking on as I sat down. The glass was actually a slightly tilted horizontal computer screen, which no doubt flashed readouts of my bios. "And you can smile, Alan. I'd expect nothing less. The room set-up is all so obvious."

I laughed. "Yes. Isn't it though?"

"Well, it does unnerve some."

I nodded my head.

"Alan, everybody is impressed with your read on Dr. Quirk, which together with your astute analysis of Reborn Village shows particular … talent, if I may use that word, for some of the thorny problems in contemporary intelligence work." He paused for a moment. "But, you seem reluctant to … grab the brass ring, as it were."

"You mean, putting off another borny village assignment?" I asked.

Klaus stared at me for long a moment. "Well, there is that."

"As you've no doubt read Dr. Bowman's notes, I had a severe reaction to their high-feeling level, and we're working to understand it."

"Alan, everybody in our techno society, especially our community, has this kind of reaction. Our technological world, while offering amazing benefits and safety to those of us at this level, does tend to suppress the feeling function, as Jung would say." He sat back in his chair. "I've consulted with Dr. Bowman, and he agrees that this kind of therapy could take another year."

"Really. I thought we were making good progress."

Dr. Klaus shrugged his shoulders. "I'm sure, but I take more of a hand-in-the-fire approach to such … dilemmas."

"Such as," I asked reluctantly.

"Reintroduction to the same set of conditions, to consciously deal with what arises, or recreate the stimulus and deal with it in a controlled environment."

"Put me back in the field, or …"

"Or, put you in a psyche ward for a week where the emotions

run quite high." The doctor glanced at his monitor screen and frowned, apparently not getting the desired reaction.

"It's the feeling, not emotions, we're talking about, and I don't believe you can … simulate that," I said.

The doctor gave me a rather odd look. "Well, there's always sexual therapy?"

"Really. Twenty women and a water bed?" I joked.

"More like Reichian therapy, or an extreme form of it," Klaus added with a cynical laugh. The Nazi was coming out of the closet. "It tends to bring repressed feelings to the surface."

"I thought Wilhelm Reich's work was totally discredited?"

"It just took the right conditions to find it relevant." He had a thought and smiled. "A hundred years ago, any red-blooded male would've jumped at such an opportunity. Shows how far we've come … or not."

I started to wonder if Sherry's little tizzy fit and the subsequent rededication of our sexual life wasn't orchestrated by them. These thoughts and the attendant emotional reaction were apparently lighting up Heir Klaus' monitors, much to his delight. I took a deep breath, closed my eyes for a second, and brought the reactions under more control. When I opened my eyes, Klaus was staring at me with clinical interest.

"Where did you learn to do that? Yoga? Mediation? Some other Eastern practice?"

"You mean reeling in my emotions?" I asked.

"It's different than that. From your brain-wave readings, it was more like a shift from one mode to another." He thought about this observation, and then hurriedly added, "Well, let's not go there, yet." He sat forward in his chair. "I'm not saying these are the only alternatives, but you're an asset we need to use and we have to figure out how to speed up this process."

"I see. Can I have some time to think this over?"

Dr. Klaus stood up. "Why, of course. Just don't take too long. There's a … pressing need for the evaluation of a certain critical situation in the field."

"Okay. Give me three or four weeks." I turned and walked out without an exchange of goodbyes. As I passed the receptionist's desk, she stuck out her finger and my portable registered the electronic transfer.

"Your next appointment is in three weeks."

I didn't stop for further pleasantries. This meeting had been definitely unsettling, and I needed to get out of there and think things through for myself. Mostly I was concerned that my little therapeutic process had been recorded. It was a technique I had picked up in college, from a survey course on twentieth-century experiential psychotherapy, and had used ever since to deal with feeling and emotional upsurges. But, when I got back to the office, there was an emergency that needed my full attention.

Gene quickly briefed me. "It's another recombinant viral plague, some wacko scientist was fooling with in his basement lab."

"He released it?" I asked in alarm, looking around for my bio mask.

"No. Didn't plan to, he says. Just part of his legitimate research, although he stepped outside the boundaries by bringing it home."

"What about all the bio monitors at these places?"

Gene just shook his head in frustration.

"And his neural processor?" I asked.

Gene shook his head. "The basement has lead-lined wallpaper."

"Okay, so where are we?"

"Well, before undercover could contain him, the police stepped in and pushed him to the wall. Now he says there's a sample hidden at the university, which will be released if he doesn't retrieve it."

"Let's see the vid footage," I said. The man, in his late twenties—a big guy for a research scientist—was in a fortified basement bunker, in a high-rise apartment building they were still evacuating. All we had currently was his tense face speaking into his vid screen.

"Sci-fi has run all the visual and auditory tests, and the readings are mixed, but he could be telling the truth."

The video was on the big screen and everybody was watching him make his declaration and then step back from the screen. He was wearing long pants and a sweatshirt, and with our 60 degree daytime winter temperature, it must've been really hot down there. There is no air-conditioning allowed for winter months.

"Any other footage on him?" I asked.

Carl, Bart's replacement, uploaded his interview with a science magazine. He was a PhD microbiologist doing independent research on recombinant viruses and their threat. It had been recorded in his basement a year ago about the same time. He was wearing a T-shirt and shorts.

"Anybody see what I'm seeing?"

Beatrice asked for a split screen of the two images. "It's hot but he's overdressed."

"Check for blood stains on his clothes or any bloody utensils within view," I said.

Billy ran the visual analysis. "No. Nothing."

"So you think he's cut himself up to create a biological reaction to fool our readings?" Gene asked.

"Ask the police what the temperature is outside the door?"

A moment later, Gene looked up from his com-link smiling. "Guy says it's at least 90 degrees."

Jeffrey did the mathematical computation. "Given all the variables, the statistical program rates this call as at best 50/50."

"Beatrice. What's his psych profile?" Gene asked.

"A little off, but not psychotic or anywhere near it, but who knows these days."

We all stared at each other. Gene finally said, "I'm going to tell the police chief he's bluffing."

"That's a big risk," Jeffrey said.

"Well, while we don't get paid big bucks for it, it's the kind of assessment we're asked to make."

Twenty minutes later, we learned that the police had stormed the basement and taken the guy into custody, and that, as I had guessed, his legs were pretty cut up and bandaged, to disguise his bio readings to back up his bluff. We don't exactly celebrate such calls, but we did close down shop half-an-hour early.

As I was getting ready to leave, I asked Gene, "This wasn't a difficult read. Why couldn't they handle it?"

"These city cops are the worst of the lot; they think like computers; it's all option-driven, no imagination or intuition whatsoever. That's why they need us." As we were heading out the door, he asked, "How did it go with Klaus?"

"Something similar to our wacko. He put a gun to my head, but I don't think he's bluffing."

Chapter Two

4.

On Friday evening, coming out of the underground station near our condo on the Upper Westside, I spotted a woman standing across the street. She lit a cigarette, which was almost unheard of in public these days, but immediately put it out once she had caught my attention. She was wearing a black and purple exercise outfit with a hood, so I couldn't see her face. The woman then stepped over to the corner receptacle and threw in a cigarette pack and jogged off. I walked to the corner, waited for the light to turn, then headed across the street. On the way I took out a notepad—the only recording device that couldn't be hacked—wrote something and continued down the street to a coffee shop. I wanted to establish for surveillance that I was using a writing pad.

Inside I ordered a cup of coffee, sat at a booth, and turned on the viewing screen scanning through the day's news. There was something unusual in the daily mix of political and financial posturing: some anti-tech militia group had blown up an Internet hub in the Midwest and interrupted service in the region for eight hours. There were also reports of another workplace rampage, leaving several people dead. I knew this was happening on a daily basis, but the government usually suppressed the reports. I continued making notes, again for surveillance purposes. By mandate all commercial businesses had surveillance cameras, all street corners, and all government offices—and those having to do with tech or biological research had work station surveillance as well. Given the "explosive" downside to high-tech malfeasance—like a viral plague or self-replicating nanobots—most people accepted the loss of privacy in exchange for safety.

I left the coffee shop and headed back to my street, continuing to make notes on my pad. At the corner, I shook my head, tore the page out of the notepad, stepped over and dropped it in the receptacle. I noticed the cigarette pack; took it out and smiled in apparent amusement. I also palmed the note stuck to it before throwing the pack back and walking off. Once inside my condo, I unloaded my tech pack and went into the bathroom. I looked at the note: $E=MC^2$. I immediately knew that it was Emma who was contacting me. She was a real fan of Einstein and his work, and used to refer to us as $Emma=AR^2$. I could only assume that she was in some sort of trouble with our employer, or she would have contacted me through normal channels. I also assumed that the next point of contact would be at the Einstein exhibit at the New York Museum of Communication Technology, tomorrow, my next day off. I felt the texture of the paper: it was definitely IP, "invisible paper," that would dissolve on contact with water, so I just flushed it down the toilet.

I slipped on a light jacket and went out to the patio to think about this dilemma. As a rule, any contact with compromised operatives was to be reported to the company's security bureau. Emma knew that I wouldn't automatically report her, but she was being cautious and would no doubt watch me at the Exhibit, to see if I was being followed or was setting her up. Upon further consideration, this approach had dangerous ramifications. Did I really want to jeopardize my position and standing in the community with this kind of illicit contact? The other possibility was, given my recent talk with Dr. Klaus and my upcoming deadline for fieldwork, that I was the one being set up. Bart's profiling was along this line. I really liked Emma and felt that I owed her the benefit of the doubt and would assume the best. I also missed the level of intimacy we had shared on our borny village assignment and that bothered me more than any breach in protocol. It was the trigger for my current "self-exploration."

When I stepped inside our apartment, Sherry was cooking dinner in the kitchen, or I should say, heating up a prepared meal which actually wasn't that bad. I'll have to admit they couldn't compare to the freshly grown fruits and vegetables at the borny village and the chemical-free chicken and beef that was almost impossible to get in the city.

"I was thinking Chinese," she said as I came into the kitchen.

"Sounds good to me." I took a fruit drink out of the refrigerator.

She turned around. "So, what's up?"

"What do you mean?" I asked, feeling just a little guilty.

"Well, I come home and find you out on the patio, staring off into space, and I'm thinking something is bothering you." The quick-oven alarm went off, and she pointed toward the dining room table. I sat down while she served dinner.

After she joined me, I said, "Oh, just the normal conflicts at work. Clipping the wings of people who just want a little freedom. That sort of thing."

"Well, why don't we go out and catch a period play or movie about the good old days."

I had to laugh. This was most unlike my wife. I wondered what was on her mind.

"Or, we could … stay home and see what develops," she said rather coyly.

I laughed. "Rough day, huh?"

She closed her eyes, nodding her head.

"Sure, let's just stay in," I said.

"Good. I'll wear something retro, just for you," she said with a leering smile.

I nodded my head, thinking of Emma the whole time. Well Sherry was definitely in one of her "moods," and so I let her play the dominant role in our little sexcapade that evening, but while the Bluie kept me functional throughout and certainly satisfied Sherry, I had to fake it at my end. She must have sensed something, because when we finished and I stood up to leave, she said, "What's up with you tonight?"

I shrugged my shoulders.

"Getting tired of me, Alan?"

"No. Just think this head job is getting to me," I said in all sincerity.

"Maybe you ought to talk with somebody at work about a transfer," Sherry replied, and I could detect real concern in her voice.

I snickered. "That's the problem. I did, and they want me to go back into the field."

"With that woman?" she asked, sitting up in bed and covering her chest with the sheet.

"No. Emma's out of the picture." I couldn't say more than that.

This seemed to be a relief to her. "Well, can't Dr. Bowman help? Earn a little of his money."

"Look. I'm tired. Got to go in to work tomorrow. Can we talk about this later?"

"Sure. I've got plans too," Sherry said, reaching over and turning off her bed lamp.

"Well, good night." I closed the door behind me and walked down the hallway to my bedroom. If I didn't know any better, I would've thought that Sherry had sensed, at some unconscious level, that I was planning to meet with another woman, although it wasn't a romantic tryst. After slipping into my sleep briefs, I sat up in bed and thought about her reaction. She was mostly closed off to deeper levels of herself, hardly ever dreamed or wanted to remember them, and wasn't really interested in the psyche at any level. Or, maybe it was my own psychological tells in a less-than-fully-responsive lovemaking session.

In our post-techno world, where one's individuality was assaulted from every angle, people adopted new behaviors and watched for those in others, like teenagers adopt hairstyles to express themselves. Few people wanted to delve deep inside and find that expression there. I mean most younger couples today didn't even sleep together to prevent unconscious merging. It was one of the most difficult parts of my borny assignment, the fact that couples there slept together like the bornies, and the company insisted that we did the same as part of our cover. But, I'd have to admit, if I were watching my own reaction, I would have detected a heightened feeling level at the prospect of catching up with Emma and discovering why she had contacted me.

5.

In the morning I took the same underground as if I were going to work, just in case Sherry was following me. She had already left the apartment when I woke up, and so I was being cautious. Sherry hated traveling on them since they made her claustrophobic. The Museum of Communication Technology was located in Greenwich Village, near Washington Square Park, where the New York hacker community had congregated in the early twenty-first century. So, I got off at mid-Manhattan, strolled through the entrance to K Industries, in case she had taken a cab there and was watching for me, and then headed out the east side of the building. I walked twenty blocks to the Museum, the collar of my overcoat pulled-up, wearing a Yankees baseball cap and sunglasses. No underground or cab fares to note my travels, other than the street surveillance of a guy who matched the description of a thousand other male pedestrians that day.

At the Museum I paid in cash and took the visitor's tour through the ground-floor exhibits, and then an hour later rode the escalator to the second floor, where the Einstein Exhibit was located. I didn't go directly there, but took a roundabout route and finally arrived around noon. The outer studios, concerned with his life and times, were fairly under populated, but would give somebody watching me for tails ample room to detect them. After a while, I moseyed over to the studio on Relativity that attracted most visitors. At some point, somebody bumped into me. It was a blond-headed woman wearing a short black skirt, leather leggings, a see-through blouse and a hat—Emma's height and built. After a while, I headed for the lavatory, went into a stall, and checked my coat pocket. There was a pack of matches for the "Kitty Kat" club in the bowery. I had to laugh. I assumed it was a sex club without surveillance cameras, since too many people in our line of work frequented these places, on and off the job.

I ate lunch in the museum's cafeteria, browsed their bookstore, and then left and walked south to the club. I arrived around 2:00 in the afternoon, which would be early in times past for this kind of activity, but our world was definitely 24/7. I stopped across the street and watched the place for twenty minutes. There was some club traffic, mostly stevedore types, and my hand-held snoop scope didn't detect any camera frequencies, and so I strolled across the street, paid my $50, and stepped into the club. It took a moment for my eyes to adjust to the darkened room. A 20s something hostess, in tight black satin pants and no top, sidled up against me, her ample breasts with nipple rings brushing my arm.

"What's your pleasure?"

"Whatcha got?" I asked.

"Well, there're private rooms for shows and intimate encounters, and in the main room, strippers in cages at either end, and a live sex show in about twenty minutes on the main stage."

"I think I'll just get a table and watch the show for now." This definitely didn't suit her.

"We have booths where the girls can 'serve' you, or tables. Your choice."

"I think I'll take a booth in the back over there," I said, pointing to a dark part of the cavern. This was more encouraging for her. "And I might have someone joining me." This definitely marked me as a low-income prospect.

"Well, no pros and no sexual activity with outside girls or guys," she said, rather sternly for someone with her breasts fully exposed.

I nodded my head in agreement and followed her through the club to the back row, weaving our way through a most unsavory group of customers.

I took a seat and watched the dancer in the cage to my left. She couldn't be any more than fourteen years old, which was perfectly legal, but from the way she moved and her provocative poses; you'd think she'd been doing this for years—maybe at some illegal "kiddie" club. A topless waitress came over and asked for my order. I glanced down at the illuminated menu on the tabletop and ordered a light Heineken. She left.

I'd been sitting for ten minutes, when a tough-looking Asian girl with a blue wig, short but well-toned and fit, with dark expressive eyes, stepped over and slid into my booth.

"Sorry. I'm waiting for someone."

"Honey. I'm someone." She put her hand on my thigh, her fingers inching toward my crotch.

"No. Really. She should be here anytime now."

The girl smiled at me, her hand rubbing my crotch. "She's come and gone, and gave me this for you." She removed a note from her black-laced bra and handed it to me. I put it in my pocket. The girl started to unzip my pants. "She also paid for a BJ, to get things going for you."

I pushed her hand away and zipped up my pants. "Then you got a freebie, because I'm good to go."

The woman looked at me as if I were slightly unhinged. She licked her big red lips. "Really? Nobody's ever turned me down, free or not."

The waitress came over with my Heineken. I laid some cash on the table. "Then, honey. You need this more than I do." I stood up and hurried away. Outside I glanced at the note—all it said was: "Around the corner." I turned left, since our training told us that right-handed people, given such directions would go right 90 percent of the time. At the corner I spotted a sleazy hotel halfway down the block. I walked over to the hotel and stood outside. A moment later, the woman in the black skirt strolled past me and said, "202." I waited five minutes and then stepped inside and climbed the stairs to the second floor. I knocked on the door. No answer. I tried the knob; it opened, and I stepped inside.

Emma was standing behind the door; she shut and locked it. "Alan. Thanks for coming."

We stood there in the middle of the room, unsure of how to greet each other. Emma was taller than average, thin, a brunette with a heart-shaped face and green eyes. After a moment she gave me a full-body hug and led me over to a tattered brown sofa, its stuffing spilling out from behind the buttons. I sat down next to her. As she removed her blond wig, she said, "And I'm sorry for all the cloak-and-dagger protocol, but I had to be careful."

"I assume there was a good reason for it."

"What've you heard about me?" she asked, and then added, "if you don't mind telling me."

Technically, I was breaching my confidentiality agreement by sharing any information with her, but I was, as we say, already totally exposed. "Not much, but I assumed you were compromised, or you would've just called me."

She thought about this for a moment. "Well, I didn't renew my contract, so it was all legal."

"You mean that after your probationary period, you didn't choose to sign up for a five-year stint?" I asked.

There was a flash of anger in her eyes. "Yes, if you want to put it that way, Alan. But, given the cost of our training, they think they own you."

"They put pressure on you?"

Emma let out a sigh, closed her eyes. She was too well trained to cry, unless for effect. "They threatened me. They said, given the current level of anti-government activity, anybody with borny-village experience could have been turned. They said it was within their rights to 'interrogate' me; I agreed but didn't show up for it, and have been underground ever since." She paused. "I mean. I didn't commit a crime; there's no indictment against me."

"If you had nothing to hide, why not go along with them?" I asked, but knew the answer.

"Aggressive chemical interrogation can really fuck up your mind."

"Yes, I know. That's what they threaten to get people to reenlist, but the alternative ..."

"Well, I could hire a lawyer and fight them. Some people have won their case against reenlistment, but I just don't have the resources to 'fight city hall.'"

"So, what's the statue of limitations on this kind of holdout?"

"Five years max, but that depends on your status. It's usually two years for rookies like me, but I don't know and they won't tell my father."

I could see what was coming. "So you want me to find out?" I asked.

"Alan, I know that's a big favor, and you can't just ask them, because that would be admitting to illegal contact."

"I assume you've figured out another way."

Emma smiled. "You're so smart. That's what I miss about you, besides being really ... nice to me on our assignment."

This sounded sincere.

She took a thin metal disc from her pocket. "One of the old-time tech guys, who went through this reenlistment tango himself, gave me this high-tech scanner. It's totally undetectable; you put it under your watch, and all you have to do is get someone to call up my file, and it'll scan what's on the screen, page by page from twenty feet."

This sounded very dicey to me. "I don't know, Emma. That's pretty risky. I could not only lose my job, but go to prison for it."

"I know. There's no rush. Think about it. I'll contact you in a couple weeks, and if you decide against it, just don't show up at our meet."

"Okay," I said.

"Alan, I have another big favor to ask."

"If you need money, I don't have much, but I can help you with that."

"No, but that's sweet of you. I'm fine, but I've been on the lamb for six months now, mostly by myself, with little human interaction, always on my guard." She shed a tear. "Alan, can we get ... intimate, just this one time. I'm simply going to die without some kind of caring physical contact."

She reached over and took my hand and looked me in the eyes. I held her stare for a long moment, and then I let her lead me over to the bed. We sat there and kissed, slowly and gently, nothing rushed and forced like with Sherry. We slowly disrobed, kissing each other's bodies, and then we made love with our eyes never losing contact, and this stirred me to my core. And later, as she fell asleep in my arms, I knew that I would help her.

6.

By Sunday night I had ruled out using Emma's tech device to copy her employment file. I knew Dr. Klaus had that kind of access, but he would be too crafty to manipulate for the information. Also, even if I did succeed, Emma would have me in a compromising position with hard evidence. It wasn't that I didn't trust her, but she could be compromised at her end, or even running a sting operation for the company to settle her case. No, if I were to help her, it had to be a situation where I was covered if I got caught and could reasonably explain away the inquiry.

However, I didn't have time to consider my options, since I was hit with a high-level emergency detail first thing Monday morning.

Gene called me and Beatrice into his glass, office cubicle while everybody was just getting situated to start their day. "We have a high-level leak in the Communications Ministry, and the FBI has asked us to review their case."

I glanced over at Beatrice and then back at Gene. "Us?" I asked.

"Yeah, we think Minister Kohn may be the leak, or the source of it, so they told us to put together a two-man task force to help keep the inquiry contained."

"Did you pick us or did it come from them?"

"Are we being paranoid, Alan?" Gene asked. I laughed. "Beatrice was recruited because of her political background, and since they've run into a dead end with their thinking, they wanted some unorthodox or creative approaches."

Beatrice snickered. "You mean Alan's screwball thinking."

Gene nodded his head. "Yeah, that's the tag they use to save face for them being so unimaginative."

"Well, it's always nice to be appreciated. So, how do we work this without everybody questioning what we're doing?"

"We'll use the satellite office in the basement that has everything you'll need: full tech, a private link to the Bureau and one to me."

So, Beatrice and I took an early lunch together, and didn't go back to the 10th-floor office afterward. When we went to the basement, there was an FBI receptionist and a plainclothes guard out front. Inside, however, we had the whole office to ourselves, with the same level of sophisticated computers and linkups as upstairs. To start off, the agent in charge interfaced with us from the FBI via a video linkup. Agent Musgrave, a thin guy in his forties, with a bushy mustache—not one of the Bureau's muscle-bound types—gave us a rundown on the leaks and their investigation of everybody in the ministry with the needed access.

"Well, our conclusion is that only Minister Kohn had all the access for these leaks, but nobody here believes this 30-year pro has anything to do with this kind of treason."

"I assume you've delved into his personal life and checked the pillow-talk angle?" Beatrice asked.

"Yeah. No girlfriends, no hookers, no compromising friends he'd share this kind of info with."

"What about his wife?" I asked.

"Well, her clearance is as good as his; she worked in the government for years before retiring. All bank accounts, all communications, everything has been checked out with no apparent breaches from either of them."

"What about kitchen help, gardeners, and the like? Beatrice asked.

Musgrave seemed to be getting impatient. "Yeah, all staff members, at the office and all the help at the house and vacation home; everybody's been vetted. Believe me, no stone's been left unturned."

"Thanks for the briefing, Agent Musgrave. You certainly seem to have covered all the angles," I said.

"Yeah, well we suspect that there was another leak this weekend, so you tell me." He smiled wearily and then cut the com link.

"Not a happy camper, and certainly unhappy about our involvement," Beatrice said. I nodded my head. "So, where do you think we should start?"

"Let's download the raw data and then just study the footage and see if we can spot anything, like we did with Dr. Quirk."

The data feed, at fifteen pages a minute, flashed across the screen. Then we scanned through the footage of the minister, his wife, and their staff and help over a three-month period, our processors isolating and making quick data comparisons, but nothing jumped out at us. No smirking giveaways. At the end of the day, before we called it quits, Beatrice said, "Well, I don't see anything odd, not that I know what I'm looking for."

"Yeah. The only thing I noticed is that Barbara Kohn certainly has a great mane of hair for a woman her age."

"I caught that," she said. "Seems she goes out of her way to keep up her appearance. Maybe she feels threatened, or there's some female competition at the office we don't know about."

As we came out of the operation's room, the receptionist, Agent Silvia Moore, asked, "Any updates?"

"Nothing yet. Tell Agent Musgrave that we'll be back at it in the morning," I said.

"And I don't need to remind you of the confidentiality of this inquiry?"

"Thanks for reminding us, dear," Beatrice said sarcastically as we walked out.

As I headed for the underground, I check my messages—all outside communication was banned, given our access to highly sensitive materials—and learned that Sherry would be late and asked that I fix dinner for myself. She said that she tried calling me at the office but nobody knew where I was. After Saturday's tryst with Emma, my level of sexual interest was low this week, and Sherry might have sensed that and suspected something. This was only the third time I had been unfaithful, but while our contract did not forbid outside liaisons, we had agreed to keep each other informed. I didn't consider an afternoon tryst as a liaison, but that was a matter of interpretation.

I was in bed by the time Sherry came home. She knocked on my bedroom door.

"Come in."

"Getting to bed early?" she asked.

"Yeah, got a long day ahead of me tomorrow?"

"At the office?" she asked tentatively.

I didn't overreact, given my recent indiscretion. "I've been assigned to a separate task force this week, and am operating out of our satellite office."

"Oh, and they don't forward your emails?"

"No. All outside communication was closed down."

"Is that where you were Saturday?"

I paused. "Yes."

"Well, you certainly seemed preoccupied when you came home, and yesterday ..."

"What's bothering you, Sherry?" I asked.

"You don't seem very happy with me these days, and I was just thinking that if you want out of our contract ..."

"I don't; I'm just, as you said, preoccupied and not happy about going out into the field again."

She nodded her head and smiled. "Can I sleep with you tonight? No sex, just cuddling?"

This was so unlike my wife, but I could sense her vulnerability and it was very appealing. "Yes, of course." Well, she quickly changed into a new black negligee; she must've gone out shopping, which was endearing. I held her in my arms as we drifted off to sleep and I really liked the intimacy of our sleeping together. I had to again wonder if her intuitive side, which in most moderns was repressed, was indeed active and sensing that I had committed an indiscretion. Maybe there was hope for us as a techno subspecies after all, and for our marriage. Halfway through the night, Sherry kissed me on cheek and went back to her own room.

When I woke up in the morning, still in a semiconscious state, I rolled over onto Sherry's pillow, hugged it, and got a good whiff of her hair scent. I suddenly realized that she had gone to a hairdresser the night before, and then, instinctively, I sensed from the deeper recesses of my unconscious mind that Barbara Kohn's hair did have something to do with this leak.

When I got to the basement office, Beatrice was already there looking at more footage. "Sorry, didn't want to wait, given everything we've got to go through."

"Bea, do we have a list of the leaks and some kind of timeline?"

She did a search through all the mounts of electronic data and found such a list. "Okay, what about a list of Barbara Kohn's hairdresser appointments?"

Beatrice laughed. "You're kidding me."

"No. Can't explain my reasoning. I just know her continued hair maintenance has something to do with this breach," I said.

Beatrice quickly scanned the download of data from her neural processor but couldn't find any such list. She shook her head. "We don't have it."

"Okay, let's gather all the information about her hairdresser and look at any footage we may have on them."

The guy turned out to be Chinese-American, his family here for several generations, and he and everybody in his shop were vetted. I thought about my hunch, and it was looking less and less promising. "Well, I'm going to call Musgrave and get that appointment list; you don't have to go along with me on this."

"And get cut out of the credit afterward," Beatrice said. "No way."

Musgrave wasn't impressed with our request, but said he'd get it to us shortly. He called back as the list popped up on our main vid screen and its correlation to the timing of the leaks. He was considerably less annoyed since there was a connection. "So, what's this about?"

I winged it. "Well, it appears we have two unimpeachable individuals that have been compromised. I assume the house, the office, and the car are electronically secure, but not the bedroom?"

"Our net would pick up any active devices from anybody going in and out of that house," Musgrave said, looking doubtful.

"There are neural implants that are inactive but can have timers. It seems that the only outside electronic device coming in contact with either of them, from what I gather, is the hair dryer at Mrs. Kohn's hairdresser. I suspect some incredibly sophisti-cated technology was employed, to implant a sliver device that reads her husband's neural processor while they sleep and downloads it at each appointment." I paused, and then added. "I assume they sleep together like many older couples."

Musgrave just stared at me for a long moment. "Certainly, an … original idea. Let me run this by Tech and I'll get back to you."

After he broke the com link, Beatrice looked at me in amazement. "Where did you get that?"

"Well, I suspect the hairdresser and that's my best reasoning for how they could do it."

"Boy. Talk about hanging your … our asses out there."

I just shrugged my shoulders again.

"So, what do we do? Just wait for the guys in white jackets to pick us up?" she asked.

After our lunch break, Gene came down to the operation's room. He looked pleased, so we were both relieved. "Well, appears Alan's cockeyed idea passed the tech muster, and so they raided the hairdresser, his house, and all of his family. Found the hairdryer with the device in his brother-in-law's shed. Mrs. Kohn is having a medical checkup this afternoon to remove the implant."

Beatrice started laughing so hard that we had to wait for her to recover. "Gene, it was all Alan."

Gene stared at me. "Okay, you got to tell how you figured this out, since I have to write a report that makes sense."

I shook my head. "I woke up this morning and smelled the lotion from my wife's hairdo and some part of me figured out that it was the hairdresser."

Gene put his hands to his face. "I can't put that in a report."

"Just put what Alan told Musgrave; it sounded, if not reasonable, at least possible. I'll write it up for you."

"Well, you're both getting a bonus out of this one. Don't spend it in one place."

"I think I'll buy my wife something nice," I said almost to myself.

Chapter Three

7.

The only other person who might have access to personnel files, besides Dr. Klaus and Gene, who I wasn't about to compromise, was Bart Caruthers. It was obvious that he was an IA plant, looking for compromised workers or those susceptible to being turned. I also knew from his stint in our office that he was single and had dark sexual proclivities, or his off-colored jokes suggested as much, and he might frequent places like the Kitty Kat club. The approach was that, since I was going into the field with a cover wife, which would require intimate contact, I wanted to be sure I was placed with someone that would make this more pleasant. If he informed on me, this was rather an innocuous inquiry that shouldn't have any major repercussions. Of course, if he caught on to my inquiry about Emma and I was followed to a rendezvous with her, that would be more serious and could cost me my job.

Gene told me that Bart had been transferred to the group that specialized in foreign operatives on North American soil. This was perfect since last week's assignment and its exposure of an Asian spy ring should have given me credibility with their division. It was located across the street, in the building that housed human resources, which I had a good reason to visit, given my possible deployment. I made an appointment to talk with a counselor about my assignment and my reservations. It had been scheduled for 4:00 so that I would be heading out of the building at 5:00. Bart was notorious for being punctual on both sides of his workday. He wasn't in the lobby so I window-shopped for a minute, then I spotted him exiting an elevator and walking outside.

I caught up to him as we both left the building and headed up the street. "Bart, how's it going?"

He turned my way. "Alan Reynard, as I live and breathe. Your name came up this week. We've been talking about your call on the Asian spy ring."

"Oh, really. Yeah, that was out there."

"I'd say. Care to talk about it over coffee?" he asked.

"Sure. This falls into your area?"

"Yeah. Working on foreign operatives, so I'm interested in how you figured it out."

At the corner, we crossed the street and headed for *Maxi's*. We took a booth in the back, away from the main bar and quieter. The waitress took our order, or I should say took mine and asked if Bart wanted his regular: a low-fat Latte.

After she left, I started up the conversation. "So, how do you like working the foreign desk?"

"Easier. The operatives are mostly on assignments, and so there's usually more logic to their operation. No Dr. Quirks wanting others 'to see God.'"

I laughed. This would be a better fit for somebody like Bart, whatever his assignment, who was mostly mentally oriented. The coffee came and we sat back and had a few sips. "Do you mind if I take out my portable and take notes?"

"Oh, I'm being interrogated?" I said with a smile.

"No, just had a long day and want to make sure I get your line of reasoning down."

"Well, there wasn't much reasoning involved. Everybody checked out, and the only thing that caught my attention was … the lady's hairdo."

He nodded his head. "Yeah, no names. But, what did that have to do with anything?"

"I had a hunch that they were using an electronic implant on a timer and the hairdresser and his hair dryer seemed to be the only loose end."

"A hunch? Yeah, well that's what we get paid for … out of the box thinking the suits can't figure, but even so that's really out there, even over the edge. I can see why they want you going into the field; you think like the bornies."

We both exchanged a knowing look. "Yeah, I figured you have pretty good sources," I said.

He was quick to add, "Just good ears, my friend. You hear things."

The waitress refilled our cups and we sat there, trying to ease ourselves over this unintentional revelation. "You know. It's interesting I should run into you. I need some help."

This definitely caught Bart's attention; I could see him figuring the angles already. "With what?"

"Well, as you've surmised, they're sending me out into the field, and that means intimate contact with a cover wife, and I'd just like to make sure that I'm with someone I can live with."

Bart didn't say anything for a long moment. "Well, don't know how I can help you with that, buddy."

"Well, if you could, I'd be really grateful."

Bart nodded his head. He understood.

"Maybe this isn't the right … place to discuss … this," I said. "I agree."

"There's a club in the village, the Kitty Kat, kind of an off-limits place—no cameras."

Bart nodded his head. "Meet you there at eight o'clock. Don't bring your wife." He stood up and left me to pay the bill. A good sign.

Afterward I walked down the block and stepped into a jewelry shop. Since I would have to explain a cash withdrawer and couldn't transfer the funds, I would have to use merchandise—something I could justify on my bank statement. I bought a $500 woman's watch. I called Sherry and told her that I would be late, still working an assignment, and I ate dinner at a Chinese restaurant halfway between our offices at Midtown and the Village. I just happened by it; the restaurant looked low-end, but I was somehow drawn to it. While waiting for my dinner and sipping my green tea, I thought about my last trip to the club. And as the Chinese waitress served my dinner, I remembered the blue-haired Chinese girl who passed me Emma's message. She seemed very bright and I wondered if she was a undercover plant, working the customers for information. The only other indication was my happening upon this restaurant and the feeling that I needed to eat here. Again, nothing the rational mind could wrap itself around, but my intuitive side was definitely sending me messages and I needed to listen.

At the club, later, I asked the hostess, "Is the Chinese girl with the blue hair available?"

"You mean, Wu?"

"I didn't catch her name."

The woman nodded her head and escorted me to a back booth. "I'll send her over."

Wu, if that was her real name, walked over, wearing a green wig today. She was topless with rings in her nipples. She scooted over next to me, placing her hand on my thigh, moving it closer to my crotch. "How nice you asked for me again. We did have such a good time."

She started to lower her head but I lifted her chin and looked directly into her eyes. "I have a friend coming shortly. Treat him well, and you might find him of interest." I handed her two hundred dollars.

This stopped her for a moment. "I find all yummy guys of interest."

"There's yummy and then there's … dummy." She gave me a knowing look, stood up, and walked back to the bar. Bart strolled into the club about fifteen minutes later, and the hostess knew to escort him to my booth. On the way I could see him ogling her breasts, and then watching the live sex act on the stage. This was definitely his kind of place.

The hostess took our drink orders. Bart was still getting accustomed to the low-light levels. "Well, Alan, I never suspected you of being a provocateur."

I laughed. "Well, I wouldn't jump to conclusions. Just trying to make a difficult situation more pleasant."

He smirked. "I see." He stared at me for a moment, and I passed him the watch case; he didn't open it and placed it in his inside coat pocket.

"Yeah, I can imagine a borny village can be a real snooze without some … entertainment." I nodded my head. "I think Jean Whatley might be a good match for you. She's a new recruit trying to make her bones, if I may use the term."

"Got a picture of her?" I asked. He looked askance at me. "Well, the undercovers don't have their own websites."

"I'm to provide pictures as well?" he asked, rather bemused by my insistence. I nodded. He pulled out a portable, keyed in his code, and called up Jean's picture and profile. He handed it to me and I stared at the girl. She was definitely pretty and looked eager, and just what he would order for himself. I quickly scanned her file and didn't catch any red flags, or that she was more than what she seemed.

"Yeah, not bad. What about Emma Knowles? She went out with me last time, but I haven't kept in touch."

I handed the device back to Bart; he looked her up and flinched when he saw her status and tried to shut down the device. I reached over and grabbed his wrist. "Come on, Bart. What's up with her?"

At that moment, Wu sauntered over, swaying those marvelous hips of hers and caught Bart's attention. She sat down next to him, leaned over and kissed him on the mouth, her tongue halfway down his throat.

This was enough of a distraction for me to quickly scan Emma's file. No wonder Bart flinched; she had a five year hold on her activities. Emma was definitely on their compromised list. Finally, Wu released Bart.

He caught his breath, but immediately shut off his device and pocketed it. "Wow. That's some welcome."

"Honey," she said, reaching over with both hands and cupping his face, "that was just the appetizer."

I could almost feel him shudder. I also noticed that Wu was now wearing a watch, probably with Emma's scanner, and that her timing couldn't have been any more perfect. She was definitely a pro in more ways than the obvious.

"And what will the main course cost me?" Bart asked rather bluntly.

"Don't worry honey. Your friend here bought the first course."

Bart turned to me. "Well, how nice of you, Alan. Maybe Whatley won't be enough after all."

I stood up. "I'm sure she'll be just fine, but I think you have better things to do than find me another cover wife."

By now Wu had unzipped Bart's trousers and was mouthing him. He could only nod in reply. I left the club and hurried uptown to catch the underground at a more appropriate location for its time stamp locator.

8.

My meeting with Dr. Klaus was at the end of the week, and I had to make a decision about accepting the field assignment or not. I didn't have much choice if I wanted to continue in this line of work, but after recent events, a stint at a borny village, despite its challenges, seemed like a welcomed respite from my own harrowing world. This became even more obvious on Tuesday afternoon, when a malfunctioning neural processor seemed to trigger another psycho rampage, but this time within our own company. I arrived back from lunch to see a live feed from a local hospital on our main screen. Brain surgery was being performed on an accountant who had gone berserk that morning and killed three co-workers with a light pencil. They had already tested his processor and determined that it was defective and were removing it. Beatrice updated me on the gruesome details, but I was still baffled by why we were viewing this operation. When I asked, there was a round of titters from my co-workers.

"Actually, it's for your benefit, Alan. Too bad you missed the bloody extraction through the skull portal; it was rather interesting," Gene said with a smirk.

"What does this have to do with me?"

"Dr. Klaus wants you to interrogate him before they replace his processor."

"I thought the switch had to happen within hours to prevent severe migraines."

Dr. Klaus had stepped into the room behind me. "Yes, and that's a short window, so we better get started."

Everybody shuddered at the sound of his faintly metallic voice, as we all turned around to face the curmudgeon. Finally, I said, "I can't imagine why?"

"But, Alan … if you can't figure it out, who can," he snickered. I didn't reply. "I'll brief you on the ride over to the hospital."

I followed Klaus out of the office, as we took the elevator down to the basement maglev commuter station. There were only a few people on the platform between shifts, who were no doubt curious about why the train had been held up. Klaus keyed us into the VIP's car, and we took a private room. I sat across from him, on black-cushioned benches, with a ceramic table between us. He slid over his portable device, which had a long document and a place for my thumbprint.

"This is an above-top-secret security agreement; no need to read it; it's pretty standard."

Nevertheless, I quickly scanned the whole document in thirty seconds and saw the same kind of language from my previous security clearance. I placed my thumbprint on the last page; my identity was acknowledged and the document closed. I slid the device back to him.

Klaus began to brief me. "This sort of malfunction has been happening more frequently, despite great improvements in the neural processors and their interface with the neocortex. The results vary; some people just melt down into a ball of cringing flesh; others, like this guy, become violent."

"Did he have any violent tendencies as a child, before his processor was implanted?" I asked.

"No. And that's the heart of the matter; did the malfunction cause the behavior, or did the brain and/or the repressed psyche cause the device to malfunction?"

"And, given my right brain or borny tendencies, you feel I'd be a more sympathetic interrogator?"

"Yes, in a nutshell." Klaus saw my hesitation. "You were a psych major in college; I feel confident you can draw him out."

This was a little disconcerting. I closed my eyes and tried to still my mind and its anxiety, and to focus on the task at hand. I opened them. "Okay, I'm ready."

"You do need to show me how you do that interior thing of yours."

I smiled, not in this lifetime.

The maglev arrived across town at the hospital in five minutes, and we were quickly escorted to the patient's room by a security contingent. Without further instruction, Klaus pointed to the door. "I'll watch from the viewing window." He paused and placed a reassuring hand on my shoulder. "Don't worry; I won't barge in on you. It's your show."

I stepped inside as the patient's doctor was checking his pupil response, with a light scanner that projected a holographic image for him to check. The doctor turned to me. "I'm lodging a protest."

"Doc, lodge it with the guy in the hall; I'm just the front man."

This was even more demeaning, and he shook his head and stormed out of the room, waving his hands in the air. I pulled up a chair. The patient, Boris Harkum, turned to me. It took a moment for him to focus his eyes.

"Mr. Harkum, sorry for this intrusion. This will only take a moment."

"Okay, I'm feeling ... up to it."

"But, in the past few weeks, you didn't feel ... well?" I asked.

"No. I felt very agitated. All these fucking numbers, the meaninglessness of it all."

"Was this a recent feeling, or had it been building up?"

He tried to probe his mind for an answer to my question, but he was painfully slow without his neural processor. I smiled sympathetically and patiently waited for his response that took over a minute.

"Kind of both. I used to like my job; numbers are finite, nothing arbitrary about 2,000 + 2,000 = 4000. No bullshit or personal bias. What's made of the results is not my problem. I was the number cruncher, but something ... happened."

"A sense of ... hopelessness?" I asked.

He looked startled by my question, and then nodded his head. "Yes."

"At this point, did you feel ... agitated?"

He again grappled for an answer that wasn't readily called up. "No, just hopeless."

"How long did this feeling last before you became ... agitated?"

This took another thirty seconds to recall. "Not long ... maybe a month ..." Harkum closed his eyes and winced, then put his fingers to his temples. "Oh, this really hurts now."

The doctor rushed into the room and came over to his patient. I stepped back. Dr. Klaus waved me into the hallway and started to walk off. I followed him and caught up. "I think it's obvious ..."

"Alan, not here. We'll go back to my office and discuss this in private."

On the maglev ride back to K Industries, we had a brief

exchange about sports; I was amazed that Dr. Klaus was a tennis buff; I would've thought his short stature would be a huge disadvantage. He assured me he was just a duffer, but he liked to follow the professional sport, especially when they had switched back to wood rackets, which made it more of a volley game. Five minutes later, we were sitting in his office, at his couch and coffee table setting, more like colleagues.

After we settled in for a moment, he summarized his conclusions. "So, a feeling that his job and maybe his life were meaningless, developed into a sense of hopelessness over a period of time, and that …"

I smiled. He knew the answer, but wasn't about to articulate it. "And this 'feeling'," I added, "short-circuited his neural processor and its modulation and that made him more agitated and created the violent rage."

Dr. Klaus sat back in his seat for a long moment. Finally, he said, "I'm not sure I agree, but that's a line of speculation everybody's afraid to acknowledge, but that's my problem not yours." He paused for a moment, stood up and walked back to his desk. He pointed to the chair across from him; I came over and sat down. "Well, now that I have you here, why don't we just settle on your field assignment?"

I felt like protesting; I still had a few more days of consideration, but I knew my answer. "Okay. I'll go, but I want to pick my undercover wife."

"I assumed as much." He transferred a portfolio to my portable; I scanned through the pages viewing the agent profiles and their photographs. Jean Whatley's picture and profile were the last on the list. I wondered if Caruthers' suggestion and her "appearance" here was all part of some set-up. But I did like the soft curve of her face and her "sparkling" eyes.

"This Whatley girl seems good."

"Yes, Whatley's a good match for you and this assignment, and if you hadn't picked her, we would have insisted." He paused for a moment and rolled off one of his smirky smiles. "We'll start briefings next week; this time it's in Washington, so you'll have a few days there to … get adjusted to each other."

"Yeah, my wife will love that."

"Then don't tell her; it works for me," Klaus said offhandedly.

9.

I decided to walk home after work, to sort out my thinking about today's assignment and this new revelation that Harkum's feelings had short-circuited his neural processor. These devices, first designed and implemented in the mid-21st century, were made from one's own cell tissue, using advance nanotechnology. From the start there was no auto-immune reaction and so that couldn't account for this malfunction. The concept was that the grafted tissue would be absorbed and function like an evolutionary brain appendage; it would then interface with the neocortex and accelerate the firing rate of its neurons—a quantum leap in computing power. The processors could also be "grown" in an afternoon to replace older or defective ones, which was the case here. But, what I was suggesting was that the more they mirrored human brain tissue, the more they were subject to the same psychosomatic effects. If a lifetime of toxic emotions could cause brain cancer, they could also affect these neural processors, and even accelerate that process.

Suddenly someone walking past me on the sidewalk bumped into me. I saw that it was a woman who was now slowing down. I picked up my pace and passed her, our hands hitting and a folded message was placed in my cupped hand. I didn't look at her, and at the next corner, I walked into a restaurant and used their men's room. I unfolded the message: KKC at 6:30. I flushed the note down the toilet and headed out to the street. I left a message for Sherry that I would be working late and to eat without me. I hailed a cab and had him drop me off at

Washington Square Park. I ate dinner at a Middle Eastern restaurant that advertised all natural meat kabobs; I doubted it but the idea was catchy and the food was delicious, maybe just a little too spicy for me. At 6:30 I entered the Kitty Kat club, hopefully for the last time. I wondered if Emma was going to actually meet me here, since bringing Bart to the club might have generated a security alert, but then, how would he have justified his own presence there?

I asked the hostess to take me to a back booth, and I waited to see what would happen. I ordered a beer from the waitress, who shoved her breasts in my face and told me that one was domestic and the other foreign. I had to laugh. Talk about genetic engineering. After a while I saw one of the girls making her way over to me. I thought it might be Wu with another message, but as the girl sat down I saw that it was Emma with a purple wig, her breasts fully exposed, with nipple rings. Before I could say anything, she reached over and kissed me, with her hand rubbing my crotch.

"Act normal, Alan. Like I'm one of the girls. My name's Dorothy."

I placed my hands on her breasts and rolled her nipples between the thumb and forefinger.

"Yes. That feels good," she said.

I glanced up at her questioningly.

"Yes, Alan. I've worked these clubs before, on KI assignments, but now as a job occasionally."

"You mean, like your friend, Wu?"

She smiled. "Just a contact."

Emma paused, probably figuring out how much she going to tell me.

"I don't know who she works for, but I needed a way to reach you and get my info. I'd run into her before at another club and suspected … well, I don't want to get caught up in this game, so that's all I'll say."

I looked at her incredulously.

"I wasn't ... I'm not playing you, Alan. My tech device wasn't as invasive as Wu's and would've only got what I asked for."

She gazed at me, that question hanging in the air. "Well, sorry to say, but they have you on a five year hold."

Emma closed her eyes, and then, to hide her feelings, went down on me. "You can talk," she said between times. I could feel her wet tears on my skin.

"Guess, the only place that leaves secure is a borny village."

Emma surfaced after a minute or so, her eyes as red as her smeared lipstick. She reached over and took a sip of my beer. "Seems so."

"Well, I'm going back into the field in a couple of weeks; it wouldn't be good if it's the same village."

She nodded her head. "No. That would be awkward, especially if your cover wife's any good." Emma reached over and kissed me on the cheek. "Take care of yourself, Alan. Maybe I'll see you in five years."

"Is that it, Emma?"

She stood up. "What else could it be, Alan? I'm on the nonaligned list, and any further contact would compromise you." She touched my shoulder, then turned and walked away.

I finished my beer, paid my tab in cash—saw that Emma's services weren't included—and then headed out the door. I looked around before turning north and walking back toward midtown, where I'd take the underground home.

When I returned home, although it was still fairly early, Sherry's bedroom door was closed and the lights were out. She must've had a rough day herself; I felt like knocking on her door and checking to see if she was all right, but by the time I washed up I decided to call it a night myself. I read for an hour, and heard Sherry go to the bathroom, but she might've sensed that all was not what I claimed and that it was best to just let it settle. The next morning she was up and out of the apartment before me. I didn't actually consider this rendezvous, unlike my last time with Emma and our unexpected lovemaking, as an infidelity but women didn't always see it that way, consciously or unconsciously.

When I arrived at the office, there were no emergencies or assignments—just a load of paperwork to prepare for my upcoming fieldwork. However, there was a message from Jean Whatley, asking me to a get-to-know-you lunch. I wished I could put it off for another day and let the emotional load from my meeting with Emma and my wife's angry vibes play themselves out, but like triple plane crashes, female encounters in my life seem to come in threes as well.

We couldn't meet outside the office, so we had lunch in the company's executive restaurant on the enclosed roof. Eating there was actually above our pay grade, but Whatley had gotten Klaus to set it up. I hoped he wasn't coming. I immediately recognized her as I stepped into the foyer. She was sitting at a window table, her profile to me, so I could take a moment to examine her without equal scrutiny. She was much prettier than her photo, and looked younger than twenty-five, but for undercover female operatives that was almost a job requirement. Suddenly, she turned and looked my way. I waved and walked over.

She stood up and extended her hand. We shook. A firm grip. "Well, I'm glad it's a table for two and Klaus isn't joining us."

Jean laughed. "Yeah, I swept the table, but can't vouch for remote cameras and long-distant microphones."

There was a silent moment. I let it extend to see if she would nervously feel compelled to fill the gap with useless chatter. She didn't. "First assignment?" I asked.

"To a borny village? Yes. I've done some overseas work, so I'm anxious to get the ... lay of the land." She caught herself and smiled.

"Is that going to be ... difficult for you?" I asked and smiled, gazing into her eyes.

"I guess that depends on us, how we mesh. But, I'm sure, just looking into those kind eyes of yours, that I might even enjoy our time together."

"You know why this is required?"

"Yes. They're more sensitive and can sense the pheromone levels given off by sexual activity, which is what gave away earlier agents."

I nodded my head. She waited, her last question hanging in the air. I added, "Well, the biggest problem for me last time was choosing between the born-again church and the Zen Buddhist; I went with the born-again, since the whole concept of meditating for an hour was a stretch for me."

"Damn. I never thought of that. We'll have to go to church with the rest of them."

"And picnics, and Shakespeare in the Park."

This made her eyes light up. "Oh, that I would enjoy. I was a drama major in college."

"Yeah, kind of a prerequisite for our line of work."

The waiter stepped over with the menus; we scanned them and ordered, neither one of us drinking any alcohol. Afterward Jean peered out at the cloud-covered city—with higher temperatures, there were more rain clouds and thus more rain. "I hope the skies are clearer."

"Depends. I hear the Southwest is still sunny, but wouldn't expect the same for the Midwest Sector."

"Anything else I should know?"

"Well, you'll have to learn to be patient; everything runs in slow motion, or compared to our pace of life, and the locals are a lot slower, and the feeling level's quite high. Be prepared to get hugged by total strangers."

Jean laughed. "As long as the guys don't take advantage of it."

"Are you kidding? These guys are so … sensitive that it's amazing they get around to procreating at all."

Jean was really laughing now. "Oh, Alan. You're so funny."

Our meal arrived and we ate and talked about our backgrounds, and while it was fairly guarded, we were probably more open with each other than we had planned. Afterward the waiter came over and handed me a note.

"And the check?"

"It's on the house, sir."

I opened the note and a room key for the Waldorf fell out. Jean started to giggle like a teenager. I glanced up from the note and looked at her. She was definitely willing but despite her attractive allure, I hesitated. I guess I was feeling a little sexually confused after the last two weeks, given my tryst with Emma and Sherry's recent tender overtures.

Finally Jean asked, "Today's not good for you?"

"You could say that. Lots of … static on the home front." She nodded her head sympathetically.

"Well, I'm sure it won't be a problem, but I am looking forward to … 'a consummation devoutly to be wished.'"

I laughed. "Catch a recent production of Hamlet?" I asked.

"You did mention, Shakespeare in the park."

I smiled. "I don't know about 'devoutly,' but me too."

"Okay, so we wait until the out-of-town debriefing?" she asked. I nodded my head.

We stood up and Jean gave me a full-body hug that was very stimulating, to say the least. She turned and walked out of the restaurant. On the elevator, crammed with young secretaries in provocative apparel, I thought about today's hypersexual atmosphere. My father had once told me it wasn't like that when he was younger, and I had to wonder if sex in the modern post-techno world had become a head-game, like everything else, and that this was symptomatic of our whole deadening society.

Back at the office, I half expected to see our lunch meeting being played back on the wide-screen, grist for the mill, but it was just another psycho rampage at a sports event. Gene called me over as the guy's history flashed on the sidebar of the video rendition, which I quickly downloaded.

"Klaus said since you're available this afternoon, he wanted you to profile the perp." Gene gave me a questioning look.

"Prep work for my new assignment that can wait," I said with a straight face, knowing that we were being monitored.

"Okay, good to have you back then," he said, oblivious to the nuance of the situation.

Chapter Four

10.

Walking home that evening, I thought about telling Sherry that the schedule for my borny village assignment was set and that I was going to Washington next week to be briefed. Feeling guilty about its "perk package," I was first going to suggest that we get away to the mountains this weekend.

"That sounds great," was Sherry's first reaction, as we sat in the living room after dinner. Then, she stopped herself. "You're getting ready to head out, aren't you?"

"Well, they did set the schedule, and I begin briefings in Washington next week."

"With your cover wife, who you'll be fucking the whole time, I take it?"

This was never easy, but I thought we had worked our way through this aspect of such assignments last time I went "in country," as we called it at work. "Sherry, we'll be staying in separate hotel rooms but getting 'used' to each other, as the briefing material calls it."

"Well, I think you should store up your energy; wouldn't want you to waste it on me, when the fate of the country depends on you and your fucking cover wife."

I scooted over on the sofa next to her, but she stood up and stepped away from me. "No, Alan. I'm not fine with this; I never was, but went along with it last time because … I actually don't know why. Maybe low expectations."

"I've been putting this off for a year now, and one reason was because of this aspect and its fallout for us."

"And that's supposed to make me all warm and cuddly?" she asked.

"Look, when my contract is up with K Industries in two years, I won't renew."

This seemed to mollify her somewhat, but she still had her pride to defend. "Well, while you're away this time, don't expect me to sit home and pine away." She went over to the closet, took out her coat, and stormed out the door. "Don't wait up for me."

I figured she was going to call a girlfriend or two and go out to a bar, to get picked-up in an attempt to assert her independence. I guess I couldn't really blame her or get indignant. I could understand her feelings about my in-country assignments and sleeping with cover wives; I doubted if I could go along with it if the situation were reversed. I liked Sherry and we did get along, but the idea of love—if any of us moderns actually knew what that was—didn't seem to be in the equation any which way you figured it.

The next morning I was the one who was up and out of the apartment early. I arrived at work ahead of everybody, which as it turned out was timely. There was an electronic message from Klaus; he wanted me to take a trip out to the Bradbury Institute on Long Island, where they were holding Dr. Quirk, and to interview him. The assignment criterion was to probe his background and try to figure how this religious impulse had developed. Was it part of his early background? Were his parents religious? Did he have any spiritual experiences as a child? He had sent a further list of general questions that wasn't very elaborate, but I certainly didn't want to talk with Klaus about further amplifications. The least contact I had with him, the better for me. I assumed this was preparation for my field assignment, since our division had already done its job in regard to Quirk. I hoped this wasn't a prelude to them dropping us into some kind of religious ashram or born-again revivalist camp. That would be a real downer.

I forwarded Klaus' authorization to Gene, but by the time I closed down my workstation and headed out, I ran into him in the hallway.

He smiled. "Short day, Alan?"

"I wish. Klaus has me on assignment today. Forwarded the autho to you."

"Klaus. The two of you are getting pretty chummy." He smirked.

"Yeah, like sharks and prawns."

Gene laughed and patted me on the back as I headed for the elevator. The underground took me to Grand Central Station, where I picked up the commuter to Long Island. The Institute was located in Yaphank at the far eastern end of the island, but far enough away from the coast not to be swamped by the rising waters. It was always an eerie sight to take the train or drive out to Long Island and see all the crumbling seashore mansions, whose dikes could not hold back the encroaching waters of the Atlantic. While I was familiar with the Bradbury Institute, the state-of-the-art psyche center where the first neural processors had been developed, along with all their updates over the years, I was unfamiliar with the town and did a Web search of its history on my portable. It was amusing to find a reference to Camp Siegfried there, a summer camp for Nazis during the 1930s. This was particularly interesting, since many liberal thinkers had compared genetic and neural-implant technology to the Nazi's eugenic programs of an earlier era—culling out and ostracizing the outcasts who wouldn't accept neural implants. I had no doubt that Klaus was a board member of the Institute.

The urban sprawl of Long Island—or what was left of it—had receded by this point, and the town of Yaphank itself was fairly rural. Like most towns, it had UV protective screens over sidewalks and all the windows were heavily tinted. A car met me at the train station and drove me to the Institute outside of town, where a small city had arisen—homes and apartments for the staff and businesses that catered to them—around the ultra-modern buildings that housed the Institute, all of which were protected by a gleaming hundred-foot high UV dome.

I was met at the front door by a very pretty PR person, or so I assumed, a Sara Irving. She was more casually dressed, just a blue skirt and white blouse, than what I would have guessed for her position.

"It's a long train trip from the city without maglevs," she said as we walked down the hallway. "Would you like lunch first?"

I had eaten breakfast and wasn't really that hungry, but I was interested in hearing Sara's line of inquiry, since it could be revealing. "Sure. Lead the way."

The cafeteria was quite plush, and while they were still setting up for lunch, Sara was able to round up some roast-beef sandwiches and really good potato salad, along with some healthy chips and beverages. We sat down at a corner window table that looked out under the dome's overhang, to the sparse and largely burnt brush in the sandy soil.

Finally, after some chitchat about things in general, Sara posed her first question. "You know, Alan, Dr. Quirk's psychosis has nothing to do with his neural processor, that's been checked and found to be totally functional."

I smiled. "I never thought as much."

"We're familiar with K Industries recent ... incident with Frank Harkum."

I nodded my head.

"I believe you ... interviewed him as well?" she said.

I chewed my bite of food and dabbed my mouth with the paper napkin. "You're particularly well informed."

She smiled. "Dr. Klaus has discussed this situation with our people, and we don't agree with your conclusions: that his anxiety short-circuited his neural processor. There have been malfunctions, but few of these emotional outbursts or rampages have been attributed to a defective processor."

"Excuse me, Sara, but this is rather heady territory for a PR person."

She smiled again, a little tighter this time. "I'm sorry; I didn't mean to give that impression. I'm a neural scientist and part of the new-product development team, and as such receive and research such inquiries."

I took my last bite of the sandwich and pushed my plate aside. "Well, I'm not here to debate or justify my opinions, but to interview Dr. Quirk. It's going to be a long day, so I suggest we get on with it."

Sara looked slightly abashed. "I didn't mean to offend you; we're just curious about your assessment of Harkum. I mean, if it were proven to be correct, then we need to understand its implications and adjust our product line."

"Well, I think since you've done such a good job mirroring the brain's own neural processing, that these artificial processors might be subject to the same kind of psychosomatic pressures."

She stared at me for a long moment. "I guess I can take that as a compliment."

"You should; the fault may lie beyond your realm or your control," I said.

She squinted her eyes trying to grasp my argument. "You mean sociological factors?"

I nodded my head. I could see that this was an area that she was unwilling to explore, given its political implications.

"Well, I'm just a scientist."

"And I'm just an … interviewer."

"I suspect that's the only understatement you've made today," she said sharply and stood up, straightened her skirt.

I followed her out of the cafeteria.

11.

When Sara led me to the monitoring station for the interrogation room, I handed her an FBI mandate that my interview with Dr. Quirk would not be recorded or viewed by them, and the station, in effect, would be closed down for its duration. As Sara read the paper, she knitted her brow and couldn't mask her aggravation.

She carefully folded the document, pocketed it, and told the technician to shut down all audio and video surveillance and leave.

She stepped to the door herself, and then paused and turned back. "You know, Alan, when I first met you, I was hoping you would be staying over and we could have dinner together and get to know each other better."

"But ..."

"It's probably best that you finish up here and get on your way."

I figured that would just be a prelude to some pillow-talk interrogation, which would only further disappoint her. "Well, it's been interesting," I said.

She forced a smile. "We do hope you'll eventually share your ... speculation with us, since we want to nip this in the bud," Sara said, then turned and marched out the door.

Yeah, I thought, nip the speculation but not the problem.

Unlike standard police interrogation rooms, this one was more like a high-end living room with sofas, chairs, and soft natural lighting. Dr. Quirk, in a casual blue, one-piece jumpsuit with its metal loops, was sitting on one of the sofas drinking a beverage—I assumed something cold that couldn't be used as a weapon. Klaus had insisted that no behavior modification be used on Quirk until we had a chance to interview him.

He looked up as I entered the room and scrutinized me for a long moment. "Ah, you're not from here. FBI? DOD?"

I raised an eyebrow.

"Not the eyes of clinician," he said.

"The private sector."

He smiled. "Ahah, the think-tank guys who picked me out," he said, without a trace of rancor, as if his being caught and incarcerated was all part of some cosmic plan.

I pulled up a chair. "I'm Alan Reynard, and I have a few questions for you?"

He nodded his head. "Well, I hope they're more imaginative than some of the questions asked of me recently."

"I'll try." Quirk looked hopeful. "Doctor, maybe you can help me out. We're trying to figure out how this religious impulse arises in the population, and ..."

"So you can ... 'nip in the bud?'"

This startled me, but I quickly recovered. "I see you've been talking with Ms. Irving."

He caught himself. "She's not listening, is she?" he nervously asked.

"No. This is totally confidential, just between you and me."

"And Big Brother," he said, smirking again.

"Tell me, since you weren't raised religiously, how this ... impulse first came to you?"

Quirk snickered. "Not very imaginative after all."

I shrugged my shoulders.

"Better," he said, then paused. "Alan, we live such isolated cutoff lives, mostly in our heads and our gonads. As a scientist, I was always interested in the bigger picture, but our culture is so ... pedestrian, everybody given their little box and encouraged not to stray beyond it," he said in a plaintive tone. "All we have left is our own speculation."

"So, your exploration was a reaction to the mindset of our culture and its restrictions?" I asked.

"Yes, I realize, given the downside of high-tech hazards in the hands of aberrants, that 24/7 surveillance, even the inside of your head, is called for; but it makes some of us want to seek out 'high-end intimacy,' as someone once called it."

"And that led you to the religious philosophies?"

"Not at first. It took me years to get beyond the rationalists, the Hegels and the Kants, but ..."

"Was it a personal experience that provided the impetus?" I asked.

Quirk nodded his head and stared at me more closely,

wondering if he had found a compatriot, and then caught himself. "I assume you're recording this?"

I smiled; he got the message.

"Yes," he continued. "Hikes in the woods, walks on the beach, hang-gliding off mountaintops. I felt so ... connected to something bigger."

"And this led you to ..."

"The real classics: the Hindus. *The Upanishads*, the *Yoga Sutras, and The Bhagavad Gita*."

"But, to interfere with another's free will, or force-feed them an experience as you did ..."

Quirk almost looked apologetic. "Yes, still a product of this century and of our force-fed mechanistic culture I'm afraid."

"I assume in arriving at your formula that you ingested psychedelics yourself?"

He took in and let out a deep breath. "Please, don't reduce this to some drug-induced mania. The impulse ... my experiences were as pure as those Hindu sages of long ago, just working with less fertile ground."

"And you wanted to help others to experience this ... mystical state?" I asked.

"To help them break free and experience something ... real."

"I see." I took out my portable, and opened up a file. "Now for some really pedestrian questions."

Quirk laughed. "Yes, we all have our masters ..." He paused, stared at me intently, and added, "Some more ... expansive than others."

I ate dinner in town, not wanting to run into Sara or to get hijacked by another of the Institute's technocrats at one of the campus restaurants. I dined at a seafood place since I was out on Long Island, but the crab and lobster from the "fish farms" weren't very tasty, and I could have been dining in Iowa and it would have tasted the same. Nobody ate seafood from the polluted oceans these days, or at least not those who could afford alternatives. I was almost willing to risk it for a tasty bite, but no legitimate restaurant would serve it, given the risk of contamination and the lawsuits. So, I only ate half my meal and had some fresh strawberries for dessert to wash away the taste. Of course they were grown in a greenhouse, but I guess it was the degree of artificiality—soil was soil, unless they were hydroponically grown—that made the difference, or at least in my mind.

But, sitting there drinking my coffee and waiting for the seven o'clock train, I was in a rather sour mood. After a day at the Bradbury Institute, where the culture was as shallow as the neural implants they produced, I was in desperate need of something real to counter the effect. However, the restaurant's feeble fare, the less-than-engaging service, and the heavily tinted windows that cut one off from the sky and the early-evening dusk, all only emphasized the lifeless, artificial world we had created to keep us safe from hostile nature and from our own terrified selves. I could almost empathize with Dr. Quirk and his quest to find a greater connection to nature and his natural self, and once he found it, to share it with others. And we labeled him a terrorist.

My portable beeped, alerting me to the train's arrival. Since I had already paid the bill, I took one last sip of the coffee, picked up my portable, and headed across the street. I had reserved a private compartment, at Klaus' insistence, and was glad now, since I would be spared from riding back in a car full of unhappy people, making me even more miserable. About ten minutes into the trip, there was a knock on my door. I opened it to discover a rather pretty young woman. She was wearing a short black skirt, her blue blouse opened to reveal some cleavage.

"Hate to impose, but I saw that you were alone, and I was hoping you wanted some company."

I gave her a questioning look.

"Oh, it's not like that. I'm trying to get away from … well, it's complicated."

I was still leery.

"Please. I won't bother you at all," she said.

"Sure. If it's life or death."

She smiled amorously as she stepped sideways through the doorway, lightly brushing up against me. "Well, I wouldn't put it that way, but who knows."

Since I had been trained to be leery of such offers while traveling, knowing how intelligence agencies or even private-sector firms use pretty young things for their own purposes, I was as interested in seeing this through as I was in breaking my mood with some engaging company. The woman didn't have any luggage or a carry-on, just a purse, and she sat down across from me, her knee-length skirt hiked up to reveal a well-toned thigh.

She reached over, offering her hand. "Hi. I'm Marcy Kent."

"Hi, Marcy. I'm Peter Travers."

She smiled a little too knowingly at my cover name. "So, what brings you out to the smelly shoe of New York?" she asked.

"Quaint way of putting it. I was just meeting a business client in Yaphank, and heading back into the city."

"Me too. I had a meeting at the Institute there; I'm a graphic designer, and they want to … buff up their image."

Since she wasn't carrying a portable to display her designs, unless they were on a pocket device, I doubted her story. Then, it dawned on me: this was a set up, and some goon of a boyfriend would be knocking on my door shortly and creating a scene to compromise me. So, despite its gentile persona, the Bradbury Institute could play hardball. I immediately grabbed my portable and stood up.

"Marcy, since you need the car more than I do, it's yours."

Before she could protest, I opened the door, stepped out and slid it closed behind me. Two cars down, I walked past a big guy on a mission; he did a double take as I passed him in the aisle, but kept walking. I entered the dining car, sat down and ordered a coffee and pastry. I also asked the server to tell the train's security guy to drop by. I decided to nip this in the bud, as Sara would say. But, at least all of this maneuvering had broken my mood, and I could thank her for that.

12.

When I got home late that night, there was a note from Sherry saying that she had taken a few days off and was visiting her parents in Virginia. They lived in Charlottesville, which was only a hundred miles from D.C. and I couldn't help but wonder if this was coincidental, given that I was traveling there in two days. I really didn't like her parents very much; her father was a retired professor of anthropology from the University of Virginia and her mother, Millie, a retired PhD statistician. Needless to say, Thanksgivings were a real hoot at the Reynolds' residence, or at least until I stopped going and Sherry would spend holidays there every couple of years by herself. Both my parents were deceased, and Sherry had hoped that I would develop some kind of surrogate bond with her parents, but that never happened. I'll have to admit I was glad she wasn't home and I didn't have to deal with her resentment after another rather trying day. But, then I caught myself, saw how self-absorbed I had become. It did give me pause, but not for long.

At work the next morning, there was an email on my computer from FBI Agent Musgrave. He could have sent it to my remote, but it was coded for my office computer with no forwarding. I suspected it had something to do with my encounter on the train the previous night, but what was also unsettling was that they were sending a car to pick me up. Their New York offices were only fifteen blocks away and I could easily take a cab or even walk there. While I was thinking about my summons, Gene buzzed me and asked me to come to his office.

"Shut the door, Alan," he said as I stepped inside his glass cubicle. He pulled out and turned on an electronic bug suppressor.

"What's up, Gene?"

"You tell me. Did you notice the FBI agents staking out the building this morning?"

I sat down across from his desk. I had totally missed the stakeout. "No. But, I got a summons from Musgrave and a meeting with him across town."

"What the hell happened yesterday?"

I wasn't sure how much of my assignment I could share with him, but told him whom I had interviewed—if not the content or my conclusions—and my own interrogation by Ms. Irving, and the suspected shakedown on the train.

"Yeah, it's you they're covering. Must figure you're a target, even from within our circle," he said.

"My in-country assignment must be some hot potato."

"Alan. Watch yourself. I don't trust Klaus, or his recent dance with you. Politically things are more fragile than they let on, and they could be trolling for patsies."

"Yeah, I kind of upset the applecart with my recent call on the Harkum case."

Gene shook his head. "Don't tell me anything else. Just watch yourself." He stood up to indicate the meeting was over—very brusque treatment for my always cordial boss. This situation had unnerved him.

When I got back to my desk, there was a cryptic message from Jean Whatley, wanting to have lunch together. I told her I had a meeting across town, but would catch up with her later in the day. She replied that I should "watch my tail." I suspected that she was being followed by the FBI and was wondering if they were targeting both of us. I didn't want to alarm her, so I emailed her back and wrote that "my tail was just fine." I was sure she got the message.

The car picked me up at 12:30; I assumed this wasn't a lunch meeting, so I ate early in the cafeteria. I was somewhat alarmed when the car didn't drive across town but out of Manhattan to JFK airport. The thought did cross my mind that I was being detained and flown somewhere for "interrogation." I asked the agent about the detour, and he said that Musgrave had flown up from D.C. and wanted to meet on the Bureau's plane to save time. I also noted that it would be a more secure location.

Musgrave met me at the top of the gangway and personally ushered me into the medium-size scramjet. The interior of the plane had few passenger seats and was mostly subdivided into cubicles for a flying office. Musgrave asked if I needed anything to eat or drink; I asked for bottled water and followed him back to his office at the rear of the jet. There were several agents and some clerical staff manning the workstations.

"Well, Alan. It's finally nice to meet you in person. You really saved our ass with the Kohn leak."

"Glad I could help." There were cross-the-aisle cushioned divans on either side. Musgrave sat on one and I sat across from him.

"Imagine you guessed that this is about your little encounter on the train last night."

"Yeah. Figured as much. What did they have to say for themselves?" I asked.

Musgrave smiled. "Alan, it's always nice to work with pros like you. They were confined to your compartment and then taken off the train by our agents in New York." He pulled up a file on his remote. "They're a regular shakedown couple who've been working this corridor for a few years, but below our radar." He looked across to me. "Suppose you figured they were hired by the Bradbury people?"

"Made sense. They didn't like what I had to say about their precious neural processors, and there's a lot of money at stake."

"Well, they don't know who hired them, and believe me, chemical interrogation gets the truth out of everybody. I called

Klaus, and he's been looking into it from that end."

I smiled.

"Yeah, I know. He's on the Board and has stock options, but there's a lot more at stake here than money."

"If not them, then who?" I asked.

"Well, Alan, that's what I'm here to figure out." He paused to get just the right tone for his next question. "You involved in anything … off-the-books, that would bring this kind of heat down on you?"

"Well, there was an unauthorized contact that I'm playing out."

"Okay, we figured as much given … the holes in your work-home schedule." He paused. "Anything you'd like to share?"

Since neural processors recorded travel like old-time GPS devices, I had flushed my processor after each excursion to the Kitty Kat Club, which would show up as holes in my timeline.

"I'm not sure what's going on, but you'll be the first to know," I said.

"Okay. That's fair. I like to give people like you a wide berth."

"But then, my new in-country assignment, even though I haven't been briefed, could be the nexus point of both."

"That's what I'm thinking. A rival faction or even a leak at our end. The borny revivalists know that the political climate is changing and nobody knows what that portends. If you've noticed, there's been more anti-tech activity in the last few months."

"Is that why you've started watching Whatley and me?" I asked.

He nodded his head. "Yes, after last night." He smiled. "You didn't spot us this morning, but she did. Quite a girl. Might recruit her myself some day."

He stood up as did I. "So, until you're deployed, you've got tails, and we're flying you down to D.C. in the morning. A car will pick both of you up. We'll email the times. See you in D.C."

We shook hands and Musgrave's assistant ushered me out of the plane and to my waiting car. I was a little alarmed that they had figured out the timeline holes for my excursions to the Kitty Kat Club, but even if they had questioned Bart, I had a plausible excuse. However, it made me wonder if these "holes" were the real source of their concern and not last night's shakedown.

When I got back to my office and took the elevator, it stopped at the third floor and Jean got on. There were two other people in the car, and so she handed me a note and got off at her floor. I had no idea how she timed this rendezvous, since it would require some kind of external surveillance, or heads-up from someone else. I went to the Men's Room and opened the note in a stall: "Dinner. 202 East 72nd Street, 302. Seven P.M. Tails not invited."

This was interesting. How did she know that Emma was away and I would be free for the night? Another unanswered question. Well, after yesterday and today's excursions, dinner and its trimmings with the lovely and engaging Ms. Whatley was just what the doctor or shrink had ordered. Or was it? I had to ask myself.

Chapter Five

13.

After work I thought about heading over to Jean's apartment, but the fallout over last night's marital quarrel soured that prospective "date" for me. I called and told her it would be better to skip a rendezvous this evening, especially since we were now scheduled to leave in the morning. She sounded disappointed but wasn't insistent, and said she'd see me tomorrow. I have to admit that I was a little intrigued by Musgrave's premise that I was being targeted by the opposition, whether they were the pro-religious or anti-tech factions. So, I decided to stroll around the city, and headed south toward the village to see what other tails I could pick up. After about an hour, I went into my favorite Chinese restaurant and sat on a stool at the counter. I could see my FBI guys staying well out of sight across the street at a news stand. I ordered the vegetable dumplings, and when they arrived and I was struggling with my chop sticks, Wu from the Kitty Kat Club strolled in and sat down next to me.

I immediately recognized her but didn't say anything. She ordered the Won Tong soup and a foreign beer. After a while, she slipped her chop sticks out of their paper sleeve and reached over and took one of my dumplings. "It's done this way, Alan. Lower stick firm, with the top stick mobile between the thumb and index finger."

I looked over at her. "Ah, Wu, from the club."

"Who did you expect? Emma?" Wu paused. "She's a neutral, if you haven't figured that out."

"Well, I wasn't expecting anybody. Just eating out by myself with my wife out of town."

"And you just like walking around Manhattan on balmy nights?" she said.

It dawned on me that somebody had failed to compromise me

65

on the train, and seeing my FBI tail, they arranged this little rendezvous. "So, what do you or your handlers want, Wu?"

Her soup arrived and she quickly ate it, like a woman who was used to eating on the run. "Alan, don't go out in the field. You're not welcome, and you're compromised."

At that moment my two FBI tails entered the restaurant and hurried over to us. "Ah, Ms. Ling. How nice of you to show up." One of the guys picked up her purse and the other grabbed her by the arm. "Let's go."

The cook behind the counter yelled out. "Who pay bill?"

"I'll cover it, Li," I yelled back.

One of the FBI agents threw a twenty-dollar bill on the counter. "You might need this," he said with a snicker.

Wu, or Ling, as it turned out, didn't resist and went with them without saying another word. It was obvious that this was the Queen Sacrifice move by her faction. The stakes must be really high for them to give up such a prime operative, or so I figured at the time. After they left, my portable rang. It was Musgrave.

"Nice move, Alan. I assume this was your 'unauthorized' action?"

"Well, not … Ling herself, but somebody who used her to get to me."

There was a long pause at the other end. "Another team will be there in five minutes to escort you home. Don't leave until they arrive, and we'll talk about this tomorrow."

It was naive of me to hope this contact would cancel my borny village excursion; it just raised the stakes for them. Of course, my little off-the-books maneuver over the last two weeks was exposed, and my unauthorized contact with Emma would be highly suspect, despite Musgrave's wide berth. On the drive back to my apartment in the FBI car, I wondered if he would accept that Emma was being used by one of the factions, and I was just playing it out, like I told him, to see where it would lead before reporting it. At that moment the driver glanced back at me in the rearview mirror. I wondered if they had the car wired for brain scans. No, too smart for them.

In the morning the car picked me up first, and then swung around to Jean's place on East 72nd. She watched one of the guys load her excessive luggage into the trunk before she hopped into the backseat.

"Hi, partner," she said with a smile.

"Going for an extended vacation?" I asked. She looked puzzled. "I don't think they'll deploy us from D.C. Probably come back here first, resume our normal activities, and then we get picked up in the middle of the night."

She snuggled up against me. "Then I'll just try out my new wardrobe in D.C."

They flew us down to Washington on a small jet with a dozen seats. The flight itself was only twenty minutes, and there were only twenty pages of briefing background for us to read, which we quickly scanned. Afterward Jean was very chatty, maybe just nervous energy, but I was still enmeshed in the implications of last night's encounter with Ling.

"You seem a little distant, Alan. What's up?"

"Oh, it's my wife," I lied. "She's not very happy with me right now."

"Well, boyfriends don't mind, as long as there's enough left for them, and there always is."

"We'll see about that," I laughed, keeping up the pretense.

"That's better, Alan," Jean said and pinched my arm.

We landed at Dulles Airport, so I figure we wouldn't be doing this briefing at FBI headquarters in town. Our two-car caravan headed west and pulled into a gated and wooded compound, with somewhat desiccated and stunted trees about thirty minutes later. A mile down the road, we came upon a series of rustic cabins and a reinforced concrete building, with an array of telecommunication towers on the roof. We were dropped off at our cabin and our bags unloaded, and told the first briefing would be in thirty minutes in the main building.

"Not much time to freshen up," Jean complained. One of the agents snickered, slid back into his car, and they drove away down the entrance road. I figured they were headed back to D.C. or for another airport pickup, or other flunky work. They didn't seem very high-level.

The cabin was quite spacious and high-end, and it had two bedrooms. We looked into both of them. "Let's take this one. The windows are west-facing—less light in the morning," Jean said.

I didn't argue with the lady about sharing a bedroom; no need to keep up the pretense out here in the boondocks. I had wondered if Sherrie's visit to Charlottesville was actually a ruse to track me down at my hotel in D.C. but that was foiled now. We unloaded our luggage, and I took a drawer and Jean took two and most of the closet, which still left one bag unpacked. She slipped into more comfortable shoes and we strolled over to the main building.

The small windowless briefing room was comfortable and high-tech. Musgrave and two of his men were seated on one side of a long wooden table and Jean and I sat directly across from this group. There was a huge vid screen on the wall, and it now flashed a picture of Ling and then a vid of her walking into the Chinese restaurant last night and sitting next to me.

"Su Ling is an operative for one of the anti-tech factions; in the past two weeks they've tried to compromise Alan by having him run an off-the-books inquiry for one of K Industries former agents, Emma Knowles, and Alan's last in-country partner." Her photo flashed on the screen. "We're not sure if Knowles is working with them, or was set up to get to Alan and discredit him."

Jean turned and stared at me, no doubt wondering if she should start distancing herself.

"Together with Bart Caruthers from K Industries Foreign Bureau, they set up a sting operation on their own at the Kitty Kat

Club in the village and passed along some bogus info on Knowles' probationary period." Musgrave stopped. "Alan, this is what Caruthers told us; I assume it's on-point?"

"Yeah, that's pretty much what was going down."

He nodded his head and continued with the briefing. "Apparently they had tried to trick Alan into further compromising himself, even tried a honey-pot scheme on a train, but to no avail. So finally in desperation, Ling followed him into a restaurant last night and kind of gave herself up, knowing all of this would come out into the open."

"Was she top level?" Jean asked.

"It's hard to tell with these independent cells, but we've now been able to connect her to two past operations that we know of, so she was no new recruit."

"So I guess this pretty much cancels our operation?" Jean asked ruefully.

"Actually this plays right into our game plan, since we're asking Alan to become a double agent."

This caught me totally off guard. "You're kidding?" I said before I could catch myself.

"In our next briefing we'll get into the details, but I can say here that we're not spying on the Midwest's anti-tech movement and your last target, which Ling was trying to protect, but going after another faction based in the Southwest, with more of a shamanic religious focus."

"And given my orientation, or leanings, you think I'd pass muster for their recruitment?"

"Yes, and since Jean is quite the opposite, she's partnered with you to make sure you don't go over the edge and into their camp."

"Oh, a kind of yin/yang partnership, with me the yang element," Jean said in a perky tone.

Musgrave nodded his head.

"I like that."

"We thought you would, Ms. Whatley," Musgrave added, as everybody but me had a good laugh.

14.

After this brief introduction, a Southwest desert community expert, Dr. Justin Holmes, a professor type with wire-rimmed glasses and bad skin, continued the briefing and gave us a rundown on the Southwest sector, which included the old four corner states of New Mexico, Arizona, Utah, and Colorado plus Nevada. He told us that most of the big cities like Albuquerque, Phoenix, Salt Lake City and Denver, were still cosmopolitan centers similar to those in the East. However, given their Native American and Hispanic populations, and historically the area's independent streak, there were higher concentrations of alternative and borny villages and communities and some quite large like Taos, New Mexico and Sedona, Arizona. He briefly sketched out the economic forces and political agendas and their histories in this sector over the last fifty years.

After a brief break, Musgrave got down to specifics. "The town you'll be going to is Jerome, Arizona, halfway between Sedona and Prescott. It's an old copper-mining town, on top of a hill that's some 1800 feet above the surrounding area, one road up and down that can get dicey in the winter. A veritable fortress. A hundred years ago it was an artist community and tourist spot, but after the economic turndown or depression, it was deserted yet again and then taken over by a series of religious communes of various beliefs. About ten years ago, after some infighting, most of the others left, leaving the community to a group formed around a messianic figure, Maria Fria.

"And she's a threat … why?" I asked.

Musgrave told me, "Let's wait until the afternoon session to go into that."

"Your cover stories did take some time to flesh out. Jean, who will take the name of Brenda Howell, is an heiress from Chicago, whose family was a food manufacturer of organic and healthy food products. The family and their history are real, as is Brenda, who's Jean's age and looks a lot like her, but has been a recluse all her life, educated by her eccentric mother, a former university professor, and a series of foreign tutors. She has few electronic footprints and we've been able to alter all of them. Brenda's parents are retired and have agreed to work with us for a price, and Brenda, who's always wanted to travel to Europe, has been given a new identity and a credit card and will be escorted around by one of our agents."

"Why go to all of this trouble; why not just create a fabrication, which we've used in the past?" I asked.

"We've tried infiltrating this woman's inner circle, but she's spotted every one of them—she's very psychic, whether you believe in that or not—and we feel that Jean playing a real person, with a history, might sustain the illusion, and being an actress of sorts will help." Musgrave paused for a moment. "But, for Alan, who we want to be discovered, we got a little more creative."

"So, I'm using Brenda and her history to hide behind and slide in on her coattail?"

"And she's so in love with you that she can't see she's being used," Musgrave said.

"I can't wait to hear whom I'm playing."

"Lewis Hargrove, an eccentric author of messianic novels that are quite popular on the Internet, but who has no electronic footprint and no available picture, bio, or location—just a name that most considered a pseudonym. He can't be found because the guy cold-drops hard copies with his e-book publishers and the proceeds are donated directly to various charities. We located the author, who lives with his mother in Maine, and all of his activities are being closely monitored."

"So you want them to discover I'm a fraud and a freeloader,

living off Brenda."

"You ingrate," Jean teased.

"No, we want them to discover that you're an undercover agent, spying on them and using Brenda as a cover." Musgrave paused. "But, you'll have to read this guy's novels, uploaded to your portable, and be able to spout long passages, which can be programmed into your neural processor."

"Hope he isn't into purple prose."

Musgrave laughed. "I think we've covered enough for one session. Let's break for lunch and we'll meet back here at 2:00."

The cafeteria was small but had windows looking out into the wooded landscape, and the food was healthy and excellent. It has always interested me, how the new techno man had incorporated some of the practices, such as healthy eating and yoga, from past generations of seekers and adapted it to their own mental mindset. While theirs was integrative, ours is more of a segmented approach, and utilitarian—exploit anything that's useful and gives you an edge to dominate self, others, and nature.

After coming back from the buffet line and eating for a while, I got the distinct impression Jean was studying me, or my mannerisms. I assumed she had studied method acting and its new school of thought, adapted from the 20th-century behaviorists, who were generally discredited, but the method still had some "useful" features. So, I started to cut my salad vegetables with exaggerated intensity. At first this caught her attention, but soon she was on to my ploy.

"Okay, so I was studying you; give me a break."

"You're not going to play my role, so I assume you're looking for inroads into my soul," I said, with a smirk.

"Well, at least you have one; it's part of your … charm."

I stopped eating for a moment and stared back at her. "And you're afraid you don't?"

She avoided the question. "Got a feeling that's the subject of our afternoon lecture and I was just … pinging the depths, you could say."

"We're too mannered to reveal much in this setting; probably need to wait until somebody points a gun at me."

Jean smiled. "Or, handcuffs you."

I laughed self-consciously. "Well, there's always that."

The other diners started filing out of the room, and we took our last bites of food and stood up and left. In the conference room, we took our seats but Musgrave was the only other person in the room. He looked over at us. "This next briefing will be by an undercover asset for one of the local universities, a religious specialist. As with all deep-cover assets, the less exposure the better, so it's just going to be the four of us. You can call him Mr. G."

He picked up his portable and texted a message. A moment later, a side door opened, and a man entered the room and stepped over to Musgrave's table. He was tall and thin, close-cropped dark hair, and dressed in black. His eyes, his most distinguishing features, were small, dark and intense. I figured he was a priest, maybe a Jesuit who taught at Georgetown.

He set down his portable and flashed a picture of a rather large, big-boned woman of mixed ancestry, but definitely with some Native America blood, on the screen. She appeared to be in her fifties, with black hair streaked with gray, but in contrast to Mr. G. had eyes that were clear, light, and you could say … bouncy. I kept staring at her, which drew everybody's attention.

"Yeah, she's a real looker," Musgrave added with a sneer.

"This is Maria Fria. While she grew up in Santa Fe, her father was from the Jemez Indian Reservation, and her mother was mixed Anglo and Hispanic. As a young girl she spent her summers at the reservation and came under the influence of a Native medicine man there," Mr. G. paused, and then flashed a dated black-and-white photo of an old Indian medicine man, in full Native attire, squinting his eyes. The picture must have been taken in a sunnier era. "Benito Cochiti. He recognized the young girl's ... mystical bent, and helped develop it, but she was too willful to be confined to any one tradition. She quickly developed her psychic ability, earned a living as a psychic in her 20s, and then suddenly dropped out of sight about twenty years ago. She probably traveled to Central and South America, where there's less tracking in the smaller, indigenous groups and further developed her ... psychic reach. The only picture we have of that stay comes from the CIA." It showed her, younger and much thinner, standing outside a medicine hut with native women. "And then, ten years ago, she showed up in Arizona, as a mystic leader with a following, and soon moved to Jerome and took over the place."

"Strong-armed tactics?" I asked.

Mr. G stared at me for a second and showed just a touch of annoyance. "No. Her followers are totally nonviolent but she has a very powerful ... energy and those coming into contact with her seem to align with her or leave."

Musgrave said, "What caught our attention is that she trains healers and sends them out across the country, and many of her students have had spectacular results. Prominent people, some politicians and their families, with debilitating diseases have been cured, and of course this only adds to her influence and sway over people."

All three of us turned and looked at Mr. G. He shook his head. "Well, don't expect me to explain it. We know enough now about energy medicine, chakra alignment, and hands-on healing to know it's totally legit."

"Yeah," Musgrave added, "our doctors have analyzed the medical histories and post-healing recoveries, but they can't explain how 4th stage cancer and bone disease and whatnot can be so completely ... healed."

"Have you detected any ... energy cords between her and her patients?" I asked.

Mr. G. glanced over at Musgrave who nodded his head. "Well, we've used a slew of advanced imaging technology to detect anything along this line, but haven't turned up anything … yet." He paused. "But then, that's the point: what she and her students do is undetectable, outside of its effect."

"Nobody's getting brainwashed, if that's what you're asking," Musgrave said. "This isn't a cult, in the old twentieth-century model."

"Then what's the threat?" Jean asked.

Musgrave smiled and looked over at me. "Tell her, Alan."

"It's how this energy affects neural processors and chemically maintained psychological functioning, especially if people start healing themselves."

Musgrave added, "The advances in all areas of our lives over the last fifty years, including safety from aberrant individuals and their harmful use of technology, are largely based on our neural processors and how they bestow increased intelligence, psychological conditioning, and …"

"Allow for surveillance and monitoring," I added.

Musgrave frowned. "Well, we can't read your thoughts, as you know, but we can read brain-wave frequencies, and the new models are harder to flush, so hacking the devices can reveal a lot."

Jean looked over at Mr. G. "So she's not some messianic religious leader with a cult that threatens us politically?" Jean asked.

"No. She has followers and the ranks are growing, but she's shown no tendency to exert such influence."

"Which would be a relief, since we could then discredit her, or compromise her in any number of ways? But this …" Musgrave said.

"Is far more insidious," I added.

"Yes, Alan. But, fortunately, it's still early on and something can be done to determine its effects and if needed, stem the tide, as it were." Musgrave paused again and turned to Father G. "But now, we need to cover the ins and outs of her group, and the broader unity philosophy she espouses and which you, Alan, need to be familiar with."

Jean yawned. "Boy, I'm going to … sleep well tonight."

Mr. G. didn't know how to handle this remark and so he ignored it; I just wondered if I'd packed my bluies.

15.

When we returned to our cabin after dinner, Jean wanted to go for a walk in the woods before dark. I told her that the trees were probably bugged. She laughed. "Well, I wasn't thinking about a covert conversation, if that's what you're getting at."

"Okay, I'd like to get out into nature, clear my head too." We put on light jackets and headed out. There were some good trails and the one that we took, wound up the side of a large hill in a switchback pattern. I was hoping that the top would afford a clear view of the countryside. Jean talked about a family trip she took to the Southwest when she was a teenager. I didn't pay much attention, only giving her a nod now and then. I was still preoccupied with our assignment, or so I told myself, but it was clear that the image of Maria Fria and her "bouncy" eyes was hard for me to shake.

"Alan, where are you?" Jean finally asked.

"A little distracted by our last briefing and just mulling it over."

She looped her arm through mine and snuggled up to me. "Don't worry. I won't let her get to you."

"Well, I doubt if sex alone will be enough of a countermeasure but, with Emma, it did keep me grounded."

"Are you sure it isn't Emma that concerns you, or her popping up here, and not this Indian babe?"

I had a good laugh. "Talk about retro slang, as Sherry would put it."

Jean raised her eyebrows. "Oh, so we're talking about your wife now."

I nodded my head and picked up the pace. "Yeah, it's the intimacy issue, not that this woman ... attracts me."

Jean had a good laugh and snuggled closer. "There are all kinds of attractions, Alan. You know better than most about that."

We reached the top of the hill, and there was a gorgeous sight of the sun setting behind the Appalachian Mountain range to the west. The clouds were painted in red and orange hues. It was breathtaking. I could've stayed until dark, but Jean reminded me it was time to head back or we'd lose our way. I felt safe; I doubted that Jean ever lost her way in any terrain—part of her charm and her great lack.

Our first sexual coupling was intense and quite exploratory. Jean had few inhibitions and liked great variety, the scope of which kind of intimidated me. After we fell asleep, I woke an hour later and slipped out of bed and into the other bedroom. I didn't want to mesh with her this evening and I quickly fell asleep. Of course I dreamed about Maria Fria—my psychologist would dismiss the dream as a trouble daytime obsession working itself out, but there was something very "present" or real about the encounter. We were sitting in the living room of a large Southwestern house on a mountaintop, with a twenty-foot ceiling and a spectacular view of the surrounding terrain. I had to wonder if this was really her house in Jerome, which was revealing and might indicate the ability to monitor our briefings as well and know our plans. Of course this could have been my fear working itself out, given Musgrave's insistence on her psychic reach. In the dream I kept looking toward her bedroom, which seemed to amuse her and finally she said, "You can't handle my energy yet." I didn't react to her statement or feel diminished in any way, but we just sat there across from each other and stared, and pretty soon I had a waking dream, or a dream within a dream, which made me think of Christopher Nolan's classic film, *Inception*. I just couldn't get a handle of what was transpiring, but at one point I was looking down at the previous scene from above.

I suddenly woke up with Jean straddling me and making love. It was perfect timing, or an unconscious counter to Fria's dream intrusion, if that was what it was. Jean was really taking her assignment seriously, or was this just her own programming unconsciously protecting me? Either way, I thought that if the genders had been reversed, and I was a man making love to my sleeping girlfriend or wife, I'd have hell to pay but guys are supposed to like it any way they can get it, as the old retro song goes.

Well, my timing was also perfect, since Jean was having a shattering orgasm, which was telling in that it was a solo performance, as they say. She collapsed onto me, her blond hair covering my face.

"Well, I'm glad it was good for you, my dear."

She sat upright. "Oh, I woke you."

"You think."

She actually looked guilty, which was something I'd never expect from her.

"Sorry, didn't mean to … take advantage of you. But I woke up and you were gone and came in here and saw your absolutely gigantic erection, and I couldn't let it go to waste."

She rolled off of me and cuddled up next to me in bed. After a while her alarm went off in the other room. We lay there for a moment, letting her heavy breathing slow down. Jean slid off the bed. "Well, at least we can shower together, now that you're awake."

We quickly showered, since we had to pack our bags as well. Just one more morning briefing and we were heading back to New York. Musgrave was alone when we entered the conference room. He had a smile on his face; it occurred to me that our rooms were being bugged and probably videoed. The room darkened, and a video began to play on the scene. Jean glanced over at me, thinking the same thought and waiting to see our private moment going public. But, I was the one caught short. What played out was a blurry reenactment of my dream: it wasn't very clear, other than the image of Maria Fria. Jean let go of my hand.

The short clip finished and we all sat there in silence for a moment. Finally, Jean asked, "Was that a dream of some sort, and that was Fria, right?"

Musgrave stared at me almost apologetically. "Sorry, Alan. But this is why we're up here and not briefing you in D.C. Your cabin is wired—one of the few labs in the world with this kind of technology—for dream recovery."

This took a moment for both of us to compute. "So, you figured if she can plant dreams, she can remote-view this compound?" I asked.

Musgrave nodded his head.

"Aren't you afraid ...?"

"No. This entire room is encased in a psychotronic field that's impervious to remote viewing or any other kind of psychic reach."

"But this suggests that she's seen me here at this compound and must know what that means," I said, and then added, "if it wasn't my own dream, which given my fears about her influence does seem more likely."

Musgrave nodded his head. "But hypothetically, let's assume it wasn't and she did implant it." He paused. "So, what would that mean, Alan?"

"She would know that I know she's aware that I'm a plant, if not our strategy, and if I still show up, it means that I'm personally compelled to go through with this, so I'm susceptible to being turned."

Jean shook her head. "This game strategy is way over my head."

Musgrave smiled. "Tell her Alan."

I tried not to sound too condescending. "It gives her power over me and makes turning me an easier proposition for her and her crew."

But again, I had to wonder, what if this was my dream and she was innocent of such manipulation? Then what? She'd be compromised either way.

Jean nodded her head at my explanation and Musgrave smiled. "Unless of course, Alan is really turned, and this is where Jean comes in."

"Yeah, I'm impervious to her kind of persuasion," Jean added.

"Yes, that's what we're hoping," Musgrave said, but sounded less than convinced.

He closed down the screen monitor, opened his computer and voiced a command, and the doors opened and the rest of the team entered. We spent the next several hours going over the specifics of our assignment. Well, I was glad that my neural processor recorded this session for a future playback, because I was somewhere else, no doubt back in that gorgeous mountaintop home "viewing the scenery."

Chapter Six

16.

We were back in New York for only a few days before Jean was whisked away in the middle of the night, to the Howell's lakeside mansion and compound in Chicago. As our last briefing had noted, Jean would be outfitted there, and while she was just a bit smaller than Brenda, her clothes would be altered to fit Jean to help maintain her cover. For my end, I was taken a couple days later, when it became evident that Sherry was flying back to New York from Washington. They didn't want me interacting with her before my assignment. Interestingly enough, I was then flown from New York to Bangor Maine, where Lewis Hargrove lived, and spent several days observing him as he went about his daily routine.

There was an all-night diner on the outskirts of town where he liked to write and where I spent several late nights eating, reading the news on my portable, and observing him. He was a weird-looking guy in his late forties, tall with a long narrow face—his left ear was missing its lobe, as if someone had bitten it off—very van Gogh. He always wore a baseball cap pulled low on his forehead, which accentuated his sharp features as he hunched over his portable and typed. He looked like the kind of guy who lived with his mother and wrote apocalyptic sci-fi novels. We even exchanged a few words, when I left early one night and he asked me what the latest news was on the storm heading our way.

"Yeah, supposed to hit at dawn," I said, stopping at his table, but well back from it to protect my earlobes.

He glanced up at me and had trouble focusing his eyes. "Not from around here?" he asked.

I nodded my head.

"Well, these northeasters can be a real bitch," he said, with a sneer. "Like everything else in life."

"Yeah, tell me."

"We should all move out West," he said, with a sly smile, and then turned back to his portable.

I hesitated, a little taken aback by his reference, and then thanked him for his heads-up and walked out. I had to wonder if Fria wasn't the only psychic rattling my cage, or if the Howells weren't the only coconspirators in our cover story.

After our Washington sojourn, I continued to dream intermittently about Maria Fria. What I couldn't determine was whether these dreams were actually projections from her, or my own subconscious fears working themselves out. At some point, after I bought a local car with Maine plates and drove to Chicago, where I hooked up with Brenda/Jean and we started sleeping together, they stopped. I wondered if sleeping with Brenda formed its own kind of psychic shield, or was my libido getting its release and my subconscious was thus preoccupied and not fixated on Fria. The plan was for us to head out in the family's touring car after a week or so and drive to the Southwest as a kind of getaway vacation from Chicago and her parents, who lived in another wing of the mansion. I'll have to say that Jean was quite an actress and had adopted a whole new set of behaviors playing the part of Brenda Howell—softer and more feminine in some ways, but no less a voracious lover.

On one of our last nights in Chicago, we dined at an expensive lakeside restaurant frequented by Brenda Howell. When I tried to pay for the dinner, which more than my weekly salary, Brenda was insistent. "No, Lewis, save your money. You impress me in other ways, dear."

The waiter extended his electronic check pad and Brenda used her retail fob to pay it. He must've seen her name come up on his screen because he looked down at her more closely. "Is anything wrong, Claude?"

"No ma'am, you just look … younger than I remember, Ms.

Howell."

"Well, great sex can take years off of you."

He laughed, glanced over at me. "I'll remember that, ma'am."

"Well, I hope you do more than just remember it," she said leeringly. Brenda turned to me, no doubt expecting me to slip into my own altered ego.

"I wish you wouldn't embarrass me like that, Brenda," I said as the waiter walked away from the table with a smirk on his face.

"You must allow me to take care of you, Lewis. I'm hoping this trip will spur on your creative efforts. I did so adore your last novel."

It was at that point that my Lewis Hargrove persona seemed to gel. I had wanted to leave for the Southwest earlier, but Brenda insisted that I wasn't ready, or that I hadn't taken on my role yet. It was clear that she was in charge, and from then on I started calling her Brenda and thinking of myself as Lewis. The dinner performance had apparently convinced her and two days later we headed out—after a shopping splurge, in which she bought me a Southwest wardrobe to go with my "Maine duds," as she called them.

I knew this wasn't going to fool Fria, nor did we want it too, but the idea was to maintain Brenda's role as the duped lover. I was concerned that, if Fria had remote-viewed me at the compound, she could have spotted Jean. Musgrave's experts said that was unlikely, given that she had so quickly acquired me as the target. It probably helped that from the moment I arrived in Chicago, Brenda was in character and never deviated for a moment, even her orgasms were more ladylike. One had to be impressed with this degree of role playacting, and it made me wonder if her previous role as Jean Whatley wasn't just another persona as well.

As we drove through Oklahoma and then into New Mexico, the wide-open spaces and endless expanse of brown prairie grass and sagebrush really opened me up, after living in the confined cages of big cities and our modern straitjackets: from work to relationships. However, it turned Brenda from Ms. Chatty to Ms. video game, as she shrank down to the size of her portable and blocked out the surrounding landscape. I recalled a quote from a twentieth-century Western author, about how the expanded horizons frightened structured people who are afraid their essence will leak out. It had quite the opposite effect on me: I could feel myself, or my real self, as the Jungians might say, busting out of its seams. I even rolled down the window to smell the sagebrush and feel the biting cold winter air. Brenda activated her passenger-side climate control and kept focused on her game playing. At one point I pulled into a diner in Tucumcari, New Mexico for an early lunch, just because of the city's name. It suggested an exotic locale, even if the diner was a dilapidated old railroad car.

Brenda called up the roadmap on her portable. "Why don't we wait until we reach Albuquerque? Better selection, I'd imagine."

"Brenda, dear. Our destination is a mountaintop in the middle of the desert. Get use to the wild."

I stepped out of the car and she reluctantly followed me, zipping up her rather expensive, teal-colored, ski jacket, which did look smashing on her. She took two quick steps into the interior; since unlike most modern establishments, the diner didn't have a UV-ray awning. We sat down at an old-fashioned booth, with red vinyl benches right out of the twentieth century; the windows, by federal regulation, did have darkened UV screens, if peeling in places.

The restaurant also had a white & gold-chipped Formica counter with bar stools, where a mixture of local Hispanics, Anglo cowboys and rift-raff hard cases sat drinking coffee that could probably hold up spoons. Since they were used to tourists, and there were a few others here this morning, our presence didn't make much of a stir. Brenda quickly scanned through the tattered plastic menu and ordered something safe: a taco salad. I ordered the Huevos Rancheros with green chili sauce.

Brenda looked down to my selection, which didn't have a description. No doubt they figured most locals knew what they were getting, and tourists could ask if they dared. "Ma'am, what is that?" she asked the waitress, a fiftyish Hispanic woman with pockmarked skin, as she stepped over.

"Fried eggs on black beans and tortilla chips smothered with green chili sauce," she said, shaking her head, grabbing the menus, and walking off muttering "gringos."

"Lewis, have you ever had this before?"

"No. But, then I've never been in Tucumcari, New Mexico." She gave me one of her new disapproving looks. "Think globally, eat locally," I added.

"Well, if you get sick, dear, don't expect me to drive that car of yours."

I had to laugh, as did half the guys at the counter. She was really playing her role. Well, the food came, and I was both pleasantly surprised by its quality and taste. It must've had homegrown ingredients and not the frozen precooked meals we were used to eating, even in East Coast restaurants, or the less pricey ones.

17.

We had to take a roundabout route to Jerome from Flagstaff, to avoid driving through Sedona, one of the more notorious borny villages in the Southwest, or maybe we were thus instructed to avoid the so-called energy vortexes there. Anyway, we headed south on Route 17 and then turned onto the road to Prescott and backtracked to Jerome. We got there in late afternoon the next day and drove up the icy road to the top of Cleopatra Hill. There was a sign outside of town, welcoming visitors, signed by Mayor Maria Fria. We had made reservations at a small hotel, The

Sliding Sands, and since we weren't married, they made us both sign in. We then went to our room. While Brenda was showering, I checked out the room with my bug sensor: there were several that I disabled, as well as one vid feed. If Fria knew I was coming and knew of my affiliation, I wouldn't need to hide my identity from her, just Brenda's, and while I wasn't really sure about Musgrave's scenario, I wasn't taking any chances.

After a little nap, we headed out with our UV-protective attire and strolled up the 30-degree slope of the street, to the west side of town and viewed a spectacular Southwest sunset. It was really breathtaking, what we city dwellers hardly ever see back East. Then we walked around town for fifteen minutes, with no fixed destination and after passing up several restaurants, chose one on Verde Avenue at the south end of town. We didn't know what to expect here, whether there would be many tourists or if the whole city was "zoned" for her followers, who might be easy to detect by their flaky attire or blissed-out stares. We were pleasantly surprised that our servers and fellow diners were as normal as they could be, if a little slow, or at least on the surface. We had a table off to the side and could have talked about our assignment, but had agreed to stay in character in public settings. We just didn't know the level of surveillance, electronic and otherwise. We ordered dinner, their combination Mexican combo plate, with a burrito, enchilada, and taco and drank bottled water.

"Well, Lewis. This is a perfectly delightful little town," Brenda said at the end of our meal. "I think we should stay for the week, at least."

"It would make a great setting for a novel," I added.

"Yes, dear. That was what I was thinking too. Maybe a messianic shamanic novel set in the high desert."

"I should have you write my back cover copy."

"Well, you're not the only creative one," she said, reaching over and caressing my hand.

"Well, I'll have to do some research. I wonder if they have a library."

"You mean with real books," Brenda laughed, like Sherry would have at such a retro concept. "I'm sure you can find reams of material on websites, and stay closer to home. You know I do need your … constant attention, dear."

I had to smile. What an actress. The waitress, a woman in her 20s, with short-cropped blonde hair, handed me an electronic check pad. Brenda began to reach for it but I gave her a look. She sat back and I used my own e-transfer fob, which identified me as Lewis Hargrove.

The waitress glanced at her e-pad and then looked up with a more solicitous attitude. I wondered if that was because she recognized my nom de plume, or had been alerted to watch for it. She now asked us, "So, are you passing through town or staying on for a while?"

"Well, we were just talking about that." Brenda turned to me. "What do you think, Lewis?"

"There is my research."

"Then it's settled," she said, glancing up at the woman.

"Reason I asked … tomorrow night there's a … gathering you might want to attend."

"Oh, really. An Indian powwow?" Brenda said facetiously.

"Well, nothing that traditional, but whether you know it or not, one of the country's best healers lives here, and she's having an … open healing at the old Methodist church on Main Street."

"Oh, how exciting. Anybody can attend and … get healed?" Brenda asked with feigned enthusiasm.

"Yes. That's the idea."

"Oh, thank you. We'll be there."

The waitress nodded her head and then stared at me, her eyes narrowing. She wasn't very good at hiding her tells. Again, I wasn't sure if my e-transfer had triggered this inquiry, and if so, whether it was for Lewis Hargrove or Alan Reynard.

Afterward we walked out in the cold air and saw a really

spectacular clear, night sky, the likes of which I had rarely seen; the Milky Way's band of stars clearly discernible. As we strolled back to the hotel, Brenda leaned over and kissed me on the cheek and then whispered in my ear. "Phase one, complete."

We didn't dare use electronic communication for contact purposes, so we were pretty much on our own, or at least within the confines of the town. The other consideration we discussed walking back to the hotel, was whether either of us should participate in the healing ceremony, given how her energy was reported to affect neural processors. Of course that was part of the assignment, but we decided to just observe this first healing ceremony but decline to participate. That night Brenda was really sexually primed and nearly wore me out; in the shower, which we figured was off-limits to even psychic prying, I probed her and she confessed that this dual Brenda/Jean role was creating tension that intense sex seemed to relieve. Being more integrative, and not as invested in my dual role, it didn't affect me the same way.

In the morning, Brenda woke up with a throbbing headache, that didn't go away as the day progressed. On our morning walk, we wondered if they hadn't slipped something into her meal last night, causing the headaches to make her a more willing participant that evening.

"Interesting that they would target me and not you, if that were the case," Brenda said.

"You're my ballast, as it were, and maybe affecting you would make it easier to compromise me."

"Well, we'll see about that."

"So, you think you should step forward tonight?" I asked.

"Let me play the sucker and see where it leads us."

Musgrave had set up a remote contact facility in Phoenix with full tech capability, so if Brenda's neural processor was affected, we could have it checked out fairly quickly. It did seem too obvious for a first move on their part. Maybe they just wanted to make sure we attended their little get-together, or maybe this speculation was just unfounded.

I spent the afternoon at the library, reading dozens of Native American, shamanic, and energy medicine books and some e-book editions that weren't available from booksellers on the Internet. Brenda made a show of being bored and went shopping, taking advantage of the government's unlimited expense account. While viewing their archives, a very attractive young woman saw my interest and started up a conversation with a lot of enthusiasm and way too many sexual undertones. Maybe this group wasn't as sophisticated as we had assumed about their recruitment tactics, or maybe they underestimated me. After a while, I told her I needed to get back to my research, and she asked if I was coming to the healing tonight. I said yes, and she replied that maybe she'd see me there. I had no doubt about that. I just hoped Brenda wouldn't get territorial about her interest.

18.

The Methodist church where the healing ceremony was conducted had high, stained-glass windows, depicting the Stations of the Cross, but the pews had been replaced with padded folding chairs, that could be easily moved around on the wood floor to form various configurations. Tonight they were spread in a semicircle around the front of the elevated sanctuary, where a rather large ornamental, high-back chair sat. There were about a hundred people in attendance, in an audience five rows deep. The chairs were half-filled, and we were shown by an usher to the second row from the front. I assumed the locals filled it in from the back forward, to give first-timers a better view. After we were seated, the other chairs were quickly filled and the organ began to play *Ave Maria* and the small choir sang the hymn. After a while, most of the attendees started meditating, and we took that as a cue and at least closed our eyes and pretended, but Brenda's form was suspect and it showed.

At some point I sensed a shift or a slight disturbance in the air, and I squinted my eyes open to watch Maria Fria enter the sanctuary from a side room and take her seat. She was dressed in a flowing turquoise gown that was understated, and she wasn't as large in stature as I had supposed from her old photos. She closed her eyes in meditation and I was able to examine her features: her skin was lighter than either her Indian or Hispanic heritage would suggest, indicating that she was probably more than one-fourth Anglo. She had a high forehead and prominent cheeks, and one would say that she was an attractive woman, but unlike many of these messianic female leaders who tended to be quite plump, she was just a big-boned woman and well-toned. The choir finished their hymn and the organ music stopped, and we sat in silent meditation for at least fifteen minutes. I could sense Brenda's restlessness but wasn't about to nudge her.

A young woman in a blue, ankle-length dress walked into the sanctuary and stepped up to the old pulpit. I was interested as to just how far they would mirror their "church" or healing service after Catholic ritual, which was the faith that Fria had been raised in. The woman cleared her throat and began.

"I welcome all of you to our healing ceremony tonight. Many of you are part of our ministry, but I see several new faces and assume that you're curious tourists visiting our elevated city, or maybe the infirm from the surrounding region who have learned of Maria Fria's healings. We ask the curious to be respectful of our service and to at least entertain the thought that they may have been drawn here by some higher aspect of themselves.

"Whether your ailment is physical or emotional, know that all disharmony begins from a misalignment with one's totality and thus they are spiritual in nature. Maria will draw energy from the Godhead to your God-Self, which will direct that energy along the appropriate channels. Know that she can only provide the opening for healing and that you must be willing to rise above your belief system, psychological or mental framework, and surrender to your God-Self to effect a change.

"Also know that this charge of energy will affect neural processors and other kinds of modern 'enhancement' devices or tissues, but you should not be alarmed for we are all one in our totality, whatever our makeup. If your desire is to be healed, you must surrender and allow all parts of yourself, be they natural or enhanced, to be adjusted by the flow of this energy. If you come here to heal your cancer or heart disease, you must be willing to come away with your IQ lowered or raised, or your psychological adaptation altered, depending on what the God-Self so deems.

"Maria will prepare herself, and when she is ready to receive you, please stand up and form a line in the center aisle. If you're unable to stand, allow your mate or surrogate to stand in place, and when they're called, our ushers will assist you and bring you forward. Also know, that this charge of energy may temporarily render you unconscious, but again don't be alarmed, for most this will be experienced as a brief bout of dizziness. But, know that if needed, we have a medical doctor present to assist you. But unlike most medical treatments by drugs or invasive surgery, this is the energy that animates every cell and organ and is the intelligence that directs the body and knows better than any doctor what is needed to affect your healing.

"Thank you and bless you and may you all be healed."

As the woman stepped over to a waiting chair, sat down, closed her eyes and began to mediate, a hush descended on the chapel. I watched Maria Fria and noticed the glow of energy that seemed to surround her, and looked up to see if there were any lighting fixtures that would account for it, but saw none. I must say that the prologue and set up of this healing by the young preacher or facilitator were very effective. While we had planned for Brenda to step forward, I wondered, given this introduction and her previous trepidation, if she had changed her mind. I turned and she looked at me and shook her head. She wasn't about to "surrender" to her God-Self. As the line formed, I hesitated and then started to stand up to take my place; Brenda, or was it Jean, grabbed my hand.

"It's all right, Brenda," I whispered to her. "I'm ready to accept my healing."

"Well, I do hope it enhances your creativity and doesn't destroy it," she added with a wry smile.

I smiled at her and stood up, circled around the row of chairs and took my place in line. There were two fairly disabled attendees and stepping aside, I watched their healings and reactions and was fairly impressed that after their initial dizziness, they walked away and appeared to be much better off. Many fainted and slumped down in the "receiver's" chair, that had been set up in front of Fria to facilitate the movement of her hands, acting like a funnel to channel the energy from above, down into the body of the receiver.

Then, it was my turn. I stepped up, bowed my head, and as I lifted my gaze, stared directly into Maria's and was struck by the love emanating from those dark eyes, and as I sat down I was actually looking forward to this transmission. After several moments, I felt an intense warmth spread from the top of my head downward. It first stopped and seemed to collect around my neural processor for a moment, but without any disruption or enhancement, or so I felt at the moment, but it did seem to affect other areas of the brain before it moved throughout my body, jumping from what I assumed was one chakra center to the next. Again I could sense it stop and collect around organs or exterior parts that needed "alignment," like my right wrist which had been broken as a child, and then move on. What seemed like an hour was only a minute or two before two hands grabbed my arms and lifted me from the chair. After a moment of disorientation, I was able to walk over and sit down in my second-row seat. I remained silent for at least five minutes as this peaceful feeling settled in.

Finally, a nervous voice said, "Please say something, Lewis. So I know you're all right."

I turned and stared at Brenda and the look on my face must have alarmed her. "I'm fine, Brenda. It was quite … exhilarating, really."

We sat there for another half hour as some of her devotees also stepped forward, exchanged greetings, and sat down for their healings. And then, it was over. The facilitator had some closing words. Maria Fria stood up, smiled at the group, and slowly walked back to the side room from which she had entered earlier in the evening. In silence, everyone stood up and walked down the aisles and out. Unlike church services I had attended in the borny village that I and Emma had infiltrated, the "preacher" did not greet us as we walked out nor draw strangers into conversations or light interrogations.

We strolled off heading back toward the center of town. "I don't know about you, but I'm starving," Brenda said.

I was a little distracted and still not completely back in my body—as my research that day had informed me. "Yeah, I could eat something."

"Are you sure, Lewis? You look and sound quite out of it. Maybe we should just go back to the hotel and let you rest for a while."

"No, the noise and activity should help 'bring me around.'"

"Well, I think we should go back to the same restaurant, and see if we're 'approached' again."

"Yes, that's a good plan," I added, half-heartedly. I wasn't really focused on my government mission, but on this new sense of … integration, I guess you could call it, and what it portended for me and my assignment.

Chapter Seven

19.

When I woke up the next morning, I was surprised that I didn't remember having a dream. I figured that after the "healing," and being in such close proximity to Fria, that I'd have another marathon dream-share with her, or if it were only my subconscious activity, it would be processing the interaction. Was I disappointed, I wondered? Before I could consider this feeling, I found Brenda packing overnight bags for us. I just stared at her.

She noticed that I had woken up and looked back at me. "Well, welcome back." I nodded but didn't answer, still pretty much in a fog.

"We're going to Phoenix?" I asked.

She stopped packing her bag and stepped over to me, her face etched with concern. "Our orders are to bring you in after your first healing with Fria, for a checkup."

I'm usually a little quicker in the morning; I wondered if this meant anything. "Yeah, but we just got here. I think we should hang around a little longer. We might spook them otherwise."

Brenda shook her head and stared at me. "We're definitely going. I called Musgrave and he agreed. Get up and get ready. Twenty minutes."

I didn't like being ordered around and especially when I felt so mellow, but I also didn't want to fight with her. She had operational control for now, and I was after all just a soldier. "But, we're leaving the rest of our stuff and coming back tomorrow?"

"I've rented the room for a month, but when or if we come back is up to Musgrave."

I crawled out of bed and headed for the shower. Brenda watched me as I stripped down and opened the stall door. The hot water was soothing, it was slowly bringing me around. The door opened and a naked Brenda stepped inside.

"I've got a better way to wake you up." It didn't take long for my body to respond to her touch, and while some part of me enjoyed the vigorous early-morning sex, as I always did, another aspect just watched. I had never experienced such a split perspective, watching myself perform or act from a distance. It definitely had something to do with this healing, or whatever you would call it, but did I really want to tell them?

Before we left the room, Brenda did one more circuit, to make sure nothing sensitive was left behind for prying eyes. In the lobby the desk clerk waved and told us to have a good trip. The car, which we hadn't used in a couple days, had a light coating of sand, which we easily brushed off. I was actually hungry, but Brenda insisted that we wait until we reached Prescott, which was only thirty miles down the road, to eat breakfast.

As I drove down the hill and then onto the two-lane highway heading west, Brenda kept an eye on any cars pulling out and following us, or those ahead of us that were driving slower and could be waiting for us to catch up. I knew the protocol, but seemed less interested in maintaining "operational integrity." I figured that Fria wouldn't have anybody following us, when she could keep tabs in more subtle ways or so I assumed—if she were so inclined, which I doubted. Seemed like this "exchange" of energy gave me a window into her as well, and I now felt a lot more comfortable about the assignment and less fearful of her. Of course, Brenda and especially Musgrave might consider that attitude part of my brainwashing, but even in psychological warfare, a little transference was encouraged to "get to know the enemy."

We ate at a diner in Prescott, which like many smaller towns had been shrunk down to its inner core, where sidewalks could be placed under environ screens to allow people to walk about and shop like they did in the pre-UV-collapse era, or at least in sunny areas like the Southwest. The diner was a chain, and the food was not nearly as authentic as our Mexican breakfast in

Tucumcari, but the blandness seemed to suit Brenda just fine. I wasn't in a very talkative mood and scanned the local newspaper while we ate.

"So, are you mad or something, Lewis?"

I glanced up from the newspaper. "No. Just feeling mellow and kind of quiet."

"Well, you certainly don't seem to be yourself this morning," Brenda said.

I smiled. "And that's a bad thing?" I joked.

"Yeah, I thought we were meshing well. That I was liking you the more I got to know you."

"But, not now?"

"Well, maybe this is just another side of you I'll need to explore." She picked up a section of the newspaper and made a show of burying her head in it.

"Or, maybe we just need to learn other ways of communicating, dear."

Brenda laughed with a huff. "No way I'm letting that witch 'heal' me; not after what I'm seeing."

I put the newspaper down and looked at her fondly. "I did enjoy our shower this morning."

This was more to her liking. "Good. We'll put it on our wake-up routine."

After breakfast we headed north, instead of south toward Phoenix, until we reached Interstate 40, west of Flagstaff. The protocol was for us to drive up to the Grand Canyon as a tourist trip, spend the night there, and then drive back through Flagstaff and down Interstate 17 to Phoenix. This would give us plenty of time to lose any tails, not that we had spotted any yet.

As we got closer, I'll have to say I was fairly excited. I had never been out West, and needless to say had never seen the Grand Canyon except on vid clips. Brenda was again oblivious to the beautiful scenery and focused on her game cassette. As we drove up to the park entrance and paid, I pulled the car over to the Welcome Center.

"Why are you stopping here?" Brenda asked. "I thought we'd go straight to the hotel."

"I want to pick up maps and talk to the rangers about where we can get the best views."

"You aren't actually thinking about touring the place?" Brenda said, having set down her portable after viewing the hotel's website.

"Of course. I've always wanted to come here, see one of the natural wonders of the world."

Brenda added, "Oh, Lewis. You can be so … antiquated at times. The hotel has a viewing theater, with live camera feeds of every nook and cranny of the big hole, without exposure to the elements."

"Well, you stay in the car, and I'll get the maps and drop you off at the hotel afterward."

"Well, dear, as much as I would love to let you go traipsing off on your own, until you've been checked out and cleared, you're stuck with me."

Brenda followed me into the center and took a bathroom break while I viewed the wall pictures and collected maps of the area. I was disappointed that they had long ago discontinued the mule runs from the rim down to the floor of the canyon, due to UV exposure, which was hard to shield against in confined open spaces like ledge trails. But there were a series of safe viewing shelters along the rim, and you could drive from one to the other. Since it was mid-afternoon, I decided to take the tour before heading over to the hotel. Brenda sat in the car but did call up descriptions and histories from the Internet at each stop, to fill me in while we drove around. This was so typical of us moderns: most preferring a mental experience over tactical contact, even if it was one stage removed, in the viewing shelters, from an actual experience of the natural world.

At one point I got frustrated with the remote access and

walked over to the railing and gazed out over the wide expanse of red buttes with their serrated edges and deep canyons in shadow. I then found an old mule path with its clear cliff drop and hiked down a hundred yards. After a while I could sense Brenda's panic, so I soon scampered back up to the rim.

She had gotten out of the car and gone into the shelter and now stepped outside. "Lewis, wasn't that dangerous? I mean, there aren't any handrails and the wind can be treacherous."

I stared at her for a moment before I realized that her concern wasn't personal but operational. She had been told to keep me in view at all times until I was cleared. As we walked back to the car, I had to shake my head. This Fria woman really spooked them.

20.

We drove to the Maswik Lodge on the south rim of the Canyon. The rustic cabins hadn't changed much since the nineteenth century, but a massive opaque UV dome now covered the entire area, with a tinted green hue from years of UV bombardment. This seemed appropriate, since the whole natural world was now seen from behind tinted glasses or shields of one sort or another. At some point it dawned on me that our roundabout route to the Grand Canyon was as much to check the effects of the natural world on me and my "sensitivities" as it was to shake any surveillance. Maybe there was a correlation here.

We checked in, swept the cabin for listening devices or bugs, but didn't find any. At dinner we kept an eye on any possible intruders, but nobody caught our attention. They were just a typical group of tourists, mostly elderly, who seem to yearn for this natural world contact more than the younger moderns with their hi-tech absorption in artificial worlds.

The restaurant and its fare were fairly typical, but the huge overhead screen with its live picture of the night sky was truly spectacular. I had picked a seat with the best angle, and Brenda one with her back to it. Since there was no need for pretense or to make an impression, we could settle back into our own selves, but we discovered there wasn't much to talk about, or any great correlation between us outside of the mission.

"Getting tired of me already, Alan?" she asked. This was a question that Sherry had also posed not long ago.

"No, dear. It's just that I'm more affected by the natural world; feel kind of expanded for a moment, and not as concerned with the minutiae."

"Which you feel I'm only concerned with?" she asked.

I looked down from the screen to my consort of sorts, I guess you could say. Staring at her, I could see just how emotionally fragile she was and in need of reinforcement. I liked her and certainly enjoyed our sexual dynamic, but we didn't have much in common otherwise. I glanced around the room and noted the always ubiquitous surveillance cameras. "Seems like a conversation for the road."

She glanced up to the ceiling and then back down at me and smiled. "That's what I like about you, dear … your cognizance."

"Well, let's pay the bill and let me cognize you back in the room."

"Oooh, that sounds delicious."

Back in our cabin, with a fire going, we made love on the rug in front of the fireplace, me using the brickwork at its base for leverage, with my response more vigorous than expected. Afterward Brenda fell asleep in my arms lying there and seemed content for the moment. As had been the case, the sexual contact between us seemed to form a barrier to Fria's outreach to me in my dreams, or again was it just my libido getting its fill. The contact made during my healing session seemed to reveal someone without the kind of guile our side had assumed. Was it just my subconscious working out its issues? But Brenda was right; I was acting a little off, and wondered myself whether I had been overly affected by this "healing."

The next morning we drove back through Flagstaff, taking Interstate 17 all the way to Phoenix. The previous night's question was left hanging in the air as neither of us felt inclined to explore it. The Metrocenter Mall bordered the Interstate and we pulled off the highway and into the parking garage. Like many shopping malls, this center had been greatly expanded after the environmental deterioration into a small city in itself, with apartment complexes, grocery stores, health clubs, etc. under one domed environ roof. It even had a monorail to take you from one sector to the next.

I accompanied Brenda as we shopped, or she shopped for more Southwest clothes for us. At one point we moseyed over to an electronics shop, with all the modern devices for home protection and surveillance, besides all manner of other electronic gadgets. Since one of their top sellers was a device to knock out electronic probing and video surveillance, we called ahead and all surveillance of the store was temporarily blocked as we strolled inside. After the manager showed us several items at the back of the store, the curtain parted and we slipped into the back room, walked down a hallway, and took a private elevator to the basement.

A junior field agent named Rob Sanchez took us back to a small conference room where Musgrave was waiting for us. There were two more experts, or so I assumed, flanking him on either side.

"Ah, the prodigal pair returns," Musgrave said with a smirk.

Brenda immediately switched back to her "Jean" persona and tensed up, as if we had done something wrong. "Which means what, sir?"

"Calm down, Whatley. It's just a figure of speech, since this is the Wild West and your assignment isn't exactly pedestrian." Jean forced a smile and took a deep breath. Musgrave turned to me. "So, Alan. You stepped forward and had a 'healing,' I understand."

"Yes. We had planned for Jean to test it first, but ... seemed like a waste of time, since I was planted there to gauge Fria's effects on me, or I should say, my neural processor."

"Well, you have operational latitude. So, tell about your reception in town."

I proceeded to fill in Musgrave on our hotel, the restaurant where we made first contact, and the library where I was first approached. This ruffled Jean a bit since I hadn't shared this flirtation with her, and she tried to make it an issue. Musgrave waved her off, wanting me to continue with my assessment. I moved on to the healing ceremony—that grabbed everybody's attention. I gave a detailed report of what happened there and my own personal experience.

"Excellent. Of course, we'll download the recording from both of your neural processors, but this incursion is as much about your personal reaction as it is the nuts and bolts of what occurred." I nodded my head. "Don't worry, Alan. Besides the testing, we'll conduct a more thorough debriefing, including a psyche evaluation with Klaus."

"But he's not here, I take it."

Musgrave looked curiously at me. "No, Alan. It'll be a remote session."

"What exactly are you looking for?" Jean asked.

Musgrave smiled. "Tell her, Alan."

"Well, they've certainly checked out the effects of Fria's spiritual healings, via her students, on other subjects or plants, but probably never one with a high degree of ... integration, if I may say so."

"Exactly," he said.

"Which will tell us what?" Jean asked. She was definitely out of the loop on the science end of this operation but didn't like being left in the dark.

I looked over at Musgrave, who nodded his head. I turned to Jean. "Harkum, the accountant who went berserk and killed three people, had a great deal of anxiety and it appears that his state of mind short-circuited his neural processor and opened a floodgate that led to his rage."

"And you're quite the opposite, I take it, and they want to gauge how it affects or expands you?" she asked.

I nodded my head.

Jean turned to Musgrave, "Then why don't you just test a Buddhist monk or something?"

"Haven't found one with a neural processor, and the idea is exposure to this particular healer's energy since it is so pervasive, and with someone who can better gauge its effects," Musgrave said.

"Which may give them an idea of how it would affect larger groups of people, if this healing modality is generally applied by individuals," I added.

Musgrave's eyes narrowed at this description. He turned to the mirror on the wall across from us. "Delete that statement from the record." He turned to me. "We need to keep focused on the task at hand, Alan, and rein in your personal speculation."

I nodded my head; Jean shook hers in consternation. What was that about? She must've asked herself.

Musgrave opened a folder. "Okay, before your testing, let's run through some operational directives."

"Okay." I assumed they figured that the testing might further space me out and they wanted to go over details now, so Jean could drive us back tomorrow. It was hard to keep my focus; I kept thinking about my interview with Klaus.

21.

The first test in their makeshift clinic was a remote examination of my neural processor, which they could test separately from my normal neo-cortex reactions. However, they had to redo the test several times; I assumed there was more integration of my processor with the neocortex than they had expected and separating the two feedback loops was difficult. I was then given a battery of IQ tests, emotional response tests, and finally an intuitive or psychic test. No doubt its inclusion was Dr. Klaus' brainchild, if I can use that term, which seemed counterintuitive here. The testing took some three hours; at which point I was given a half-hour of sleep time to clear my mind for the next round. I had no trouble falling off to sleep.

Afterward I ate lunch alone; apparently they didn't want any contact between me and the others, including Jean, until after my interview with Klaus. I was now ushered into a living room setting in which one wall was a huge screen; after I got settled on the sofa and someone brought me some water, the screen blipped on and there was Dr. Klaus in his New York office.

"Alan, hear you've had an interesting start to our little adventure."

"Well, I've made an intensive first contact, if that's what you mean."

Klaus gave me one of his Cheshire cat smiles; this was appropriate since in this case he had my test results and did know more than me. "Okay, Alan, run me through the actual healing experience. Close your eyes and relive it, if you will."

I sat back in the chair and closed my eyes. "She put her hands on the top of my head, or just above it, and after a while I felt this warm current of energy spread across the top of my head, and then seep down into the cranial cavity. At first it seemed to collect around my neural processor, or that's what it felt like. I do know its location, unlike others you've tested, and so I think I can make that statement. I didn't feel affected in any way, and then it moved on to other areas of the brain but seemed to affect them. This I felt. Then, it leaped from one chakra center to the next, or that's what I assumed they were, radiating out from each one, until it left my body through the bottom of my feet."

I opened my eyes and Klaus was staring at me, his right hand stroking his chin, thinking intently, or so it seemed. "Excellent description, Alan. Almost worth all the effort put into this op on its own."

I didn't know how to respond to this praise, so I just nodded my head.

Klaus looked down at his glass table computer screen, no doubt reviewing the test results. "Normally, I wouldn't share test results with a subject, but in this case you're an active collaborator in this venture, and frankly we need you to monitor your own reactions in the field, since it's not something we can safely do without detection in this case."

This sounded promising; I did want to know how this energy would affect me but needed feedback to get an overview. "Okay, I understand, and I assume this would be on a 'need to know' basis."

"Yes, Alan. Your new security agreement would cover it, but you're not to share this aspect of your assignment with Whatley or even Musgrave. I'll keep him informed." Keeping Musgrave out of the loop was unusual and made me wonder who was running this operation, since Klaus was from the private sector, or so I had always assumed.

I instinctively looked at the mirror on the side wall, which was no doubt one-way and wondered if we were being monitored. I turned back to Klaus. He shook his head to indicate I wasn't.

"Your intuitive test scores are quite high, much more than your entry test score of several years ago. Whether this has been accumulative, or a spike due to this contact, we don't know. It's not a test we administer on a yearly basis like some. I assume the latter."

"I think that's safe to say."

"So, you've noticed a difference, or heightened awareness, I should say."

"Yes. Nothing too dramatic, but you could say that."

"So, Alan, this is the question. Does this energy integrate

cognitive-intuitive functionality across the board, especially in regard to neural processors, or just in isolated advanced cases like yours?"

"You mean ..."

"Alan, I think it best that you keep your speculation to yourself, as Musgrave said earlier."

"So I assume you'll want to expose Jean as well, to gauge her reaction as a comparison."

Klaus nodded his head. "One reason she was chosen. Although we have readings from others at her level; she's been 'conditioned' and we want to gauge the reaction."

That was interesting and made me wonder just how that was done or to what extent.

"Well, I hope you're telling her, not me."

"She's being informed as we speak."

I shook my head, as if trying to shake off her coming reaction to this twist in the assignment.

"Don't worry, Alan. She's a trouper." Klaus glanced down at his computer screen for a moment, then back to me. "We'll want you to monitor your intuitive reactions or progress. I mean, reports on dreams, intuitive flashes, heightened sensitivity and also cognitive functionality or its lack." I nodded my head. "Normally we'd have you make notes in your neural processor and download them, but given the heightened psychic reach of our subject, we'll provide you with a secure recorder for your notes."

"Okay. I can do that, and I assume I'm to keep this operational detail from Whatley, so as not to contaminate her own log."

"Yes, Alan. Perceptive as always." He smiled, as if making a mental note to himself. "I look forward to your progress reports, and if I may say, be careful Alan. This is a hazardous mission, more so than you can ever imagine."

He let this last statement hang in the air for a moment, and then the screen went blank. Talk about a counterintuitive break in the flow of our conversation. Maybe Klaus found himself stepping over some operational line with this last warning, and this was the only way he could reestablish his detachment, for himself and others.

When I left the interrogation room, Jean was waiting for me. She was definitely tense and preoccupied, but soon her lead role took over and we quickly left the clinic as previously instructed. We took the elevator up to the electronics store, picked up our packages, including I assumed, my recorder, and headed out into the mall. We had reservations at a hotel/spa northeast of Scottsdale in the desert and so we didn't linger here. As we drove east from Phoenix, Jean's "Brenda" persona took over again, maybe a self-preservation mechanism.

"Well, Lewis, I certainly hope this spa has private hot tubs and some good tequila. I definitely need to get drunk and fucked good." She looked over at me and blinked her eyes. "But in no particular order, dear."

"Sounds like what the doctor ordered," I said in a rather off-the-cuff tone. Brenda, however, gave me a penetrating look, as if I had been given separate instructions from hers. I reached over and took her hand. "Why don't you call ahead and reserve that private hot tub."

She put her other hand over ours. "Lewis, you can be so thoughtful," she snickered. She pulled her hands away, picked up her portable, and made the reservation.

The hotel/spa was located in the desert and our room with its balcony had a spectacular view of the chaparral and the McDowell Mountain range to the east. It was after 7:00 when we pulled in, and already the daytime temperature had cooled off and would become cooler still in the desert at night. We had a fast meal in the hotel dining room, since our hot tub reservation was for 8:30. What was really great was that the private hot tub rooms all had views of the desert and its night sky with its starry Milky Way band. As soon as we got settled in the tub, Brenda caught me staring at the sky.

"So, Lewis, is this what it's going to be—stargazing and not body gazing?"

I looked down at Brenda, her lovely breasts floating on the bubbling water, which immediately grabbed my attention. We made out in the tub, and then I sat on one of the steps in shallow water, while Brenda sat on me and we made slow passionate love, her getting all my attention. Afterward she sat across from me in the tub, so she could see my facial expression.

"So, I take it that Klaus told you about me having to get a healing from Fria."

"Yes. They want comparative test results to check."

"My low readings with your high ones," she said with a bite to her words.

"Why assume the worst? It's your own individual reaction, whatever it may be."

Brenda stared at me, and I met her gaze. "Well, you're more comfortable with your feelings and I've expended a lot of effort to 'manage' mine for career and operational purposes."

"Trust me. Integrating them will work out better for you than repressing them, and make you more competent."

"Unless, like Harkum, I go on a rampage."

I shook my head. "Won't happen. Two different cases. You're fairly well adjusted; he wasn't; it should only work better for you."

Brenda reached over and kissed me. "That's what I like about you, Lewis. Always the optimist." She rolled over and started kissing my chest, moving downward. "Or one of the things I like about you."

Chapter Eight

22.

We drove back to Jerome the next morning. Brenda was unusually quiet and played her game console most of the way. We had eaten a large breakfast before heading out, so this was going to be a port-to-port trip. As we approached Jerome, her level of anxiety seemed to increase and she started up a conversation.

"So what do you think our next move is?" she asked, probably hoping it wasn't us going to their next service and her getting a "healing."

I felt my way through a response. "Seems like they'll contact us under some pretext. They're going to want a one-on-one with me and Fria so she can work her 'magic' on me, if Musgrave's scenario is correct."

"Which you doubt?" she asked.

"Let's just say there could be another explanation and she's not what we think, or at least her motivations aren't."

Brenda paused. I could tell she was making a mental note in her processor log, and this reminded me to be less open with her about "my speculation," as Musgrave termed it.

"So you don't have the same trepidations now?" she asked.

"I don't believe in mind-control, or I should say, the garden variety. And, during the healing, it seems like I got as much of a handle on her as she on me."

"Did they give you any drugs to close down invasive avenues?"

I smiled; she really was spooked. "The whole idea is borny on borny, or my borny side at least." She nodded her head, but her body was as tense as a board. I reached over and grabbed her hand. "Don't worry, Brenda. I'll just quote some passages from Hargrove's books and bore her shitless."

This did seem to mollify her somewhat, or it at least allowed her to more easily slip into her Brenda persona. "Your readings always turn me on, dear." Then she caught herself. "Well, let's hope it doesn't have the same effect on her."

"'The sun slipping behind the ancient volcanic rock affected those in its shadow, drawing out their own shadow selves, releasing them to the coming night and the havoc it would hasten.'"

Brenda started to laugh. "Yeah, I see what you mean." She leaned over and grabbed my arm, snuggling up against me. "I've grown quite fond of you, Lewis, and I'd hate to lose you."

I didn't know how to respond to this expression, and so I just smiled—given that my own feelings toward her were more ambivalent.

When we got to our room at The Sliding Sands, there was a message left on our room phone recorder from the Center for Planetary Healing—Fria's umbrella organization. A Ms. June Caldwell asked that I call the Center in the morning, to schedule a follow-up for my healing. Brenda was going to say something, but I took out my bug-detector and swept the room first, then shook my head.

She now told me, "That was pretty intuitive of you."

"Not really. What else were they going to do? Wait until we came to one of their weekly services, or invite us to tea."

That night, since the quick two-day trip had worn us both out, we just went to sleep without any sexual conjoining. I did have a dream of Maria Fria wearing a business suit and conducting a job interview with me. When I woke in the middle of the night and went out to the balcony, I realized that this wasn't an intrusive dream but one summoned up from my subconscious, which again made me wonder about the other dreams of her. I remember reading somewhere about compensatory dreams: you have a conscious attitude and call up a dream about a situation that is quite the opposite to give you a more balanced perspective, not that either one is literally true. As I looked out over the plateau at the surrounding desert revealed in the moonlight, I realized that I had figured this next encounter would be more insidious or undermining, when it could be just a friendly inquiry from a naïve spiritual woman, just interested in the welfare of others.

In the morning I called the center and asked for June. The woman from the library picked up the call. "Oh yes, Lewis Hargrove. You're not the novelist, are you?"

"Yes, I am."

"How interesting. Maria loves your work." I didn't respond. "Well, we'd like to do a follow-up to your healing. Just pretty standard stuff: how you felt afterward and any changes you experienced."

"We can't do that over the phone?"

"We prefer to do it in person. One of our healers will conduct the interview and be able to scan your energy body which can be just as productive."

"Okay, I understand."

"Would eleven o'clock this morning be all right for you?" she asked.

"That's fine. I take it that the Center is in the brick building behind the church?"

"Yes. See you then." She paused, then added, "Oh, and we prefer that you don't eat ahead of time."

"Okay."

Brenda listened in on the conversation. "Well, I'm going along, even if I have to wait in some reception area."

"I agree. Harder for them to waylay me, if that's on their mind."

We showered separately and got dressed, and while Brenda had a breakfast croissant and coffee in the dining room, I just drank some grape juice. It was sunny but cold and the UV quotient was quite high, so we wore large hats, gloves, scarfs and sunglasses. At the Center, June Caldwell met us in the small lobby. June was small and delicate with clear blue eyes. She was curious about Brenda's presence but was very accommodating. I introduced her as my companion.

"Well, the interview of course will be private, but since you're being so wonderful, why don't we treat Brenda to a therapeutic massage. I could check and see if Claude is available. Best hands in the West."

"So he's a massage therapist and not a healer?" Brenda asked.

"Massage can be quite healing, as you no doubt know, but he works strictly with a body modality."

"Well, that would be just great. Thank you."

"If you'll wait here, I'll set everything up." We sat on a nearby sofa with a red-and-black striped Native American pattern, while June went over to the receptionist. I instinctively tried to gauge if the sofa, like Klaus's chairs, had sensors but couldn't detect anything. Guess my concern was kind of presumptuous. They probably used much more subtle means. June came back and gathered me, telling Brenda that she was scheduled for 11:30, and that Jill, the receptionist, would take her to the massage studio.

June escorted me down a long hallway with offices on either side, with designations like Outreach, Magazine Subscription, Membership, etc. This was a worldwide ministry of sorts, so this made perfect sense. We exited the building through a back door, walked through a clear-plastic connecting tunnel and entered what appeared to be a private residence. We walked through a kitchen and to a living room, similar in some ways to the one in my dream, but definitely not picture perfect—I could easily have seen it in a magazine photo spread, or maybe it was something I dreamed on my own.

Musgrave would say this confirmed his suspicions, but I wondered. What was the same was the spectacular view of the surrounding desert, if from a different perspective. What grabbed my attention, however, was Maria Fria sitting on a futon sofa. Apparently I was right about them arranging a one-on-one between us.

"Oh, Ms. Fria. I wasn't expecting to … see you. Are you conducting the interview?" I asked rather ingeniously.

"Yes. Please have a seat, Lewis, and call me Maria." She pointed to a sofa across from hers. "Thank you, June. That will be all."

June smiled, bowed her head, and hurried out.

"Would you like something to drink?"

"Water would be fine."

Maria pushed a button on her arm console, spoke into a speakerphone, and had two glasses of spring water brought out to us. The server was an Anglo in her late twenties. I could see Fria watching my reaction.

After the woman left, she said, "You didn't expect an Indian or Mexican servant, I hope."

"I didn't expect anybody, least of all you," I added with a feigned smile.

"Well, your healing was quite curious, and I wanted to conduct this interview myself."

"How so?"

"You have a neural processor, but the energy just bypassed it. That's fairly unique in my experience," she said.

This was of some interest or concern to me as well. "What usually happens?"

She gazed at me and smiled. "It makes adjustments of sorts, since they're composed of brain cells and are susceptible to … energy, like any organ."

"'Adjustments' covers a lot of possibilities."

Fria stared at me more intently, and it felt like she was gathering a remote sensor reading, like one of the apparatuses in my world.

"You're the novelist … Lewis Hargrove?" she asked.

"Yes."

She smiled. "I always thought it was a pseudonym."

"Well, it is, but I had introduced myself to Brenda as such and just kept using it ... or for now."

Maria nodded her head. "So, given the messianic focus of your novels, you would have a clinical interest in healing modalities."

"I do."

She smiled, and it was like one of Klaus' Cheshire cat smiles. "Well, I guess an ... exchange of information is only fair." She closed her eyes, as if she were channeling the response, and then opened them. "As you know, neural processors are meant to increase one's intelligence by the greatly accelerated firing of its neurons, with the help of high levels of neurotransmitters from drug conditioning and the greater plasticity of its synapses. And this can create a mirroring effect in the neocortex and accelerate it for the same heightened results."

I nodded my head. "Very textbook correct ... I would imagine."

"Well, I did go to college, and this subject was covered, and it is of interest to me," she said.

"But ..."

"But, like the neocortex and its evolution, which supplanted the reptilian brain and modulates some of its impulses, it can suppress other functions, some of which, like intuition, are needed for greater awareness of self and one's connection to others and to the divine, if that doesn't offend your sensibilities."

I shook my head.

"And, of course, the feeling function, which according to Carl Jung allows us to ascertain proper values."

"And the adjustments?" I asked.

"Well, the energy can slow down the neuron firing or redirect it, or spread out the effect to include other areas of the brain, for instance."

"And in my case?"

"Well, leaving it alone but affecting other brain centers, could mean that an integrative process had already begun to spread out the effect and accelerate other functions like intuition, which should be more heightened."

"Which I've experienced since the healing."

"Excellent." She smiled. "Would you mind if I conduct my own examination?"

This sounded particularly dicey given my mission, but I did need to engage her. "Another healing or strictly an examination?"

Maria sat back in her chair and stared at me with a kind of eerie focus that made me feel ... exposed. "Why all the suspicion?"

I tried to settle down my overreaction. "Well, I'm a little paranoid, which infuses my fiction but does complicate personal relationships."

"I can assure you my intent is totally benign. I only wish to help you with your ... adjustment, but I can only do as much as you allow."

"So, it will further adjust me?" I asked.

"Given that this energy has its own ... mind, as we say. I only intend to examine you, but adjustments might be made."

"Okay. I trust you, Maria."

Fria stood up, walked over and around to the back of my chair. She placed her hands over the top of my head, and I could feel a less-pervasive energy move through my cranial cavity and this time spread through my neocortex. It was a pleasant sensation, and then I passed out.

23.

I must have quickly dropped down to the REM state, because I had an instantaneous dream. I had walked to the edge of the Cleopatra Plateau and jumped off, but instead of falling I spread my arms and flew out across the desert like a hawk on the wind streams. It was quite exhilarating. I then turned back, saw Maria standing on the edge of the cliff and glided back and landed next to her. I woke up. I wasn't groggy at all, and looked across from me to see Maria sitting on the sofa.

"That was interesting," she said.

"What happened?" I asked, trying not to sound too suspicious.

"I just laid my hands over your head to read the energy flow within the brain cavity and you just … well, you didn't pass out as much as altered your state of consciousness."

"I had a dream," I said, which probably broke protocol, but I wanted to understand what had just transpired. She gave me a questioning look, and I told her the dream.

"Well, I don't think it was a dream, but an astral projection."

I just stared at her; I knew what they were, but for me to have one would be strange, even alarming. "And it wasn't anything you did?"

"No, Lewis. I just added a bit more energy to the mix, and you did the rest."

I was dumbfounded, to say the least.

"I assume nothing like this has happened to you before?" she asked.

I closed my eyes and tried to remember anything similar. "The morning after the healing, I woke up and … engaged in something, and found myself watching me doing it, as if from a distance."

"You were making love?."

I stared at her, wondering if this was an inappropriate inquiry.

"Lewis, do you want to get to the bottom of this, or not?"

"Yes, in the shower."

"I asked because a split perspective, or what we call the 'watcher,' is a 6th chakra occurrence, as is astral projection, and can be triggered by an upsurge of Kundalini energy."

"Well, I'm not really into mysticism, so it's all techno-speak to me." I also had to wonder if her presence behind me hadn't "triggered" this incident.

"Your mind or ego may not be, but you're so much more than that, Lewis. And you just got your wake-up call."

I didn't like where this conversation was headed. "Is there anything else we need to talk about?" I asked.

"No. I wanted to see how fast this integration was happening, and I got my answer."

"Well, I'm not sure I'm at all pleased with this development."

Maria stood up. "Nobody ever is, Lewis. I certainly wasn't, but then I was much younger and less fixed than you at the time."

June appeared at the door seemingly without a summons. "So, if the interview is over, I'll take you back to the lobby. I believe Brenda has finished up by now," June said.

"Thanks." I turned back to Maria who remained on her side of the sofa ensemble. I wasn't really up for a hug. "It's been interesting, Ms. Fria. I hope we stay around a little longer and can catch another service."

"I look forward to it, Lewis." She paused, and then with a mischievous smile, added, "Happy flying."

I didn't reply and couldn't wait to get out of there. I wasn't sure what had actually happened: her story of my astral projection, or if it was a dream implant, but I needed to get outside this vortex—to borrow a term from the Sedona bornies. I found a rosy-cheek Brenda in the lobby, and before June could bid us goodbye, I grabbed her by the arm and hurried us both out of the building.

As we walked up the street, Brenda pulled her arm free. "You're hurting me, Lewis."

"Sorry. I just needed to get out of there."

She glanced over at me as we walked along. "Can't wait to hear about it."

"Well, let's get off this … rock, and take a spin, so I can get some perspective," I said.

"Lewis, you're in an absolute panic. I don't think you should drive in this state."

"Okay. Then you drive."

"You really do have a death wish." Brenda grabbed my arm and sidled up against me. "I bet I know what would calm you down."

I had to laugh. "I bet. But, I need to get out on the land, as they say, and ground myself."

We got back to the Sliding Sands and packed a few things in case our outing became an overnighter. Brenda drove and I sat back and just enjoyed the landscape. Once we were down the hill and heading west toward Prescott, I felt a lot better. I pulled up a territorial map on my portable and decided we should drive southwest, maybe as far as Yuma, a town whose old West heritage had always intrigued me.

"Well, okay, but we can't cross over into Mexico. Musgrave would have a fit," Brenda said.

I nodded my head.

"Anyway, he'll probably get pissed off about you not updating him immediately." She paused. "And what exactly did happen, if I may ask?"

I didn't know how much I wanted to share with Brenda, not only about my astral projection experience, if that's what it was, but my sense that Maria Fria really didn't know me and had not remote-viewed us and knew nothing of my real identity and our intention. This suggested a scenario of my being setup by Musgrave and the FBI, Klaus and whoever else was in on this sting operation, including Ms. Jean Whatley.

"You were saying," Brenda said, as we drove into Prescott and stopped at a diner for lunch.

"I'm not holding back, but need to let it all settle in before I can get a handle on what transpired and how to tell you about it."

As we walked into the diner, she nodded her head. "Well, maybe a good meal will help."

Well, the meal wasn't that good, but again Brenda again seemed to like the blander Mexican food here but that was the least of my concerns. "What do I tell Brenda" was first on my list? Finally, I decided to give her a sanitized version of what occurred. I told her that I allowed Maria Fria to examine me and that I blacked out for a few minutes and had a weird dream.

"And you don't think you should update Musgrave and his team now?" she asked.

"Of course, but I don't want to get pulled in before I figure this out, and maybe initiate more contact."

Brenda just stared at me. "I guess if I insisted, or pulled rank, you wouldn't go along with me anyway."

I smiled. "Trust me on this, Brenda. I don't need more readings; I need to monitor my reaction over a period of time, and if anything weird starts to happen, I'll call it in." I started to eat again.

"Well, this contingency was covered, whether you know it or not." She paused while I put down my burrito. "Musgrave told me in Phoenix to cut you some slack and let you play out your contact with Fria, and not run to Mama at every turn."

"Nice of them to inform me."

"I think this goes beyond that, but unless you get really weird, I'll go along ... for now."

"Great. Let's hit the road."

Clearing the air with Brenda was a great relief and driving through the desert and its arid brown landscape really renewed my spirit, in a manner of speaking. After a while, I web-searched the city of Yuma and discovered that the Colorado River ran through on its way into Mexico, and it was still one of the few remaining big rivers in the country, along with the Mississippi. This did it for me; I wanted to be around water and the ocean was too far away, so I convinced Brenda to drive us there.

It took us another four hours, and we pulled into the city just after sunset. I had booked a room at a hotel in the historic district, a beautiful two-story pink adobe structure. Even though it was winter, it was quite warm, somewhere in the mid-80s. Brenda complained, but I told her average daytime temperatures were 120 degrees in the summer. This put it into perspective for her. We checked in, dumped our overnight bags and ate a really good Mexican dinner in the hotel cantina, as they called it. By the time we finished, it was night and we could walk out from under the UV screens, and strolled around the historic district for a while and did the river walk. This really seemed to settle me down. But, when we got back to our hotel room, my portable rang.

"What the hell are you doing in Yuma, Arizona?" asked Musgrave, more bemused than angry.

"Well, how the hell did you spot us? Are we being sat-tracked?"

He explained that, given Yuma's proximity to Mexico, the FBI had license plate scanners at all major roads into and out of the city from the north and south. And we just happened to be on their list.

"Look. We're tired. Let's take this up tomorrow."

Musgrave laughed. "Well, this better be good." I assured him that it would be.

24.

That night, while Brenda slept, I tried to figure out just how much I could tell Musgrave, given my new suspicions, but also knowing that I had already confided in Brenda about the blackout and the dream, which would be shared with him. I just couldn't get a handle on it all, still very confused by my session with Fria and tired from the long drive. I decided to get a goodnight's sleep and figure this out in the morning. Of course, Musgrave called me at 5:00 a.m. to throw me off balance. I answered my portable before it woke up Brenda, and took it into the bathroom.

"So we're going to do this now before I'm fully awake."

"Best time for a debriefing, and you know that."

Yeah, if the subject was under suspicion. He did allow me to put some clothes on and get a bottle of water.

"First of all, why didn't you contact us immediately?"

"We decided on no electronic communication on the hill."

"I mean, once you got on the road."

"It was all a little confusing, and I wanted to get a handle on it before I called it in," I said, stalling for time.

"So, I assume you have a handle on it, so read me in," Musgrave said in an even tone.

I told him about them wanting to interview me about my healing experience, and that Maria Fria had conducted the interview, but didn't disclose all the conversation and made it sound more pedestrian than it was. Musgrave must've of sensed that or had the conversation screened for voice stress patterns.

"What are you holding back?" he asked cuttingly.

I decided to reveal a little more. "I haven't gotten there yet," I said. "So, after the preamble, she tells me that I was called in because the energy she directed at me bypassed my neural processor, which was fairly unique in her experience."

There was a pause at the other end. "Now that's interesting, so she wanted to check you out?"

"Exactly. I allowed her, and I blacked out and had a dream of me flying across the desert like a hawk, and then I woke up."

"That's great. Just what we wanted. I'll pass this along to Klaus." He paused again. "So, how did you leave it?"

"Well, I was a little freaked out and couldn't get out of there fast enough, and so I just left it open: maybe we'd come to another service, if we stayed."

"Let me put you on hold for a minute." I assumed he was consulting with somebody else. "Look, there's an army advance training center in Yuma, used to be for desert warfare during the 2020s, but across the board now. We'll arrange a pickup; I want a specialist there to download this session from your neural processor."

This threw me into dismay. "Sorry, in my panic, I flushed it afterward." There was silence on the other end. "And I've got this pounding headache, which would distort the readings anyway."

There was another long pause at the other end. Finally Musgrave recovered. "That was a real breach of protocol, and I'll have put this on record." He paused. "So, no need to bring you in. Just head back to Jerome, and pick up where you left off."

"Hey, I'm sorry about that. But, you got the gist of it."

"Well, Alan, that would've been for us to decide, not you. Keep us updated." He now broke the connection. He was pissed, and rightly so from his operational point of view, but I just didn't trust him or the mission objectives anymore. I was very curious as how this would play out with Fria, and so I would hang in there with her.

There was a knock on the door. "Lewis, you're not taking a shower without me, are you?" I wondered if she was listening in on the conversation.

I opened the door to find a totally naked Brenda, who pushed me into the shower stall, turned on the water, and got our early-morning riser off to a bang, as the retro expression goes.

Chapter Nine

25.

On the drive back, I talked with Brenda about writing the next Lewis Hargrove novel in Jerome as part of our cover. Musgrave had suggested as much when we first talked about my new identity. Brenda liked the idea and agreed to act as my assistant and spend time at the library researching various subjects to keep her engaged in the project. Since I couldn't just sit down day after day and type something bogus, I decided to actually write a novel. I had studied Hargrove's work and figured we could come up with a plausible concept, based in Arizona and set in Jerome as the starting point. One of my minors in college was English, and at one time I had thought about becoming a writer, so this wasn't a great stretch for me. Since I didn't need to share the story with anyone, and nobody could hack my portable, who would know better. And given its pseudo spiritual premise, I might even interview people at the Center, or Maria Fria herself. What it did was give us an excuse to hang around town and see how this relationship with her would develop and allow me to complete my mission.

To actually engage me at various levels, we hashed out a story on our drive back, with not only a spiritual premise but spy novel of sorts, since this was the world we were both familiar with. So, Lewis Hargrove's next novel would be a cultural-political spy novel. Brenda really entered into the spirit of the project, given her drama studies, and said I should really write it and maybe it would even get published sometime in the future. Like most good cover stories, especially extended ones, it needed to be a mixture of fact and fiction and one that engaged the agents and utilized their own talents and predispositions. Well, needless to say, Brenda was really fascinated by this scenario and when we pulled into town, we headed for the café to further flesh out the story and our strategy.

We sat down and ordered nacho appetizers, deciding we'd take our time before ordering dinner. I thought the story should be set sometime in the past, maybe twenty years ago, so as not to draw on the current spiritual landscape of the city, but more of its dubious past. This would keep us clear of Maria and her followers.

"Well, we'll need to do some research, but I think back then there were a lot of competing groups here, artistic and spiritual, and so my archetypal Hargrove antagonist gets drawn into the rivalries and maybe gets caught between these factions."

"Okay, but what's the spy angle, if that's the subgenre?" Brenda asked.

Our waitress brought our vegetarian nachos, and we waited until she left before turning back to the subject. "Well, Jerome may be the battleground, but it's too claustrophobic a setting for the whole novel, so the story needs to be spread out across the territory."

"Well, don't you usually write about a fight between good and evil?"

"Okay. Well, what if the battle is between the forces of commerce and spirituality. After the economic turndown, the territorial government wants to promote the state's artistic appeal, to brand it and update that image, and to downplay all the spiritual borny activities."

"And Jerome becomes the focus point of that battle, since it was an artist colony at one time," Brenda added.

"And our hero has a dubious spiritual background, growing up in a family with religious fanatics, and so he's working for the territorial government to undermine the spiritual side of the battle."

Brenda looked around and then turned back to me. "Well, that's pretty similar to our mission," she said without elaborating.

"Nobody's going to see it, and it may even give my subconscious a way to objectify these issues."

Brenda laughed. "You really do like to cut it close, don't you Lewis?"

"The Razor's Edge," I said, but Brenda didn't get the literary reference.

So, for the next few weeks, we really jumped into the routine of me writing and Brenda researching and taking notes, and us conferring at the library or at the Iguana Café that I had staked out for my writing site. The idea was to make a public display of my activity, so it didn't make sense to write in our room at the Sliding Sands. What we did notice was that when I was alone at the cafe, June would sometimes show up and talk with me, and when Brenda was alone at the library, Claude, the masseur showed up once or twice. It was obvious that they were trying to keep an eye on us, or maybe they were attracted to us. Neither of us readily engaged them nor did we run our cover story by them. But, one day, we did drive down to Prescott and I called Musgrave to ask if we should be more forthcoming.

"Great spy craft," Musgrave said about me writing a novel, without mentioning his earlier suggestion to do as much.

"Should either of us tell them the cover story or readily engage them? I asked.

Musgrave thought this over for a moment. "No. They're trying to get information from you, but if you hold out, then Fria will be forced to engage you."

"Okay, that makes sense."

"Oh. Klaus wants to know about any changes or intuitive leaps."

This was Klaus's way of reminding me to keep up with the log, which I had been doing, but nothing substantial had shown up and I was slacking off. "Nothing big to report, outside of the so-called astral projection I mentioned. Let's see what happens, but after I meet with her next, I should get a spike."

"Brenda," Musgrave said. "Don't forget that we'll be needing you to get a healing for comparative numbers."

"Probably best to wait until after Alan's next contact. It might affect … the treatment."

"Yes. Good thinking." Musgrave paused. "But, afterward, we'll want to draw you both in for more testing."

Neither of us responded.

"Okay, see you then."

Brenda turned to me as we drove into the parking lot of a new restaurant. "I was hoping he'd forget."

"No chance. I mean, with Musgrave staying in Phoenix this long, it tells you how much they've got invested in this operation."

We decided, given the need for Brenda's future healing, to attend the next service. We sat in the back and neither of us came forward for a healing, but we certainly seemed to draw a lot of attention. At one point, during the preamble, Maria stared at me for a moment and smiled. It wasn't catty, as one might suppose, but sweet and soulful. Maybe she was as genuine as she appeared, and the only agendas here—as I've suggested—were Musgrave's and his people.

Well, several nights later, I was sitting alone at the café drinking a mild grain blend of coffee and writing on my portable, when June walked in and came over to my table. She sat down across from me wearing fairly alluring clothing.

"Hate to interrupt you, Lewis." I glanced up and tried to look annoyed. "But Maria asked me to … see if you'd like to stop by and talk with her."

"Right now?"

"Yes. There's a full moon, and the view from her living room is quite spectacular." The way June added this last incentive, blinking her eyes seductively and smiling, definitely indicated that the next level of contact was upon me.

I decided to go along with them and debated on whether to

take a bathroom break to contact Brenda, but knew that would be countered by the urgency of the request. Maybe the moon was getting ready to set.

"Sure. Let's go." I closed down my portable, stood up, put on my jacket, and followed her out.

26.

June and I entered Fria's house through a back entrance and she escorted me to the living room. Maria was there, standing by the window and gazing out over the desert. She heard us and turned our way. "Oh, Lewis, you decided to come."

"I'm a sucker for moonlight views."

She laughed. "June, thanks for … fetching Lewis. I'll show him out."

June bowed and left and I stepped over to the window, captivated by the view even from across the room. Maria turned and stared out again at the desert landscape. I stood next to her and viewed the scenery. It was surprising how clear the desert was in the moonlight, and one could see the faint silhouette of the distant mountain chain as a backdrop. I was going to say something when Maria spoke.

"It's the high altitude and the dry air that make the moonlight so bright."

"Well, it's certainly spectacular. It's a shame it blocks out the night sky."

"Yes, nature doesn't often give us a two for one, unlike the lures of our world."

She turned and offered me a seat. I discovered that two padded chairs had been pulled up to the window and set catty-cornered, so we could face each other and view the landscape as well. I also noticed that there were glasses of water set out on the end tables. So much for my surprised acceptance of her invitation.

"So, Lewis, any more dreams?"

"You mean astral projections?" I asked.

"Some say dreams are a form of astral projection, or causal plane encounters, but I was referring to the normal symbolic variety."

"No. But, I started writing another novel, and that's probably drawing off all my juice."

Maria smiled. "Interesting phrase." She paused. "Yes, June told me she's seen you and … Brenda, I believe it is, doing research at the library and you writing at the Iguana Café."

I took a sip of water. "It's my next novel, and I'm setting it here, in Jerome and Arizona." She raised her eyebrows. "It's set twenty or thirty years in the past, and it's totally fictional, so nothing of you and your group is referenced."

"Maybe not directly, but I'm sure your experience here is working itself out in your creative efforts."

I nodded my head and looked across at her, neither of us seemed inclined to talk for a while. My mind had stopped its rambling and I was just in the moment with her, sharing whatever was occurring between us at whatever levels. Finally, she said, "Just being here, without the need to talk, is a trait not many from your world can tolerate."

"My world?"

Maria smiled again. "The East Coast intellectual artistic world." She peered at me. "Your accent speaks of the eastern region, or sector, as they now call it."

"And those of us with neural processors," I added.

"Yes. Whatever the level of one's integration, there is a kind of separation between those with and those without them." I nodded my head but couldn't help but wonder about this summons.

"I was thinking, if you were open to it, of sharing an … expansive exercise with you, that might speed up your integration and hone your intuitive abilities and … connections."

127

I just stared at her and tried not to be too suspicious. Before she could note that, I said, "Sure. Let's do it." Her kind smile drew a further response. "And thank you for sharing this with me in advance."

The instruction was for me to close my eyes and visualize a web of millions of micro-fine strings of light passing through me, both vertically and horizontally, like something out of the multi-dimensional string theory that was scientifically verified in the mid-21st century. This made the whole exercise much more palatable and less esoteric. I was to "grab hold" of these colorful vertical strings passing through my head and body, and to pull them out sideways until the opening encompassed the entire room, then the city, the western region, this half of the globe, then the whole globe, and the whole solar system, and then the Milky Way galaxy, and step-by-step to expand my astral body, I guess you could call it, to include the entire universe.

At its furthermost point, it felt like every atom of my body was the size of a basketball. Finally, after this feeling settled for a period of time and I experienced an immense joy and connectivity, we gradually reversed the process from the universal expansion, step-by-step, back to me sitting in Maria's living room atop this plateau. The experience must've lasted an hour or so, and I sat there for another ten minutes before I opened my eyes.

Maria was patiently sitting across from me with her eyes closed, but opened them at that moment. "So you're back with us."

I took a large gulp of water. "Yes. Wow. Talk about expansive."

"You did well for your first time."

I closed my eyes and could still see the billions of galaxies and their stars that I had just expanded across. It didn't feel like a visualized experience but real and visceral.

"Yes, Lewis. It wasn't in your imagination, as some would claim."

"What? Do you read minds?" I asked a little peevishly.

Maria laughed. "No. I've just instructed so many people in these techniques that I've catalogued typical responses or rationalizations."

"Sorry. Didn't mean to question you or this wonderful exercise."

Maria stared at me for a long moment. "Seems like you need to integrate this experience, so let's not dilute it with more talk."

I stood up. "I think you're right. I'm feeling quite sleepy."

Maria stood and walked me to the rear entrance of her house. "If you like, I can call June and have her walk you back."

I shook my head. "I'm all right," I said.

Maria smiled. "Okay, but I do suggest you take your shower alone tonight."

"No kidding." Maria stepped over and gave me a hug. Hesitant at first, I allowed my arms to wrap around her and the energy of this contact was nearly as powerful as her healing of me. We held it for at least thirty seconds before I stepped back. "Whoa. That's some hug."

"Be well, Lewis."

I opened the door and walked outside; June was waiting for me. "I figured you might need some … assistance."

"I thought not, until Maria … hugged me."

"Maybe a cup of tea at the café?"

"Yeah. Sounds good."

When we got to the café, Brenda was sitting there, no doubt waiting for me.

June turned to me and smiled. "Well, looks like you have your guide home." With that she turned and walked back toward the Center.

I stepped inside and sat down across from Brenda. She gave me a questioning look, but not at all jealous or even personal. I took out and turned on a portable bug/video suppressor, which was part of our last tech upgrade. "She came to fetch me for a get-together with Maria."

"How did that go?"

I told her about Maria's expansive exercise, and I could sense her inwardly cringing at the prospect. I mean, if Brenda didn't like viewing the expansive Southwest landscape as we drove through it, she certainly wouldn't want to expand across the universe. And I did elaborate more than needed to further provoke her, for whatever reason.

"Well, the exercise seems fairly neutral, and I doubt if the 'hug' qualifies as substantial contact," she said.

I stared at her. "So you don't think we need to contact Musgrave?" Brenda cringed further. "You're afraid he'll think otherwise and want you to get a healing at their next service, and then bring us in?"

"Yeah, I guess that's why I'm reacting this way."

"Like I said, Brenda. It'll be fairly benign, just adjusting your processor to integrate some of your repressed feelings."

Brenda closed her eyes. "Easy for you to say, since you're way head of me in that regard."

This left me with a possible opening. "So, we just dismiss it, and go on as if this new contact never happened, given it was minimal as you said?"

Jean/Brenda actually considered the prospect for a moment. "No. We have to call it in at some point." It seemed that sticking with operational protocol was at least some solace or provided structure for her.

"I see," I said with a questioning look.

"Don't worry, Lewis. I won't bring up your suggestion."

Or, at least until it services a purpose, I thought. We headed back to the Sliding Sands, and while I slept well, Brenda tossed and turned all night long, waking me up on one occasion.

27.

The rest of the week went pretty much as it had been going with our new focus: I would write at the café in the morning or afternoon, and we'd spent time at the library each day, either together or alone. After dinner one night, we walked past the center to check their schedule of upcoming services, which were usually every two weeks and due this week. But there was a notice that Maria would be out of town, and so the service was postponed until the next Thursday.

As we were walking back to the Sliding Sands, Brenda asked, "Should we notify Musgrave that she's out and about?"

They apparently didn't have the community staked out, since we were able to get all the way to Yuma without detection. It was late but we drove into Prescott for dessert, not that we had to explain our movements to anybody, but it was always good to have a cover story for all of our excursions outside the community. There was an old-fashioned bakery with booths on the outskirts of town, so we pulled in there and since it was fairly deserted at this time of night, I called Musgrave while we ate slivers of pumpkin pie.

He thanked me for the update and said they'd use a recon satellite to check the cars going in and out of Jerome, but that she may have already slipped out. Since I had him on the phone, I told him about the late-night rendezvous and soaring through the universe. His reaction was similar to Brenda's—not the expansive type either. He was however interested in the "hug."

"Usually these healers are hands-off, but full body contact for that long could be as invasive as one of her healings." He paused for a moment. "Any effects?"

I hadn't had any great intuitive leaps, if that's what he was asking, but this week I was particularly mellow and more within myself, something that Brenda pointed out before I caught the behavior. I told him as much, and I thought he'd let it pass, but this seemed to bother him more than expected. He didn't respond for a moment.

"The next service is Thursday," he said, as if to himself, "so tell the hotel that you're leaving for the weekend on Friday, to do some research at the Old West Library in Phoenix."

"Okay," I replied. It seemed like a plan.

"And Jean, you're up to bat." She didn't immediately reply. "You there?" Musgrave asked.

"I'm here until Thursday when I get my ticket punched."

"Work with Alan. Let him walk you through it. I'm sure you'll be okay."

"And if I'm not? What about the op?" she asked.

"I like the way your mind thinks, Jean. We go to Plan B; an aunt dies and the two of you have to return to Chicago for a couple of weeks." He paused. "There we could grow another neural implant for you, and you'd be … restored."

"Okay, that's reassuring."

"Let's see how it all falls out," Musgrave said. He said his goodbyes and we headed back to Jerome for the night.

On Thursday, we attended the service, and Brenda stepped forward and had a healing from Maria. I carefully watched her walking back to our chairs, and she appeared to be all right. She smiled at me, and said it was more benign than she had figured. I suggested we stop by the café afterward and talk, but Brenda wanted to get back to the Sliding Sands and either rest for a bit, or go to bed early. Well, as soon as she lay down, she fell fast asleep. It was a little early for me to retire, and I didn't want to leave her alone, but didn't feel like any video stimulation, so I went out to the patio, pulled up a chair and just sat there in silence staring up at the night sky. I was really peaceful, and I had to wonder if this new level of integration was due to my last contact with Maria, as insubstantial as it seemed. Then I heard Brenda calling out from the bedroom and I stepped inside.

She was still asleep but seemed to be having a nightmare, thrashing about and crying out. I thought it best not to wake her, but pulled up a chair and sat there until she settled down twenty minutes later. I decided not to sleep with her. I wasn't afraid any further violent thrashing of her arms would hit me, but was more concerned about subconscious contamination. The padded chair was fairly comfortable; I rigged up a footrest so I could stretch out a bit and fell asleep in the chair. I had a dream, definitely symbolic, of us caught in a bramble bush maze with its prickly thorns. I was following Brenda, but she kept running her arms across the bushes and cutting them, but unlike my close encounters, she wasn't bleeding from her prick wounds, and we just couldn't find our way out. I woke up; it must've been about four o'clock in the morning, but Brenda was already up and packing our bags.

I watched her for a moment from the darkened corner of the room. She seemed to be in a panic, her movements frantic and disconnected.

"Slow down, Brenda."

She turned and glared at me. "Slow down? Get the fuck up and get in gear, we're heading out ... now."

She had already packed a bag for me, and given her frantic state I just changed clothes and didn't shower. When we got downstairs, I talked with the desk clerk, not wanting to expose him to her condition, and we hurried across the street to the parking lot. We hadn't exchanged a cordial word since I had woken up, and I figured quickly getting her out of town and on the road might be the best temporary relief. Well, once we were down the hill and heading south toward Prescott, she finally perked up.

"Sorry, Alan, had a rough night and I'm feeling pretty freaked out."

No kidding, I said to myself, but decided to mollify her. "It's okay ... Jean. I told you this would bring up repressed feelings."

She glared at me. "Well, thanks the fuck for the warning. How about next time saying, 'This treatment could lead to a psychotic episode.'"

"Is that how you feel?" I asked.

She just shook her head. "Sorry, didn't mean to snap at you. No. But I'm not doing well."

We stopped in Prescott at a hydrogen station and while she used the ladies room, I recharged the fuel cells and called Musgrave. He was sleeping, but like a typical soldier was clear and operational on a moment's notice. I told him we were coming in, about two hours from his mall office. Given the severity of her reaction, he directed me to an air force base northwest of town with better facilities. He said that he and his team would meet us there.

Jean got back while I was finishing up with Musgrave; I pointed at the phone, but she shook her head and got back into the car. I suggested we stop and get a bite to eat, which might make her feel better. She decided on an all-night fast-food place on the commercial strip with a drive-through. We got sausage and egg sandwiches, coffee and were back on the road, eating along the way. I tried to engage her in a conversation, but her thinking was pretty disjoined and only made her condition more obvious to both of us. So we drove in silence. About an hour out from Phoenix, she told me to pull off the road. Jean swung open the door and ran into the desert, where she threw up her breakfast. I rummaged through our bags, found a towel, and walked out to her with a bottle of water.

She wiped her mouth, chugged the bottle of water straight down and we headed back to the car. I wish I could have hugged her, or reassured her with any kind of physical contact, but given my own charge, it might have just overload her circuits. When we arrived at the base gate, the guard gave us directions to the hospital building. Musgrave met us at the front door, his hair and clothes a little disheveled. Jean tried to play down her condition, but I could see from the expression on his face that he was as concerned about her as I was, or was it about a possible failed mission on his part?

Chapter Ten

28.

The base hospital had a neurosurgeon ready to extract Jean's processor, and she was rushed away with a full contingent of nurses and orderlies in blue-and-wine-colored scrubs. I stood still for a moment and exhaled a deep sigh of concern. I wondered if she would recover, or ever be herself again. I had limited experience with extractions and replacements, and the manufacturers didn't exactly publicize that contingency.

"Let's go to the cafeteria and get something to eat and let you come down from this adrenaline rush," Musgrave suggested. I suspected he needed a break as well.

"Yeah, let's do that." I followed Musgrave through a maze of hallways with their gray walls, to the hospital's cafeteria. "Looks like you're familiar with the base," I said as we walked inside, grabbed metal trays and stood in line.

"Well, Phoenix and the surrounding area have been used for the … testing of various technologies over the years, and I have been here before, but this is a first."

It was breakfast time and we were served a fairly good meal of eggs, substitute bacon, toast and fruit, and mugs of coffee. We found a window table at the back end of the cafeteria with a view of the desert, if somewhat blurred by the ionic force-field fence. We ate in silence for a minute. Finally, Musgrave sat back in his metal chair. "So, Alan, how would you describe Jean's reaction to the healing?"

"Initially, as we walked back from the church, she seemed fine. Maybe just a little unfocused, kind of soft around the edges."

"Definitely not her," Musgrave added.

"Well, not enough to be alarmed. I suggested we stop by the café for a quick bite and a chat, but she wanted to get back to the room for a nap, or to go to bed early."

Musgrave nodded. "Then?"

"I stepped out on the patio for a long while, came back in when I heard her thrashing about and crying out, but it was just a bad dream, or so I figured and I just let her sleep it off." Musgrave flashed me a more critical look. "Then, I woke up with her in a full-blown panic attack packing our bags and acting crazy."

Musgrave sat forward and took another bite of his scrambled eggs, while he apparently considered this description. "So, what do you think happened?" he finally asked.

"Well, according to Fria, the healing energy will affect neural processors, slow down the neuron firing-rates and make other adjustments to allow greater integration of ... feelings, I assume, and heightened intuition."

Musgrave stared at me for a long moment. "Or, allow repressed ones to overwhelm the conscious mind."

"I don't think that's entirely the case," I added. "The way she talks, about it has its own ... mind or intent, and works with each individual in different ways and must compensate."

"So, she's not directing it, is that what I'm getting from you?" he asked me rather skeptically.

"I wouldn't assume any malicious intent on her part. I think Jean was a little too tightly wound, and had a bad reaction."

"At some point, whatever happens here, I need you to explore this concept with Fria ... that is, what percentage of the population might react this way."

I had to laugh. "Tom, if I can call you that." Musgrave nodded his head. "She's not a sociologist; she's a healer who exposes people to a certain kind of energy and allows them to ... dance with it."

Musgrave snickered. "Let's not put that description in any of our reports." He took a sip of coffee. "But, Fria's healed thousands over the years, and she has lots of students out there giving her feedback. Let's see if we can't get some raw data on it, even if it's anecdotal."

I nodded my head.

At that point Captain Turner, the neurosurgeon, still in his blue operating scrubs, stuck his head into the cafeteria, spotted us and walked over. He was a small man with small hands, which I would think was an asset in his line of work. Turner sat down at the aisle end of the table to face both of us.

"So, how's it coming, Captain?" Musgrave asked.

He shook his head and we were both immediately alarmed. Musgrave ran his hand through his gray-streaked hair. I leaned forward as if to hear him better, but it was just nerves on my part.

"Not well," Turner said. An orderly, who had followed him inside, brought over steaming mugs of coffee. He took a long sip.

"Spit it out, Captain," Musgrave ordered—apparently he outranked the officer.

"Before an extraction, not that I've done many, the protocol is to run a few tests to gauge how my patient will react to having their neural processor removed and having 'downtime.' It takes several hours to grow a new one, and we can't start until we've harvested brain cells after the extraction."

Musgrave nodded his head impatiently.

"The results of my examination were so negative that, in my opinion, she might not survive the replacement ordeal mentally intact."

"Why's that?"

"The processor's analytical functioning seems to be all that's standing between her and lots of repressed emotions that could cause suicidal ideation, in my opinion."

"Really?" Musgrave said in astonishment. Since we were test subjects, in a manner of speaking, this didn't bode well for our little venture. "So what're our options?"

"I've heavily sedated her, and suggest that you fly her back to New York and have a full team of neurosurgeons do the operation in a more sophisticated setting. They're much better equipped to handle difficult replacements and the psychological downside."

Musgrave considered this option for a long moment. "Okay, Doc. That's what we'll do. Whatley is a valuable asset, and we don't want to lose her."

The doctor nodded his head.

"Captain, get her ready for transport now. I'll make the arrangements."

Captain Turner set down his cup; I thought he was going to salute, but he stood up and hurried off with his orderly.

Musgrave turned to me. "Alan, you're coming with us. If you need to call the hotel in Jerome and give them a heads-up on your delayed return, do so."

"Wouldn't it just be better for me to return and tell them Brenda had a … death in the family or something?"

Musgrave shook his head. "No. Even if she recovers, it's likely that Jean won't be returning with you to Jerome anytime soon, and we have to make other arrangements."

"Read in another agent as my … new researcher?" I asked in startled disbelief.

Musgrave thought about this unlikely scenario. "I'm thinking we pull in somebody you're familiar with and have … some chemistry with."

I was puzzled for a moment, and then it dawned on me whom he was suggesting. "But, Emma's gone underground, and may even be working for the other side, and we might not be able to find her."

"Well, that's what we need you for, Alan," he spit out impatiently.

"I wouldn't know where to start."

"How about the Kitty Kat Club?" he asked.

I nodded my head. That did make sense.

"We'll get K-Industries to repeal their re-enlistment claim, a hike in salary, and no contract. A one-time-only operation."

"But Emma never did anything wrong."

"See. There's the chemistry working already."

29.

Halfway through the flight back to New York, I watched Musgrave walking back from the medevac unit at the far end of the plane where they were monitoring Jean. He had two bottles of water with him, handed me one, and sat down next to me.

"Well, Jean's signs are steady, and a surgical team is ready at the hospital, once we airlift her there and rush her into surgery."

"I assume they're monitoring her via a remote linkup?"

Musgrave nodded.

"Any feedback from them?" I asked.

"No, this is an … unusual situation, and they don't want to stick their necks out without a full hands-on work-up."

I didn't reply.

Musgrave took a sip from his water bottle. "I put an undercover into the Kitty Kat Club a few weeks ago. I'm having her ask about Emma, see if we can't speed up the search."

I found this curious. He was preparing a backup plan before we needed it, or did he anticipate as much? I didn't ask him either way. "So, I go in, she sits on my lap and passes me the info?" I asked.

Musgrave laughed. "I should be so lucky; she's a real looker." He turned serious. "If she's not getting anywhere, a paying customer offering a bribe might get better results."

"And your girl …"

"Cover name, Apple."

"Would know whose hand to grease?"

Musgrave shrugged his shoulders. "I would hope so."

"And if that doesn't work?" I asked.

"Well, there's always Ling. We cut a deal with her for a

reduced sentence."

"As long as she doesn't get out before we wrap it up."

"Agreed."

I stared at Musgrave with lots of questions I was reluctant to ask. He must have read my body language.

"Spit it out, Alan," he finally said.

"Well," I tentatively started, "the more I'm around Fria, the more I'm sensing that she's who she claims to be: she's a healer who just channels the energy and lets it take its course."

Musgrave considered my statement, no doubt weighing how much he could reveal of their real intentions, or the other agenda I suspected was in play here. "So you don't think she has other designs, or one that would require double agent tasking?"

"Yeah, I just don't see me getting on the inside and finding anything worth our while," I said.

"Ever think that's what she wants you to believe?"

I could see that Musgrave was going to dance around my inquiry, so there wasn't much else to say. "Well, I guess that's what I'm there to find out."

Musgrave stood up. "Keep on point, Alan. Let us worry about the big the picture."

After we landed and Jean was put on a medevac helicopter and flown to the hospital, I was told that my wife was back in town and that I would be staying at a midtown hotel while I conducted my business. Musgrave added that I was not to contact her. At least now I wouldn't feel guilty when I didn't.

I did have one last question for him. "What about Dr. Klaus? Do I schedule an appointment with him while I'm in town?"

"No. This is a quick in-and-out, and I need you present; Klaus has a way of confusing people, or going too deep."

This was a relief, but it also made me wonder about my last phone session with Klaus and his insistence that I keep my self-review between us and not include Musgrave, which seemed odd at the time. I figured it was just a turf war between them, with me caught in the middle.

At the hotel I took a long nap, then shaved and showered and awaited instructions.

Musgrave called. "There's $1,000 in an envelope in the drawer of your nightstand. Get something to eat and head out to the Club afterward. Apple's working this evening."

He hung up before I could ask about Jean's condition. He was gruff and a little distracted. Apparently my earlier questions or doubts about the mission's goals had unsettled him, or maybe Jean's replacement operation hadn't gone well and he was in a "blue flunk," to use a retro term. Well, either way my job now was to "keep on point" and just get through this ordeal.

The Cub looked as sleazy as ever, its black walls and low lighting unable to cover up the atmospheric grime. I did notice a few more suits in attendance as the hostess escorted me to my booth. I had asked to be seated in Apple's section, and the girl snickered and asked me if I was sure. I imagined she wasn't as good a "provider" as some of the other girls. I ordered a beer and after a while, a rather attractive if not seductive woman, short but busty, with a blue-laced bra and long blonde hair, served the beer and tentatively sat down next to me.

"Hi. I'm Apple. We've 'partied' before?"

"Well, not actually, but a friend of mine who likes … horses told me to look you up," I said.

It took a moment for her to make the connection. "Oh, yes, 'Maverick.'"

"He's a wild one," was my cover reply.

Apple relaxed noticeably and started to rub my crotch and warm up to me. As she lowered her head under the tablecloth and faked giving me a blow job, she told me that she's been unable to get any leads on Emma or 'Dorothy's' whereabouts. She thought Big Mike, the bouncer, might know something but he hadn't been forthcoming. I figured I needed to talk with him.

"Okay, Apple. I'm going to create a scene, just go along

with it."

I grabbed her by the hair and yanked her up. "You call that a blow job," I yelled at her. "You use your gums, not your teeth, bitch." Heads started to turn, and I definitely got Big Mike's attention.

This huge wall of a guy, at least six-five and three hundred pounds, sauntered over. In an earlier age I might have accused him of using steroids to bulk up, but today musclemen had to do it the old-fashioned way. He came up and put his outstretched hands on my table and leaned over to get into my face. "What's the problem, here?"

"The problem is I paid good money for a BJ and this bitch doesn't know the first thing about giving one."

He glared at Apple. "Take a hike, babe."

"Sorry," she said, scooted out of the booth and hurried away.

"How about sending Dorothy over? She could drain juice out of a lead pipe."

"You want another girl, you pay for it and take your chances, buddy. There're no guarantees."

"That sucks, literally," I said in a pout. "Okay, I'll pay for Dorothy."

"She doesn't work here anymore. But, I'm sure one of the other girls can take care of you."

"Fuck."

"That's extra," Big Mike said with sneer."

"You know where I can find her?"

"Hey, buddy. I don't run a lonely hearts finder's service. Get another girl or get the fuck out of here."

I took out my wallet and laid down three crisp one-hundred-dollar bills. Mike stared at them for a moment, and then pulled up a chair. He pocketed the money. "All I know is that she was staying at some flea-bag hotel on Bowery Street near Chinatown."

"What hotel?"

He shook his head. "Just heard her complaining about the drunks and the pimps." He stood up. "That's all you get from me." He gave me his best bouncer look. "You want another girl?" he asked.

"Nope. I'll just head out."

So, I made the circuit up and down Bowery Street south of Broome. I thought these hotels couldn't be any worse than the Club. I was wrong ... wall-to-wall sleaze. Must've checked out a half-dozen in a three-block radius. I showed Emma's picture around and spent another couple hundred bucks before I found a hotel where somebody recognized her, but she was long gone. I called Musgrave to check on Jean's condition. He said the NP exchange was made and she seemed to be doing better, but they wouldn't know for another couple days. This was a relief. I told him I had struck out on my search for Emma, gave him the name of the hotel where she had last stayed, and he said he'd follow up on it and get back to me later.

The next morning a car picked me up and drove me to the FBI headquarters at Federal Plaza, on Foley Square in lower Manhattan. Musgrave was waiting for me in the lobby, dressed like a lawyer in a dark gray suit, with blue pin stripes and a white shirt. I glanced down at my herringbone sports coat and black slacks. "Am I underdressed?"

Musgrave snickered. "Nobody's going to see you anyway."

We took the elevator down to the detention facility, where they were holding Su Ling.

"I called yesterday, and her lawyer will be present to speed this up. You're staying in the viewing booth. I don't want Ling figuring out what we're up to."

Ling and her lawyer, a black woman with a short Afro, named Paula Mansfield, were waiting for him in an interrogation room.

Musgrave started off, "Ms. Ling, I'm interested in locating Emma Knowles. If you can help me, I'll have the charges against you ... reduced, and you'll serve no more than five years in prison."

There was some jockeying back and forth with her lawyer, who wanted all charges dropped, which Musgrave would not agree to, and then she asked for three years in a minimum-security facility. Musgrave agreed to the prison but wouldn't budge on the time.

Su Ling asked, "I guess you won't tell me why you want Emma?"

"No, I can't divulge any information on an ongoing ... operation," Musgrave replied. However, the use of "operation" over "investigation" was enough of a clue.

She now stared at the one-way mirrored viewing glass—not all the rooms had them—and made some assumptions. "I guess that's Alan Reynard on the other side."

"Why would you say that?" Musgrave said in a neutral tone, not giving anything away.

Ling didn't reply to his question but nodded at her lawyer, who told Musgrave to draw up the paperwork. This only took an hour. I assumed she figured that she had guessed right, and that if I was involved, it was more of a job offer than a manhunt. After the papers arrived and Musgrave delivered the brief and her lawyer read through it, Ling said, "Emma's cousin, Joyce Power, has a small cabin on Crescent Bay, on Lower Saranac Lake, in upper state New York where she's been hiding out, off and on since she went under, or so she once told me."

30.

I was in the command center at FBI headquarters that afternoon when they located the cabin at Saranac Lake and identified Emma Knowles as its sole occupant. A surveillance team was dispatched from their Albany office, to set up surveillance in the woods around the cabin until we could fly there. On the helicopter ride, Musgrave told me that he wanted me to go in first and talk with her.

"You're not actually negotiating for us, but you can tell her that you're on an important op and you need backup, and that if she agrees to be reinstated at K Industries, for this one-time-only operation, she'll get back pay and be released of any further obligations afterward."

"After you've ... interrogated her, to make sure she's not affiliated with any of the anti-government groups, like Ling's," I said.

Musgrave stared at me for a moment. "Yes, but just routine inquiries, not chemical interrogation, and you'll be present at all debriefings."

"And exactly what can I tell her about the op?" I asked.

"Nothing at this point. If she agrees to cooperate, I'll brief her ... with you present."

I nodded my head. This was unusually accommodating for the by-the-book Musgrave. I figured he was really getting pressured at his end.

Musgrave tapped his operational earpiece—he must've received a call. He listened for a moment. "She's probably driving into town. Don't approach but follow her."

He turned to me. "She's heading toward town. Hopefully, she'll end up at a café or restaurant, where your approach will be less intimidating."

"Well, if I were her, I'd want to know more before I signed on."

Musgrave thought about my inquiry. "You can tell her that it's in the Southwest Sector and doesn't involve any anti-tech groups."

"Yeah, that should ease her mind."

As it turned out, Emma was doing her weekly shopping, but afterward she stopped off at a café for coffee and to read the late news on her portable. The helicopter landed in a parking lot six blocks away. I was fitted with a remote camera and com link. A car dropped me off a block from the restaurant, and I walked down from there and went inside. Her table was facing the entrance; she spotted me the moment I strolled inside. She was thinner but looked healthier than when I last saw her.

Emma didn't panic and try to run; she must've assumed that the building was surrounded, or maybe she was just relieved that I was the initial contact. I went over to the counter, ordered a coffee and then walked over to her with the cup in hand.

"I guess Ling must've given me up?"

"They struck a deal with her, but only after she realized that it was just a job offer, and I was involved."

Emma looked skeptical. "A job offer, after what they've put me through?"

"This wasn't my idea, but you'd be with me as a kind of research assistant, separate quarters, and it's in the Southwest—no anti-tech group involvement."

"Like Ling's," she said.

I nodded.

"So, they're not really sure if I was turned, and they'll want to determine that before they agree to put me out in the field again?"

"No chemical interrogation and I'll be present for any questioning."

Emma took a sip of her coffee, stared at me over the edge of the cup. "So, it comes down to me trusting you, or I should say, trusting your assessment of the situation."

"Yeah, I guess so," I said.

She thought about this offer some more. "So, it's an established op and your current partner was either taken out, or compromised?"

I was getting feedback from Musgrave through my earpiece, but I shook my head at his instructions to stonewall her. "She was incapacitated by a fairly benign intrusion, that I handled just fine."

Emma smiled. "So, I can't go in as your wife or girlfriend?"

"No, but we'll see if they have two rooms with a connecting door," I said with a chuckle.

She laughed. "This must be really important if you're willing to sleep with me again."

"Yeah, I really did hate that," I added with a broad smile. "And you may also have to meditate—no born-again churches."

Emma sat back in her chair, took another sip of her coffee; she was really making me work for it. "I guess you're not prepared to ... negotiate the deal?"

I shook my head.

"Well, send your handler in, and let's hear what he has to say," she said.

Musgrave gave me instructions over my com link. "They want me to drive back to the cabin with you, and he'll meet us there."

"He's not afraid we'll make a run for it?" she asked and laughed.

"Guess they figure I'm not the running type."

Emma picked up her portable, and we left the café and got into her car. It was only a ten-minute drive back to the cabin. The once green trees along the road were dying, due to climate-zone displacement, creating an even more somber mood. At one point she started to say something, then stopped herself, realizing they were listening in, or so I assumed. At the cabin we unloaded and put away her groceries, as Musgrave drove up with another agent.

"Emma, this is Tom Musgrave, a bureau chief for the FBI."

She turned to me. "This isn't a K Industries operation?"

Musgrave replied, "Officially you'll be working for them, but under our supervision."

"Must be pretty critical if you're involved?" she asked, but didn't really expect an answer.

"Ms. Knowles. If you'll pack a bag, we'll fly back to the City and hold our debriefing ... and briefing there tomorrow."

"Can I call my father?" she asked.

I could see Musgrave was ready to deny her request. "Tom, she's cooperating with us, and isn't officially under arrest."

He gave me a critical look and then turned to Emma. "Tell him you're coming in to straighten things out with K Industries, and may be reinstated short-term. That's all, and we'll be monitoring the call."

Emma gave me a quizzical look, then pulled out her portable and made her call.

It was early evening when we landed in New York; Musgrave booked Emma in a nice hotel on East Broadway, about ten blocks from the Federal Building. I was told to return to my hotel, and to have no contact with her this evening. A female FBI agent would take her to dinner and stay with her, but I was on my own. When I returned from dinner, I looked up Ling's lawyer online and gave her a call; well, left a message and she called back an hour later. I told her that Ling's friend, Emma Knowles, was negotiating a reinstatement deal with the FBI tomorrow and may need her help. Mansfield thanked me for the heads-up, and said she'd just turn up tomorrow, telling them Ling paid her to represent Emma. I was sure Musgrave would figure it out, or even do a back-check on my phone logs to confirm his suspicion. But, there wasn't much he could do about it, and he might even consider it a bonding ploy on my part.

Chapter Eleven

31.

Paula Mansfield negotiated an airtight deal for Emma, although showing up and claiming to be her lawyer caused a little rift between Musgrave and me. I knew he'd figure it out. Anyway, Emma passed her debriefing, and while it didn't include chemical interrogation, he did make her take one of the modern and sophisticated lie-detector tests. Musgrave was convinced that Emma wasn't working with Ling or other factions, and I sat in on her read-in on the operation. He wasn't as forthcoming as I would've been, and I was told not to elaborate later, but he also knew that I would and so he just had to accept that to keep this op moving forward.

Emma and I flew to Chicago, and then two days later, we were to fly to Phoenix, where I would pick up my car, and we would drive back to Jerome—our new cover story required a Chicago base. Musgrave's team was hard at work creating Emma's legend, as we call cover stories for spies, and hopefully it would be in place when we arrived. An FBI team photographed her in local places and pre-dated the social media tags.

I doubted that Fria's group would do any back-checking, but I would tell Maria that Brenda had a bad reaction to her healing, needed to be hospitalized, and wouldn't be coming back. For the general public, it would still be the allergy story, but Musgrave wanted me to use Brenda's bad reaction to probe Fria further. We'd explain Emma as a researcher familiar with my novels, and that I hired her to take Brenda's place as my assistant. She had downloaded the novels to her processor and could now readily call them up. Musgrave emphasized that we needed to keep our relationship chaste, or her cover might unravel rather quickly. I assured him that since Emma wasn't a cover wife or girlfriend, that wouldn't be a problem. We were also told not to talk "business" on either flight.

After we landed in Phoenix, we took a cab to the Metrocenter Mall, and while Emma did some shopping for Southwest attire, I visited the FBI's deep-cover office there but there were no updates. Musgrave had remained in New York for the time being. A car drove us to the Air Force base where we picked up my car, and we were on our way back to Jerome. Again I took the southern route to avoid Sedona. Since we had exhausted the normal chitchat of colleagues reuniting on our two flights, Emma felt free to ask me more questions about the operation.

"So tell me about Fria. My briefing papers give a pretty dry description," Emma said.

"Well, despite what Musgrave and his people are saying, I think she's just a wonderful spiritual healer without ulterior motives."

She noted my tone and glanced over at me. "You seem quite taken with her?"

"Well, my healing seems to have helped me to expand my intuition, and I feel a lot more … connected since then."

"And Whatley's reaction?"

"Musgrave would have a fit if he heard us talking."

Emma gave me a look.

"Yes, I did check for bugs." I drove on for a few minutes as she patiently waited my reply. "Jean apparently had a lot of repressed feelings, and I figured this healing energy, which seems to have a mind of its own, would compensate for that, but it didn't."

"What's the latest word on her?" she asked.

"Musgrave said she may never be the same. For now she's been decommissioned and placed in a psyche ward."

"I'd call that a bad reaction, and just when I was hoping to get a healing myself."

"You'd be fine with it."

Emma gazed out at the desert landscape with its Saguaros,

pine cactus, and scrub brush. "It's really beautiful here. I've never been to the desert before. I think I'll like it."

"The wide-open vistas expand you," I added.

After we had driven in silence for a while, Emma turned back to me. "You know there may be another reason for Jean's reaction."

"Really?" I said rather skeptically. This was a fairly esoteric subject for her perusal.

"Well, when Su Ling was giving her recruitment pitch, she said that their scientists claim that neural processors can be used to program people, behavior modifications, or maybe it's just a special version."

"Well, I haven't heard that one, but if anybody would have a 'special version,' it would be an operative. But who can say."

"Maybe Fria can tell you more about Brenda's reaction, from her vast experience with patients."

"Well, and I wouldn't put it past Musgrave to lie about the severity of her condition, to set this up."

We were now turning north on Route 89 to Prescott and the parched desert vista continued to grab Emma's attention, at least putting a halt to her rather free-ranging speculation. But it made me wonder if she had her own personal agenda. I didn't believe she had been turned, but Emma may have dropped out for other reasons than the given one, which Musgrave didn't explore in his debriefing—maybe she shared some of my own doubts and was into a similar self-exploration. I was curious about her initial response to my work-in-progress novel, which could be telling— she had read it on the flight to Phoenix—but we couldn't talk about it until our road trip.

"So, while there's some comparison to the actual situation in the West, Fria's reaction to your storyline seems rather underplayed," Emma said.

"Well, given her unique talent, she may be able to compartmentalize and hide her true feelings from others, but as I've told

Musgrave, she seems genuine to me. But I'd be interested in your take."

"This may require more than a church service or even a healing," she said. I again sensed this was as much for personal reasons or interests as for our assignment.

"Yeah, I think I can arrange that, but for now we need to ease ourselves back into the scene."

It was late afternoon when we approached Cleopatra Hill and drove up to Jerome. Emma was fascinated by the location: the 45 degree angle of the streets, the grand vistas, and loved the dry high desert air. We parked across the street from the Sliding Sands and carried our luggage inside. Tim, the head desk clerk, was at the front desk and was certainly curious about my new companion.

"Mr. Hargrove, so nice to see you again. Your room has been cleaned." He looked over at Emma. "Will Ms. Howell be joining you?"

"Tim, Brenda won't be returning ... for now. The desert air's played havoc with her allergies. This is my new research assistant, Emma Forbes. Do you have a room for her ... on the same floor?"

Tim tried to suppress his lurid reaction and glanced down at his computer screen a little longer than it no doubt required. "Yes, two rooms down from yours." He looked up. "It's not as spacious but it has a queen size bed as well."

I had to wonder if Tim's intuition was as full-blown as some of Maria Fria's students, of which he might be one, like almost everybody else here.

"That'll be fine. Just charge it to my account."

We took the elevator to the 2nd floor. I went into the room with her and did a quick surveillance check, disabling one listening bug. Emma understood not to say anything, even after the disconnect.

"You probably need a rest. I'll pick you up for dinner at 7:00 if that's all right."

"Sure, Lewis. Look forward to it and a further rundown on the novel."

I headed back to my room and was surprised that no new bugs or video surveillance had been installed. Of course any room surveillance was against the law but when the mayor was your "research" subject, I would've expected more from them.

32.

I had decided to take Emma to the Iguana Café, and not the more formal Diablo Restaurant at the south side of town. This is where I had been doing most of my writing, and it seemed appropriate that the first outing for me and my new researcher should be there. It was also where June had come to fetch me for my tryst, as it were, with Maria Fria, so I figured the staff there might be more "connected" to her. Emma wore one of her new Southwest outfits, a white blouse with a Western motif, and a wide ankle-length blue skirt. Her retro-style jean jacket had an image of a lizard comprised of small stones. She looked beautiful, and I had to remind myself that resuming our romantic relationship might not be the best move for either one of us.

As we stepped inside the cafe, I watched Emma quickly scan the surroundings and get a fix on everybody there. Once an operative, always an operative I said to myself. I also noted that several people recognized me and their reaction to Emma was grist for the rumor mill. Since it was the middle of the week, there was a window table available and we were seated there. The waitress brought us menus; the fare was mostly Mexican and vegetarian, although there were a few meat dishes. We ordered a variety of dishes, and since you couldn't find authentic Mexican cuisine back east these days, Emma was looking forward to our meal.

After the waitress left, I took out my innocuous-looking bug suppressor and placed it between us on the table. It actually resembled an animal totem, very ingenious of the tech guys, but then they were located in Phoenix.

Emma sat back in her seat and sipped her iced tea. She stared across the table at me for a moment. "Well ... Lewis, remember that last time we went out to dinner?"

"You mean in that ... Midwest town?"

She laughed. "Those people never could figure us out. Remember that big-bosom woman, Lidia, whom you refused to hug, until she just grabbed you and pulled you to her."

I laughed, but gave her a questioning look.

"You mean we can't talk freely."

"Well, even with the bug suppressor, it's best to stay in character, or at least in public."

"You mean we're getting some private time?" Emma smirked.

I was saved by our meal coming, or was it a relief for both of us, because Emma just scoffed up her meal and ate nonstop for a while? You really didn't realize how artificial our food or modern diet had become until you were exposed to a real meal made with all-natural ingredients. Apparently, our Midwest excursion was the last time she had tasted such healthy fare.

"Sorry. Didn't mean to pig out on you, but this is so good. I'd move here just for the food."

I nodded my head.

"Lewis, it's been a while since I've ... worked with you, so it'll just take some time to get in the swing of things again."

"I know; it's an ... unusual situation, but if you're referring to your private time remark, don't sweat it. Believe me. It'll be hard for me as well."

"You mean you and Brenda weren't ... intimate?"

"Yes. Of course, but our cover story required it, and there's intimate and then there's ... intimate."

This was becoming just a little awkward for me, and again I was saved, but this time by a somewhat expected visitor. June and a friend, Brad, stopped by on their way out of the café to say hello. He was one of the masseurs at the Institute.

"Lewis, you're back."

I stood up and gave her a hug. "Yes, and let me introduce my research assistant, Emma Forbes."

The women exchanged light handshakes. June looked puzzled and I added, "Brenda went back home to Chicago; the dry dessert air was a little much for her allergies after a while."

"Oh, I'm sorry to hear that. Well, I'll let Maria know that you're back; hope to see you at our next service." June stared at us for a long moment before she and Brad headed off.

"I see what you mean," Emma said. I wasn't sure what she was implying. "Very developed intuition. She didn't buy your explanation one bit."

"Really." I replayed the exchanged between us and that long look of hers but didn't detect any tells. "You may be right. I think I've got so used to these people that things may be slipping by me."

Emma smiled. "That's not a bad thing, Lewis. You seem much more relaxed here than ... in the Midwest."

"Good. Keep monitoring me. I need the feedback. I'm looking forward to Sunday's healing service."

Emma gave me a questioning look.

"No. I agree with Musgrave—it's too soon for you to step forward, especially since I seem to be a bit compromised in terms of my own objectivity, or so he thinks."

"Again, that's not a bad thing, Lewis."

I didn't reply; the bill came and I did my e-transfer and we left. On the walk back, I broached the subject. "There's a whole other layer to this assignment and to our tasking here, and it may take a lot of ingenuity to survive this in one piece."

Emma walked on for a while, as she mulled over my warning. "I figured as much, Alan. And I'm here as much for you as I am for myself and getting out from under their thumb."

She reached over, gave my hand a squeeze and withdrew. We walked in silence back to our hotel. I dropped Emma off at her room; there was an awkward pause before she reached over and hugged me. "Pleasant dreams, Lewis. But, I'm sure that's not a problem here."

I wondered if Emma's remark acted like a subconscious suggestion, because I did have a dream about Maria that night. Instead of the desert vistas of some of my earlier dreams, this one was set in an underground cave, at the juncture of two rivers flowing in different directions. On the wall of the cave were ancient Native America pictographs, and Maria was drawing new ones that looked very similar in design, if not in intent. The one I was fixated on was of a turtle swimming with its head tucked inside, but its feet frantically doing strokes to keep itself afloat. Maria turned to me; she was dressed in Native shaman attire, with a wolf skin over her shoulders and its head atop hers.

"Lewis. You can't find your way unless you stick your head out."

"Figuratively?" I asked.

But she only smiled and turned back to her cave drawings.

When I woke up in the morning, that phrase was on the tip of my tongue. Did I need to stick my head out, and would it be cut off if I did?

33.

The following Sunday morning was the Institute's next healing ceremony. This was the first Sunday gathering I could remember, and I speculated about this switch. There also seemed to be more people in attendance than at the usual midweek services I had attended. I wondered if the Sunday setting didn't bring out more closet Christians. I was also as interested in Emma's reaction to the service, as I was to Maria's presence and the energy that seemed to emanate from her. Or maybe I was just more attuned after my own healing. Emma listened intently to the introduction, took careful note of Maria's entrance, and watched the procession of people and their sometimes dramatic reactions to their healings with interest—especially those who fainted and had to be escorted to their seats. We had a good angle—I did pick the seats for that reason—for her to watch several people's facial reaction as they shuffled back to their seats. Most appeared, at least to me, to be genuinely affected. For myself I seemed to be able to draw on her energy from a distance and it felt like receiving another healing to me, if not as intense.

Afterward, and another switch from her previous services, Maria stood up and walked down the center aisle with people following after her, then she stood outside and greeted people. Again, this was reminiscent of a priest, at a Catholic Church service, from her childhood. Today she was wearing a white gown with a turquoise sash. While we had sat midway down the row of chairs, I held Emma back and indicated we should let the others file out first, which would allow us more time with Maria. I now wondered if this was her plan from the start for this Sunday service.

"Lewis, it's nice to see you again. June said you were back."

"Maria, this is my new research assistant Emma Forbes." They shook hands and had good eye contact. Emma was not one to back down from any face-off.

"Emma, I hope your stay here will be … fruitful." Maria turned to me. "And Brenda's … allergies were acting up?"

I stared at Maria and held her gaze for a long moment. "Oh, it's not that entirely? Is it something we should discuss? I do hope it wasn't a reaction to her … healing, since you did leave town the next day."

There was a long pause. Emma broke the silence. "Lewis, I do need to hit the books to get up to speed for tomorrow's meeting with you." She stepped back. "I mean, if you two want to … discuss something in private."

"Well, that's very kind of you dear," Maria added. "I am interested, and now's as good a time as any to hear what happened."

I turned to Emma. "So you can find your way back?" I asked.

Emma raised her eyebrows. "Lewis, it's not Chicago."

As she traipsed off down the street, Maria gave her a long, steady look. "I like that woman, Lewis. Very genuine." She turned and I followed her back into the church, through the vestry, to the Institute's building and then on to her private quarters. Interestingly enough, we didn't talk the whole way, and it was hard to gauge Maria's … feeling tone, as they say here.

After I sat down on the sofa across from her chair, she stared back at me. "Would you like some tea? I don't have any coffee, but maybe some green tea will do the trick."

"Thank you. That would be fine."

She called out and her housekeeper stepped into the living room. Maria asked her to bring us green tea. Maria sat down, closed her eyes, and centered herself, I guess you would say. When she opened her eyes, she was definitely in a perceptive mode. "So, Lewis, tell me about Brenda and her … reaction."

I'd known this inquiry was coming and had prepared my little speech, but Fria's energy always seemed to undermine any deceit on my part, and I couldn't give her my operational spin on the situation. I looked away for a moment before turning back and speaking. "Well, she had a very restless night, and when she woke up the next morning around 4:00 a.m., she was in an absolute panic. Seemed to be overwhelmed by repressed feelings and couldn't string two sentences together at a time. We packed, drove to Phoenix, and took a plane to Chicago where she was admitted to the hospital. They replaced her neural processor, and she still hasn't recovered completely."

Maria sat with his explanation for a long moment. Her house-keeper stepped forward during this pause, served our tea, and then withdrew. "That's some story, Lewis." Her tone was rather neutral, but I wondered if she doubted me. "I mean, we have had reactions to healings, but this is pretty drastic," she said.

"Well, I'm sure it's a lifetime of repressed feelings coming forward."

"But, that's the point, the energy compensates, or it usually does, as I believe I've told you. And since it's in tune with one's totality, it shouldn't adjust her to the point that something like this would occur."

Maria appeared very concerned; given my own orientation, I figured she felt threatened for her ministry. "So this has never happened before?" I asked.

She took a long sip of her tea and looked across the table at me. She was definitely monitoring my energy field, and I tried to calm down any heightened emotional response. She smiled. "I like how you do that, Lewis. Pull in your emotions. Very advanced. With some training, you could ..." She stopped herself, spread out the creases in her skirt to buy time. "To answer your question, I have seen this kind of drastic reaction before, but I'm not sure you want to hear this."

I was taken aback by her warning. "Well, I most certainly do."

"While I'm not a national figure per se, my healing practice and the healers I've trained and sent out into the world have created some notoriety for me. This has in turn attracted certain ... interest by the government, and on two occasions they've tried to infiltrate my organization, and one of their agents had a similar reaction to his healing. I later attributed it to a neural processor with ... certain insidious features that wouldn't allow alignment."

"And it didn't ... compensate?"

"Again the person needs to want it, and having such a processor indicates otherwise. We don't force-feed the energy, Lewis," she said.

"So, what usually happens?" I asked.

"Well, sometimes the person's unconscious opens the flood-gates of repressed feelings, in hopes they can free themselves of the outside influence."

Talk about a panic attack. I could barely get this. "So it's not you or the energy, but them?"

Maria nodded her head. "So, does this indicate that Brenda was a government operative and attached herself to you, and guided you here as some kind of cover?" she asked.

Maria and I stared at each other for a long moment. If she had gotten this right, I wondered if she suspected me as well, and if this was my opening to confess and either start the double agent protocol, or grab the brass ring, as it were.

"Insidious features … like what?" I asked.

Again that long, piercing look, and a somewhat disappointed one I suspected. "Behavior modification, or that capability, which the person may not even know they've been subject to and could be a victim, or someone who needs the … reinforcement."

"Wow. That's really disturbing. I know my work's been … rebellious, to say the least, but not subversive and that the government would set me up to set you up is … well, unbelievable." I paused, gauging her reaction. "I mean, that they would go to this much trouble."

Maria stood up. "What's the saying—kill two birds with one stone?"

I was being dismissed, and happy to flee this testy situation. "I need to go back and think through my contact with Brenda, if that was even her name, from the beginning and see if you're right." She walked me to the backdoor. "If you are right, I'm sorry to have brought this to your doorstep."

She gave me a kind look, but no hugs today. "We're kindred spirits, Lewis. I'm sure we can work this out, and either way our contact has put you on another path that should contribute greatly to your work."

I looked back at her, in great conflict over my own deception.

"I'm more concerned about its effect on you, Maria."

She gave me another piercing look. "I'm protected in ways you can't even imagine, Lewis." She opened the door. "Be well."

Chapter Twelve

34.

I headed back to the Sliding Sands, but then made a detour to one of the overlooks. I was discombobulated by my talk with Maria and needed to settle down. There was a bench there with a green UV-ray cover for daytime viewing. I sat there and stared out at the desert at noon, with the sun's rays beating down on it. After a while it seemed to stop my interior dialogue, as I melted into the surroundings. The earth's energy was palpable, and for the first time I sensed its correlation with Maria's energy and her healings and wondered if this wasn't the true source of her power. I did notice that nobody in her group sat cross-legged like yogis, and I assumed that this was to help draw energy not only from the cosmos but through one's feet from the earth herself. As I sat there, I could feel this energy rising within myself but only so far. This was interesting, and I wondered what would happen with an even more intense exposure.

When I arrived back at the hotel, I knocked on Emma's door. She told me to come in; I found her sitting up in bed reading through my manuscript and making notes. She really was taking her assignment seriously, or maybe it was the book itself that interested her—I could only hope. Emma looked up and stared at me for a long moment. "Have a good talk?"

I pulled a chair over to her bed. "Yes, very interesting. She figured that Brenda/Jean's reaction was caused by a processor geared for behavior modification."

Emma put down the manuscript and thought about this for a moment. "Are you sure she wasn't just reading your mind ... or energy, or whatever it is she does?"

"No. She said that my description of Brenda's breakdown was similar to a reaction by an undercover agent, with a modified processor, sent to spy on them."

"Well, that's pretty close." She paused for a moment. "What I got was that this woman is for real, and I wouldn't be surprised if she can do what Musgrave and his crew claim."

"Maybe, but I doubt she's doing it, and we're just projecting a lot onto her."

"So where does this leave us?" she asked.

"On the way back from my meeting, I stopped off at one of the overlooks, and the energy coming off the desert felt similar to Maria's."

"But you've been driving around the desert for months now."

I wondered about that myself. "I don't know—could be my long absence and reintroduction to this earth energy accelerated ... something in me."

"You know, Musgrave's analysis—or what he shared with me—seems too specific to Maria and her group, and could apply to alternative energy medicine in general."

I had been wondering about that myself. "So, you think it's a ploy?"

"It's no doubt a cover, but for what?" Emma asked.

"Well, what if this effect is more pervasive or universal, but she reflects enough of the heightened energy to test Jean and me and gauge its effects on our neural processors as a general test?"

Emma stood up and went over to the window. From the second floor you could see out across the plateau to the surrounding desert. "So this is really about the modern neural processors breaking down and the government in a panic over that?"

I wasn't sure just how much of my own speculation I could share with her, but I couldn't figure this out on my own and it was time to trust someone. "Yes, I think so."

"Well, there's a way we can test that theory," she said, turning to me.

"Get another healing?" I asked.

"Not what I'm thinking, but maybe that as well."

"What then?"

"We could drive up to Sedona for the weekend and check out the vortex energy there, although I've heard the whole area is one large vortex now."

This felt like the right move, and I could almost feel my body tingling at the suggestion. "Yeah. I think you're right." Emma was beaming. "Or is this just an excuse for you to go there?" I asked half-seriously.

"Well, I've always wanted to. Ling said it's the jewel of the borny villages, or what's coming."

"Definitely then, but let's not do any research on vortexes at the library and best not question anyone. But our portables are safe to scan the Internet for info."

"You don't trust Maria and her group?"

"I trust Maria, but if she's picked up on us, then maybe the others have, and they might not be as … forgiving."

For the rest of the week, we went about the business of me writing my novel, and Emma doing research on the book at the library. Friday morning we headed out; it was interesting that Tim, the desk clerk, asked if we'd be away for the weekend. I told him we were playing it by ear. We had definitely been picking up more of a surveillance vibe from the people here this week. Somebody had even tried to hack my portable at the Iguana Café while I was writing there one night, but they couldn't crack the DOD encryption.

It was only thirty miles to Sedona up Route 89A. We had done an Internet search and were particularly interested in exploring the Cathedral Rock and Bell's Rock Vortexes; they were both south of the town and not far from each other as the crow flies, but we decided to get a room at an eastside hotel to disguise our intent. As we drove into town, we found it similar to other places in the Southwest, where the economic downturn of years past had winnowed out both the population and its tourist appeal, leaving a group of diehard residents, most of which, from what we'd heard, were now bornies. We stopped at a hydrogen station to recharge the car's fuel cells, picked up a few brochures and then stopped at a local diner for breakfast. Just getting out of the car you could sense the heightened energy.

We took a window seat and were as much interested in watching the people inside the restaurant as the landscape outside. They were definitely affected, or had these bemused smiles on their faces, like they were tapped into the Mother Lode and couldn't get enough. This was also how you could tell the locals from the tourists. The waitress took her time, and while she seemed slow, her eyes were definitely reading more than our menu selections. At one point she started smiling from ear to ear, as if she saw us as one of them. Interesting.

While we were waiting for our food, I closed my eyes and could sense the energy permeating everything and coursing through my body. When I opened them, Emma was smiling.

"Get anything?" she asked.

"Yeah, this is definitely Energy Central. Can't imagine what the vortexes are like?"

The waitress served our food and we ate in silence, just soaking up the vibe, as they say. I definitely needed to lie down and just let this energy move through me. When the waitress picked up our plates and gave us a bill, she tried to inquire about our stay, but we were evasive and she let it drop but not without an encouraging smile. We found an eastside hotel that appeared to have once been a resort for the large tourist business, but had been scaled down after the ozone collapse to economically accommodate businessmen passing through town. I tried to get two rooms for us, but Emma insisted on one with a queen-size bed and I just went along with her. The desk clerk gave us a "friend's" discount as he called it, and I paid for two days in advance. There wasn't much fight in me at this point, and no need to keep up appearances. When we got to the room, I just collapsed on the bed. Emma let me rest, changed into a one-piece

black swimsuit and went out to the tinted-glass enclosed
swimming pool.

I nodded off, if that's what it was, and had another one of
those instant dreams or astral projections, which is what Maria
called the last one I had in her presence. This time instead of
soaring through the air like a hawk, I was squirming through the
desert sands like a giant lizard or iguana, luxuriating in the feel
of the coarse sand granules against my dry skin. I woke up to
Emma lying beside me in her wet bathing suit, which was soon
discarded.

"Are you sure?" I asked rather lamely. She just nodded her
head, stripping off my clothes and climbing on top of me. I didn't
need any further stimulation; she was voracious and the
lovemaking was very passionate for both of us. Interestingly
enough, I didn't come in the usual way, but the energy just
shifted at some point and moved up my spine and exploded in
my head. And it seemed conscious, like Maria's energy as it
"played" with my neural processor and then radiated downward
through my whole body. Emma was straddling me and seemed to
be experiencing some of the same, but not as intensely.

"Did it move up your spine?" I asked. Her eyes were closed;
she shook her head but I could tell it did spread out through her
body, but maybe not nearly as pervasively or she didn't feel as
ecstatic. She collapsed on me and we fell asleep with her on top
of me.

35.

We slept through the afternoon, woke up, took a dip in the pool,
and then dressed and headed out for dinner. We found a
restaurant at a higher elevation with a spectacular view of the
surrounding desert, if not of the west side of town with a view of
the sunset. Emma was feeling very romantic after our long-
delayed hookup and wanted to sit next to me and hold hands.

But, despite luxuriating in the warmth of our body contact, I stood up and moved across from her so we could talk. We were drinking ice teas, and ordered nachos as an appetizer— something Emma had never eaten. While we got adjusted to the new seating arrangement, Emma stared out at the desert.

"You're right. The energy is certainly pervasive."

"And you can feel it … adjusting your processor?"

Emma closed her eyes to get a better sense of what was happening inside her skull. "So, what was Klaus' question you brought up on the trip from Phoenix? Does this energy integrate higher functionality?"

"Generally, or in isolated cases like ours," I added.

Emma opened her eyes, and then placed her hand over her heart. "Well, I'm not getting great leaps of intuition, but I feel some repressed feelings getting freed up."

"And it just wasn't the great sex?" I kidded her.

"Seriously, a wave of feelings is rolling in, but my mind, or is it my neural processor, seems to be slowing down and going with the flow," she said.

I nodded my head. "Interesting. Brenda—or can we call her Jean—felt the same but resisted it and it somehow short-circuited her NP."

We both thought about this process as our waitress served us our dinner of enchiladas and fried chilies and side dishes of rice and beans, all smothered with the best salsa either of us had ever eaten. The energy definitely moved from our heads to our stomachs, and we just enjoyed the meal and kept the conversation light, or at least we did for a while. Then something occurred to Emma.

"This energy here. How does it stack up or correlate with Fria's healing energy?"

"Like I said earlier, it feels similar, but I think I won't be able to really nail the comparison until we visit one of the vortexes and really soak up the energy there."

Emma looked at me questioningly. "So we're thinking of first hitting Bell's Rock, south of town and east of Cathedral Rock, and then heading over to the other?" she asked.

I nodded my head.

She pulled some printed-out information from her purse, with a map and colored photos of the area, and spread it on the table.

"Looks like a great place to get hijacked," I said.

"Well, if the energy is conscious, it should keep us safe and secure as well," she said.

I had never thought of it in that way, but she could be right: it was how Maria described this energy and how I experienced its interaction with my own neural processor—as being very conscious, as if options were reviewed and choices made. It made me wonder if this wasn't the real singularity tech geeks talked about, in regard to super human computer intelligence, which had never happened.

"What are you thinking?" I finally asked.

"About my conscious remark?" Emma asked. I nodded. "I just wonder if it acts like a sentinel or one of those guardian spirits you read about in mythology."

"That's possible," I said, not really wanting to discuss this concept in a restaurant setting. Guess I was self-conscious about its spiritual aspects.

The waitress brought us our check, and waited as if she expected us to inquire about the different vortexes and we did.

"Well, Cathedral Rock is supposed to strength one's feminine side, but Bells Rock's, my favorite, balances both male and female elements."

We thanked her for her assessment, which reinforced our preference, but didn't indicate as much because operational security—even if we were off the reservation as it were—was ingrained in us. Well, we left a little early, but the hostess recommended a spot where we could watch the sunset, and we drove to the lookout west of town and parked there with a number of other drivers. The gold and turquoise colors of the sunset were spectacular, and we stayed on as the twilight settled in and then the night and the starry heavens above us came out. You rarely got great starscape views back east, with all the cloud cover from the increased moisture in the air year round, but out west the dry air compensates and night skies were often crystal clear, and tonight's vista was spectacular. The combination of the earth energies, our increased energy exchange and this wonderful early-evening spectacle was a little disorienting for me.

"Are you okay?" Emma finally asked.

I nodded my head in an absent way.

"Why don't you let me drive back to the hotel?"

"No macho resistance on my part." I slid out and walked around to the passenger's side and let her scoot over into the driver's seat.

"Besides, I want you to save your energy," Emma said with a leer, as she started up the vehicle and we drove off. Freed from following the road, I was able to view the city and its Southwest adobe architecture, and as we drove back into town, I was also able to watch the traffic more closely. Maybe it was my heightened senses, but I noticed that someone seemed to be following us. I mentioned this to Emma; she checked it out and agreed, and so we stopped at a night spot for an after-dinner dessert, and just stood outside on the porch and watched this guy drive up and then turn his car around—once he saw that we had spotted him—and drive away.

"Curious local, or worse?" Emma asked.

"Well, we haven't been in touch with Musgrave for a while and maybe he got concerned."

"You think."

"It may be time to check in with him, but I know he'll ask about Maria's reaction to Brenda's meltdown and I'm not sure how to answer him without giving away too much," I said.

"Let's hang out here, but not talk about it until we're back on the road."

We went inside and were immediately seated—not much business tonight, or maybe generally. We asked for the dessert menu, which seemed to bum out the waiter, but he complied and we ordered a sugary treat called Canela Bunuelos with Anise Syrup, which seemed to be the Mexican version of small funnel cakes. I could only eat a few—much too sweet for me—but Emma gobbled up the rest and had to go to the restroom to wash the sugary mess off her fingers. Her diet had no doubt been more deprived than mine on her long holdout.

We didn't linger, since this was just an evasive maneuver. Outside and on the drive back to the hotel, we didn't spot our tail, but by now they had probably scoped out our hotel and knew where we were staying.

As we drove along, Emma said, "You know, it's getting late back east if you're going to call tonight."

"Well, last time I drove off the reservation Musgrave called me at 5:00 in the morning, and I plan to wake him up as well, if not tonight."

She smiled. "I guess you can't say that Maria picked up on Brenda's modified processor."

"It does put a different spin on our operation, and not one I'm sure he wants to hear."

"Yeah, but the truth cuts both ways."

"Yes, and it could cut deeper than we want," I said. "I think for now we need to be cautious about what we share with him, or he may just terminate the whole op."

Emma didn't like that prospect, for more personal—I would assume—than professional reasons.

"I think you need to first figure out what the future holds for you and your development, before you force the issue," she said.

I nodded my head. "Yeah. You're right. It's too soon. Maybe after our … excursion tomorrow, I'll have a better handle on that."

"And we can certainly shake an agent's tail."

"But not satellite surveillance in this clear air," I said.

"Well, we'll fake our reaction too, until we're out of sight."

"Yeah, let's wear floppy sunhats and dark glasses, just in case."

Emma reached over and affectionately squeezed my arm.

"You know they'll scope out our single-room occupancy at the hotel, after we've been instructed to keep it chaste," I added.

Emma turned to me. "Fuck them."

36.

We woke up early for our drive down to Bells Rock, wanting to climb it before the sun got too hot. We took Route 179 south for five miles. The elevated "rock" was soon visible with its serrated, red-hue rounded-tiered structure rising from the desert floor. When we arrived, there were only a few cars parked at the path head with its viewing station. We stepped out and were immediately hit by waves of energy. We walked over, stood under the overhang and just stared up at it. We had been told that you could climb it, but there were no set hiking paths. On the way we had stopped at a sports store and got floppy hats, UV sunscreen lotion, water bottle harnesses and gloves for gripping the sandstone—we were told our Southwest hiking boots were suitable. So, after a while, we asked ourselves whether we should climb the rock, which could be dangerous, or stay below and see if the energy was strong enough at its base to gauge its impact?

"So, what do you think, Alan?"

"Yeah, let's climb as high as we can without breaking our necks."

Emma was watching me. "Are you sure? You look blasted already from down here."

I closed my eyes, and I didn't feel, to use a retro term, "spaced out" like last night. I felt more grounded and solid, as if the energy didn't move me out of my center but pushed me further into it. "No, I'm fine now, more grounded than ever," I said.

We used our hands to climb up the lower, five-foot-tall outcroppings, walked twenty feet or so to next one, climbed it as well and continued upward. At some point, about halfway up, the climb became too dicey for Emma, so we stopped. By now I could really feel the swirling vortex energy. It seemed to come up from the earth through my feet and weave itself around my chakras, as Maria would say, and on up to the top of my head and out, as if spinning me like a child's twirling top. As we looked out across the desert, I felt one with all of it and had never felt more integrated in my life. Emma had a more difficult adjustment, but she seemed to be enjoying it nevertheless, her hand constantly going to her heart and the feelings that arose there.

Finally, she spoke up, "So, what do you think? Is this similar, different from Maria's healing energy, or what?"

"I believe it's what she draws on and is able to focus and transmit. But what's interesting is that her healers, who tour or live in other parts of the country, are able to tap into the same energy, despite its apparent low levels elsewhere … or maybe the upsurge of earth energy is spreading out."

"That would be alarming for our employers," Emma added.

"Let's head down. I don't want to get into a head-talking space on this rock; seems too contrary and it's kind of … pushing at me."

We headed back and were particularly interested in the folks we met along the way and their reaction to the energy. Most of the women seemed affected, while only some of the men, or at least as far as we could tell from just watching them. Again, I didn't want to get into a head space, unlike everybody else who kept chatting away as they climbed up the outcroppings. It was also becoming very hot as the sun rose higher and higher overhead. Once we got back to the shade of the overhang shelter, I felt better about staying longer, as the energy was able to settle in. When the other group of people there headed out, we had more privacy.

"I think you need to get a healing at the next service, so you can help judge the similarities and differences."

"I want to," Emma said, "but I trust that you're on track with your speculation, and I don't think we need to wait for my healing to figure out what's up with Musgrave and our mission here."

"Basically, I think the neural processors keep people in a mind space that cuts them off from their higher functionality and represses feelings, so they're more easily controlled and manipulated."

"But yours isn't acting that way and it seems to be helping, not interfering, with this integrative process in you," she said.

"Well, like they keep saying, it serves as an evolutionary appendage since it's made of brain tissue, and in those who can integrate feelings, it seems to accelerate a different kind of functionality, but not in those who are more repressed."

Emma thought about this analysis. "Maybe it's Maria's healing energy, since it moves through her first, that jumps people. But those just feeding off it from the land aren't as … fortunate or … that's not the word …"

"Or, as facilitated as those coming to her and her healers," I said.

"So, eliminate the healers, or the go-betweens, and you … if not eliminate the threat, put it off while you adjust your strategy."

"Well, that apparently is what they're thinking and what this whole op was about, using Jean and me and now you as test subjects."

"Yeah, and we know what happens to lab rats," Emma said.

"Let's turn off our portables, drive north to Flagstaff and do a reverse circle-run back to Jerome through Prescott, to shake any tails."

Emma nodded her head.

"I'm not talking to Musgrave or Klaus until I've conferred with Maria and have a better handle on all of this."

"Are you thinking of teaming up with her and the anti-government groups against them?" Emma asked rather evenhandedly, not pressing the issue.

"I'm not taking sides either way, at least not yet; I'm hoping there's a middle way or a way to convince 'them' that this can be helpful and doesn't need to be controlled or stamped out."

Emma just stared at me. "I doubt if anybody on the other side would agree with you."

"That's just the problem: they both think one-sidedly—an us-against-them scenario."

"Well, Ling says the history of their resistance is littered, like those of the 19th-century Native Americans, with the government's false promises and betrayals."

"Let's see." We headed back to the car and drove up Route 179 and took 89 east to the hotel. As we approached the turnoff, I kept driving. "I sense that we need to keep going to avoid tails. Hope we're not leaving anything behind you can't do without."

Emma reached over and grabbed my arm. "I've got all I need right here."

I smiled. How endearing. I just hoped I wasn't signing her death warrant along with my own.

Chapter Thirteen

37.

After we drove through Flagstaff and headed west on the interstate, I remembered my last trip on this highway, and how Jean and I had gone to the Grand Canyon for the night before driving to Phoenix and rendezvousing with Musgrave—to throw off any tails that Maria's group might have put on us. So maybe I was responding to the recent surveillance vibe I had sensed in Jerome, or the actual FBI tail we had picked up in Sedona, but as we approached Williams and the turnoff for the Grand Canyon, I turned onto the ramp.

"Doing a little sightseeing?" Emma asked, no doubt delighted by the prospect of viewing the Grand Canyon.

"Well, that too, but while this isn't a vortex or a known one, it's a huge natural formation, and I just want to check it out after our experience at Bells Rock."

Emma tucked her feet under her. "Don't need to sell me. I've always wanted to go there. Can we go down the trails to the bottom?"

"No, they've discontinued the mule rides; we'd have to hike around the rim for twenty miles or so to find a low access point."

"Too bad, but we can view it from the edge?" she asked.

"Yes, and walk part of the way down one of the long trails, which is what I want to do, and see if I can sense or even see any natural energy flows."

"Great."

Before we checked in at the Maswik Lodge, I drove to the lookout with the old trail heading down into the canyon from the south side. Since we had our hiking boots and UV-cover hats and lotion, Emma and I decided to trek down the path a little farther than I had last time. After we had dropped a couple hundred yards beneath the rim of the canyon and into the belly of the beast, as the Jungians would probably call it, I could sense a subtle shift in the energy, or my energy, I should say. This was a particularly narrow part of the canyon, with the north side maybe a mile across the Colorado River flowing below us, so it felt more like being underground or dropping down a volcano tube into the heart of the earth, and then it dawned on me that if you moved the "h" from heart to the end of the word, you got: earth. The earth as the heart of us all, which had to be a Native American or indigenous concept. I also felt an enormous rush of feeling for "mother earth" and turned on the downward-sloping path to sidle up against the side of the canyon wall, spread-eagled. Emma, who was walking behind me, stopped and gave me my moment before I broke off.

"Anything you want to share?" she asked.

I told her about my little heart/earth epiphany, which she totally understood, without making any self-conscious smart-aleck remark to deflect the feeling. I added, "Well, I certainly pick up a vibration or energy, somewhat similar to what I experienced at the vortex, but ... different or less ... projective."

Emma closed her eyes; after a short while, she nodded her head. "Yes, I see what you mean, but what does it do to your functionality?"

"Well, I don't want to get out of my body and into my head on a five-foot-wide path with a thousand-foot drop."

Emma laughed. "Yeah, well maybe we should turn back." She paused, "or that is, if you've got what you came for."

"Yeah, I'm good. Let's go." We turned around and I let Emma lead the way up the path to the rim of the canyon.

When we stepped back into our car, she asked, "Are we heading over to the lodge or heading back to Jerome? It's not that far."

I tried to get a sense of it all, then turned and looked at Emma sitting next me. "Well, it would give us some ... alone time."

She reached over and grasped my hand. "Well, there is that."

We drove over and checked into the lodge and ate a late lunch in their restaurant, with all the old-time sepia-toned pictures of the pioneers who first explored the canyon on mules. Emma looked over at me and started to say something about our dilemma, but I put a finger to my mouth and told her we were lucky the weather was so good and that we could take a hike after lunch.

When we were out on the land, or under the cover of trees and hopefully out of sight of any surveillance cameras or the earshot of any microphones—it sounds paranoid but every restaurant in the world was "bugged" these days—I felt like we could speak more freely. "You were saying?" I asked.

"Well, if this is about the earth's 'rising' energy and its effects, which they can't stop, even if they eliminate its facilitators like Maria and other healers, seems like they'd want to 'adjust' the neural processors, or adapt them to include more just to maintain their agenda, whatever that is."

It was so great to have a real collaborator in Emma along for the ride, instead of a naysayer or company agent like Jean. I squeezed her hand. "Yes, you would think so, and maybe they'll come around to that, but now they just seem to want to … hold on to all that they have without compromise, or so I assume— since we're not getting any real feedback from Musgrave or Klaus."

"So, what's next?" she asked.

"I've turned off my remote, and I'm thinking we stay here and head back early tomorrow and hopefully attend Maria's ten o'clock service, then we talk to her afterward."

"And if Musgrave has the town staked out?"

"No, I think he'll wait for me, even if it pisses him off. I mean. We do have … operational latitude."

Emma laughed. "Well, I don't think this is what they had in mind by 'latitude.'"

"No, I doubt that."

"I'm tired," Emma said with a cute smile.

"Maybe we need to take a nap?"

"Yeah, you never know when we'll get the chance again."

I glanced over at her, but she appeared more introspective than I would have expected from such a remark. Well, maybe her intuition in this regard was more attuned than mine.

We headed back to our room at the lodge and made love for the rest of the afternoon and late into the evening, until we both fell asleep from exhaustion, although the psycho-spiritual tension of our dilemma must have contributed to the strain and its need for release and the excess of our response.

38.

Before heading out early the next morning, we checked to see if the Institute had a Sunday service scheduled. It did, for the second week in a row, and again contrary to their earlier scheduling which was usually during the week. Was Maria picking up on my dilemma, or was this a seasonal adjustment? We arrived in town early, but instead of going back to the Sliding Sands, we ate brunch at the Iguana Café before heading over to the church for the ten o'clock healing service. We sat midway up the row of chairs again, so that we could linger afterward and talk with Maria as we walked out after the service. During the set-up to her healing, while Maria sat and waited for June to complete her introduction and for the attendees to line up, she caught my eye and held it for a long moment. It almost felt like a telepathic exchange. After the service, she once again broke with protocol and stood outside the church to greet people as they filed out.

We were the last out of the church, which allowed us a little alone time, as it were, with her. "Ah, Lewis and Emma. How nice to see you back again," she said rather innocently.

"Maria, we'd like to … talk with you about a pressing issue, if that's all right with you."

The woman stood there for a long moment as if she were scanning our auras or whatever it was that she did so effectively. "Sounds serious?"

"Yes, it is rather serious."

"Then by all means let's retire to my private quarters." Maria turned to head back up the aisle of the church. I noticed a rather intense and well-built man standing off to the side of the steps, who seemed prepared to follow after us, but Maria cut him off with a barely perceptible shake of her head. Nobody else would have noticed it, except someone trained to observe such nuances.

In her quarters Maria had her assistant bring out a pot of tea, rather than single cups, this time, since there were three of us. The assistant poured for us and passed the tea around and then left. Everyone took sips, waiting for someone to break the silence.

"Well, Lewis. You've certainly sparked my curiosity. I hope Brenda hasn't taken a turn for the worse."

I shook my head, all the while keeping my eyes focused on Maria. The energy directed back at me was so loving and supportive that it made my rather difficult confession easier. "Brenda's actual name is Jean Whatley, and she's an agent for K Industries that does undercover work for the FBI." I studied Maria's facial reaction or micro expressions, as we called them in surveillance, but amazingly enough, or not, there was no discernible reaction on her part.

Maria actually smiled. "I bet that was a relief ... Lewis."

I couldn't hide my own reaction, but I waited a moment to gather in my emotions before responding. "As you may have guessed, or ... seen, I'm not Lewis Hargrove, the novelist, but Alan Reynard, and I also work for K Industries."

Maria nodded her head, and then turned to Emma. "And you're part of this ... intrusion?"

"Yes, I'm Brenda's replacement, but my name is Emma

Knowles, and I'm just filling in to get out of my contract with them."

Maria sat back in her chair for a long moment. "So … Alan, since you've already broken … protocol by revealing yourselves, you want to tell me what this is all about?"

I looked at Emma who nodded her head. I turned to Maria and gave her an overview of my assignment, the government's concern about her and her healers, but also our effort to understand the underlying intent of all of this deception, and our speculation on what they were really afraid of.

Maria was somewhat flabbergasted by this whole scenario. "They actually believe that I can remote-view anything at a distance and plant dreams?"

I "felt" my way through Maria's own admission, which seemed genuine. "So my dreams were just that … dreams, even though I saw this room and its desert panorama, or something close to it?" I asked.

"Again, dreams can be like astral projections and you connect to the energy of the person you're dreaming about, and depending on how … aware they are, they can block the connection or … play with it."

I had always assumed that these dreams were just my subconscious fears playing out, but Maria's explanation made perfect sense, and was a modified version of the FBI scenario, without the manipulative intent. "So, did you actually see me, and know something of my intent when I arrived in town with Brenda?"

Maria paused for a moment. "Again, it's not like remote-viewing and more like sensing the energy. So when you came to town, let's say your energy felt familiar, but I didn't actually know why."

"Okay, so now that you know 'why'—what are we going to do about it?" I asked.

Maria again took her time, apparently allowing herself to be directed by her own inner awareness or self. "Well, that depends Alan ... and Emma, on where your true allegiance lies. You've greatly compromised yourselves with your ... employers, and it doesn't seem like you can just walk away from them, given their reach from Emma's holdout, and playing both sides sounds like a dangerous game, especially since they seem to have set you up to begin with."

We nodded our heads.

"Seems like, since our intent, mine and my healers, is benign, or aiding the rise of this earth-energy and its influence; and even if they find that threatening, you could just report that despite our facilitation of the energy for healing purposes, they're actually fighting nature herself. And they can fiddle with their neural processors all they want, but those who resist this rising energy will be increasingly compromised, unless adjustments and allowances are made to accommodate it."

It was my turn to be amazed by her summation of our situation. "Yes, in a perfect world, or dealing with more conscious individuals and interests, I could just lay it out that way and hope for the best, but these people control everything, or think they do, and they're not going to make such a ready 'accommodation' to this 'loss of control.'"

Maria nodded her head and stood up, as did we. "So it seems like you need to mull this over further, as do I, with my own advisors, but know that you're perfectly safe here, despite your less-than-benign operation, and that we would be prepared to ... facilitate your 'escape' if it comes to that."

"Thank you, Maria. I'm really sorry for having, as I said earlier, brought this to your doorstep, and I'm more concerned about its impact on you and yours than on me ... or us," I added, as Emma glanced over at me.

Maria smiled. "It's only us, not me or you, and all who've been touched by this energy and ... want to work for the greater good."

39.

Emma and I headed back to the Sliding Sands, unloaded our gear, and she came to my room to figure this out with me. We hadn't had much of a chance to explore our options when Musgrave called. I let it buzz for a moment, showed Emma the caller ID, then I took his call. Given my talk with Maria and feeling rather elevated and empowered by it, I figured now was as good a time as any to start this dance. I answered and his vid image appeared on my portable.

"How nice of you to take my call," Musgrave said rather sarcastically.

I paused for a moment, not wanting to overreact. "Just got back in town from Sedona, but then you knew that."

"Off the reservation again?"

"Emma and I wanted to check out the energy of the vortexes," I said.

"And?"

I wasn't sure just how far I should go with my analysis, but I was feeling particularly "protected" if that's the word, and figured more deception would only undermine us at this point.

"The energy that Maria channels feels as much earth-based as … I think etheric is the word these people use, and we wanted to check it out."

"So Emma had a healing?" he asked.

"No, not yet, but we've gone to two services and she picked up on the energy."

There was a long pause at the other end. "We've been thinking much the same ourselves, but didn't want to … bias your take on it."

I didn't respond, feeling it was better to play off him than offer any more insights.

Musgrave continued, "What did she say about Brenda's reaction, or how it undermined her neural processor? I assumed you broached the subject."

Since I had the call on video as well as speaker-phone for Emma to overhear, she stepped back and shook her head. I agreed not to tell him Maria's suspicions about behavior modifications.

"Fria said the energy's supposed to compensate, so people don't get overwhelmed by an outpouring of repressed feelings or emotions, but it also depends on the person's cooperation at all levels."

There was a catch in his voice. "So she's seen this happen before?"

"Yes, all her healers have witnessed it."

"And nobody warns people ahead of time?" Musgrave asked rather skeptically.

"At the services someone says that the energy will affect modern neural processors, but since they're made of one's own brain tissue, it should compensate but depends on people's willingness to work with it."

"Okay, at the next service, have Emma get a healing, and the two of you head back to Phoenix for a checkup."

"You're back?" I asked.

"Yeah, we want to get another reading on how it affects ... more integrated people—I think is the term Klaus uses—and then we'll decide if or how to approach her."

"You're still thinking the double agent ploy will work, despite the fact that I don't think she's got that kind of agenda."

"Well, whatever her agenda, one of her healers did a number on the secretary of commerce and his wife, and they're in the same psyche ward as Jean."

"You're kidding."

"Alan, I know you've got ... close to her, and that's part of the assignment and why we chose you, but there's a lot more going on here than you've assumed."

"I guess so," I said, and actually felt rather perplexed by this disclosure.

This seemed to have the effect on me that Musgrave was hoping to elicit. "Alan, play it by the book, and Emma goes home and you get a leg up on some real power brokering."

"Okay. They've been holding services on Sundays, so that may be the soonest we can get her in."

"Well, they've just posted a Thursday service this week, so attend that and we'll expect you on Friday."

I hesitated. This dance was going much too fast.

"Any problems with that, Alan?"

"No, of course not. We'll go forward as planned," I said.

"Good. And no more ... excursions unless they're approved by me in advance. Got that?"

"Sure."

"Friday then." He ended the call.

I looked over at Emma.

"He's definitely suspicious," she said, "and I bet he's monitoring the traffic going in and out of Jerome."

I nodded my head. "Well, we're just scoping this out as best we can, and Sedona was a real key to the puzzle."

Emma nodded her head. "What do you think Maria's going to come back to us with?"

I felt my way through my response. "That's just it. She's not logic-based but intuitive, and it's hard to assess her in ... customary ways."

"Then use your own intuition," Emma insisted.

I shook my head. "I can't just tap into her like she does with others, but something will come to me."

Since the stress of it all had pretty well wiped us out, we took a nap and later we went shopping. Emma fixed us dinner in the small kitchenette in my room. But we decided that it was best to maintain our previous sleeping arrangement and cover, or at least for most of the residents, so Emma went back to her room. We resumed our normal routine of me writing at the Iguana Café, and Emma doing research at the library and us conferring on the book. I felt that this outside focus would keep our minds settled and allow our subconscious mind or our intuition to feed us its insights more readily. At some point I realized that my real allegiance, as Maria had asked, was if not with her and her group, with this greater unfolding; and that once I decided to be of service to it, the path would open. I told Emma my thoughts and she agreed, and we made a kind of pact. It all sounded rather naïve, like teenage sleuths, but Emma thought the purity of that image was appropriate.

Thursday we attended the healing service, and Emma stood in line and received hers. Interestingly enough, Maria didn't do greetings on the church steps afterward, but we had good eye contact at one point in the service, and I didn't feel any tension on her part. While Emma had downplayed the possible effect on her, she was greatly moved by the energy and given that it was a night service, she wanted to return to our hotel and get some alone time. On our walk back, I could see that she wasn't agitated, but then neither was Jean at first, so I asked for her room key—in case she fell asleep—to check up on her later. I actually fell off to sleep myself and when I woke up, I went to Emma's room and found her sitting up in bed in a meditative posture.

"How goes it?"

"Just amazing. I can feel this energy running through my body like gangbusters. It feels like I'm going to jump out of my skin at any moment."

I stepped over, sat on the bed, and took her hand. The body contact seemed to work like a ground wire and the energy surged back into me. I closed my eyes as it spread out through my body. When I opened them, Emma had stripped down and told me to do the same. I lay on the bed while she mounted me and we made love, slowing down at times so as not to get too aroused. Then the flow of the sexual energy just reversed itself and sped up our spines and exploded in our heads, and we had a deep ecstatic melding like neither of us had ever experienced. At some point Emma rolled off and lay next to me. We held each other's hands and just allowed this energy to continue to race through our bodies and apparently align not only our chakras, but amazingly enough our neural processors as well, or so it seemed to us. Eventually we fell asleep lying next to each other. It wasn't a deep sleep and I felt conscious most of the time, but there was this nagging certainty that our rendezvous in Phoenix the following day, wouldn't be as elevated an experience.

Chapter Fourteen

40.

We rose early the next morning and packed for our trip to Phoenix. I suggested to Emma that we both flush our neural processors so at least these records couldn't be used against us. They hold about two week's worth of data: conversations, what we read, write and view, but not our thought processes, or at least not yet or not that I was aware of. Since we'd been hashing out our suspicions about this mission over the last couple of weeks, we didn't want them privy to it.

"And our reasons?" Emma asked.

"If it comes down to that, we'll say we've been sleeping with each other and didn't want them to know."

"So you're thinking this is going to get hostile?"

"Actually, more invasive than hostile, as they try to figure out the effects of this energy on our processors, but given the level of deception going on here, I really don't know what to expect."

Emma sat down on the edge of the bed to check her own feelings and intuitions on our prospects. "You know, we never went back to Maria and got her feedback."

"Yeah, I'm thinking it's best to leave her out of this and just go it alone for now."

Emma looked up at me. "You really care about her?"

This gave me pause. "Well, not in any romantic sense, but more like a mentor or revered teacher."

Emma reached out and took my hand. "That's what I meant, Alan."

It was my turn to get a good sense of her. "You know, you could just ... drop out again."

"And leave you hanging in the wind?" She shook her head. "I don't think so."

We ate breakfast in Prescott, at a diner I had frequented with

Brenda. The waitress seemed to make note of the switch. After she poured our coffee and walked away, I mentioned this to Emma.

She laughed. "Boy, aren't we paranoid today. I doubt if Musgrave is staking out diners along the way."

I nodded my head, sat back in the booth.

"Relax, Alan. It is what it is, and I'll trade one ecstatic coupling like last night's for ... whatever awaits us."

We headed out. It was a clear sunny day, and we were both just mesmerized by the desert drive and the sheer beauty of the natural world around us and the energy that emanated from it. When my remote buzzed, it really jolted us. It was Musgrave. He was directing us to the Air Force base, where the military doctor had earlier tried to extract Jean's neural processor.

"They have better facilities for an in-depth debrief," he told me.

I just went along with him. After I clicked off, neither of us said anything for a moment.

"So, you're thinking this isn't a good sign?" Emma finally asked.

"Well, they'd have invasive interrogation capability, and electronic brain scan equipment and whatnot."

"Alan, why set up a worst case scenario? As far as they know, we've been following through on our mission, despite our own private reservations, unless we tell them otherwise."

"Or are 'forced' to tell them otherwise."

Emma reached over and took my hand but didn't say anything. We drove on and reached the base about forty-five minutes later. We were directed to a parking space, and walked inside the main building where a military grunt escorted us down several hallways, to a conference room with armed guards outside. Musgrave and Klaus were waiting inside for us.

Seeing Klaus was a surprise. "I didn't think you liked the sun," I told him as Musgrave pointed to our seats across from them.

"Well, everybody needs to come in from the dark eventually," he replied rather cryptically. I didn't know what to say to that, so I just smiled.

Musgrave now added, "Let me explain your debrief. First, the two of us want to go over your general impressions of Maria Fria and her group, then we'll have both of your neural processors checked out. You'll be given a series of tests, and Dr. Klaus will conduct an in-depth with Alan."

Since Musgrave was looking at me and treating Emma more like an add-on to the mission, I nodded my head in agreement.

"Good. Alan, after three months, you still believe that Fria is just a healer and doesn't have an anti-government agenda?"

"Yes, but then the results of their healings could be threatening and she may be … aware of that."

Klaus nodded his head. "Good. Threatening, how?" he asked.

"Well, from my own personal experience, as I've said, it seems like the neural processors, while bestowing added intelligence, do create a kind of schism in the psyche that represses … the feeling function, I believe you called it, Dr. Klaus."

"And?"

"These healings—and possibly not just hers but this whole arena of holistic healing—might 'adjust' the processors to allow more integration of feelings and intuitions, which will make …"

Musgrave held up his hand. "Alan, it seems like we're moving into an area of speculation that I'd rather Emma not be privy to … or to our feedback, since you've no doubt discussed this amongst yourselves." He turned to Emma. "Why don't we just do your checkup now?" Musgrave stood up and escorted Emma out of the room. I didn't try to catch her eye, which might have given away too much.

"So, do we wait for Musgrave to return?"

"Yes, he does get cranky if he's left out," Klaus said with a wry smile.

Momentarily, Musgrave returned and took his seat. "You were saying."

"That the integration of repressed feelings might make people more integrated and less subject to manipulation at all levels."

"Very astute of you, Alan," Klaus added. "So, you feel more … integrated and able to better fend off outside manipulation, electronic and otherwise?"

I took a deep breath so not to overreact. "After my healing with Fria, I felt less driven and on-edge and I seem to see things more … objectively."

"A development that, while helpful for a few … overseers, we wouldn't want to generally encourage," Klaus said.

This was rather revealing, but I didn't comment. However, he must have detected a telltale micro expression or facial reaction on my part.

"In so far as," Klaus added hastily, "the social dynamics of our rather compromised ecological system dictates the need for … continued oversight."

"I understand."

"Good, Alan. So you agree with us?" Musgrave asked.

I could almost feel the walls of the room leaning closer to better hear my response. "In what way?"

"That what Fria and her healers are facilitating needs to be … countered," Musgrave added, with a rather nasty grin.

"Well, if it were just Fria and her troupe, we'd be lucky, but since they and others are drawing on the earth's energy, seems like we'd be like the little Dutch boy, trying to plug the holes in the dike."

Musgrave sat back in his chair. He turned to Klaus. "I told you. He's definitely been turned."

"But you and I just talked about this energy being earth-based," I hurriedly added.

It was Klaus' turn to raise his hand. "While we agree that the energy affecting neural processors isn't entirely … etheric, as you've pointed out, she and her 'troupe' are facilitators and for now we deal with it at this level."

"If that's what you've decided," I replied.

"Tell me, Alan," Musgrave added. "Have you had this discussion with Fria, and know that you're being remotely screened for lie detection?"

If there was ever a time to pull in my emotions, this was it. I struggled not to overreact. "I have, in a general sense, trying to explore the nature of this healing energy and its effect on me, which led to speculation about its general effect on the population at large."

Musgrave was looking down at the computer monitor embedded in his table. "Bullshit."

"Is that what your readings are telling you or what you surmise?" I asked evenhandedly. My calm and unruffled response seemed to somewhat unhinge him.

Klaus stood up before Musgrave could respond with another angry retort. "Okay, this … inquiry has gone far enough. Let me say, Alan. I think you were well within your right to explore this with her. So let's check out your processor and test your various quotients, then you and I will explore this line of questioning further."

I stood up while Musgrave remained seated. It was obvious who was running the show, but I wondered if I was safer with Musgrave and his gut reaction to things, than Klaus and his many-level approach to manipulation.

41.

They ran me through the same battery of tests that I had undergone after my first healing with Maria: IQ tests, emotional response tests and a more extensive intuitive or psychic test. I could tell from the conductor's reaction that this last one was off the scale. Again, and even more so this time, they had trouble separating the feedback loops from my neural processor and the neocortex since, I would imagine, it was even more integrated than earlier. Finally they just gave up trying, or that's what it seemed to me. I found that this time I could almost monitor these feedback loops myself and could sense the problem they were experiencing.

Again, I was allowed to rest for a couple of hours and afterward was escorted to the cafeteria for lunch. I was hoping to catch up with Emma there, or at least see her, if they were keeping us separated, but she wasn't in the cafeteria. I asked my military escort, but he didn't have any information on her whereabouts or disposition, which I should've expected. There was a fenced-in exercise yard that we headed for and he allowed me to walk around for half an hour. While the yard was empty and there weren't any orange-suited prisoners getting their outside time, the correlation to a prison was the obvious and probably the intended effect. I was sure this was Klaus' idea. I did some yoga stretching exercises as a counter strategy and was soon whisked away to an interrogation room. Unlike last time, this was being conducted with military or police protocol: no conference table and bottled water, just an iron table and two wooden chairs.

Klaus stepped into the room after making me sweat it out for half an hour. He sat down across from me and placed his file folder on the table between us, and just stared at me for a long moment. Then he opened the folder and pulled out a picture of several nondescript buildings located in a desert setting and slid it across the table to me. "Alan, given your test results, we want to try something new. Look at these buildings, or get a feel for them, and tell me what's going on there."

I looked back rather flabbergasted. "What's this?"

"Please, just work with me and I'll clarify our protocol."

I stared at the main building and after about twenty seconds got the distinct impression that it was a munitions assembly plant—I didn't actually see people building bombs, but that was my impression. "Seems like it's a bomb factory or something along that line."

Klaus nodded his head; he slid a photo of a woman across the desk to me, along with another photo of a beach with palm trees and waves lapping the shore. "I'd first like you to focus on the beach scene, and then look at the woman and try to send her this picture."

I got it. "This is a remote viewing or psychic projection test?"

Klaus just smiled wryly. "Just do it, Alan."

I wasn't sure if succeeding was in my best interest, but I went along with the test and was actually interested in the results myself. Had I become that ... psychic? I stared at the photo and then at the woman. I could feel a kind of energy transference, or something in me reaching out to her. It was all very interesting. After I broke the connection, Klaus gathered the three photos and put them back in his file and closed it. Hopefully, this was the end of the testing. A moment later, a military grunt opened the door and passed a note to Dr. Klaus. He read it without reaction and placed it into the folder. Apparently no electronic communications were allowed—no doubt thinking I could remote-hack it.

"So, did I pass?"

"As you ascertained, your intuitive scores were the highest we've ever recorded, but then we don't recruit people for this ... faculty, or at least not yet. So we wanted to test your reach." He paused for a moment. "You nailed the munitions plant and were able to transfer this image to our test subject."

"So, do I get a free all-expenses-paid vacation to the Bahamas?"

Klaus laughed; the first time I'd ever seen him laugh. Somehow I wasn't encouraged by it.

"Seems like you've become somewhat of a protégé of your healer, or should I say, target." He let that settle. "Of course, we put you in this situation to test her effect on someone with your

... propensities, and we've got our answer."

"So was this the real op, your true intention in placing me there?" I asked.

Klaus stared at me for a long moment. "Let's focus on you, not our intentions."

While I was waiting out his next question or directive, I suddenly found myself watching the two of us from above, as if I were remote-viewing myself. Very interesting.

Apparently Klaus could sense the shift. "What just happened, Alan?"

I wasn't about to confide in him. "I suddenly felt like taking a leak."

He didn't laugh this time. "You should take your situation more seriously."

"I always take you seriously, Dr. Klaus. So why don't you do the same and tell me what this is about?"

"I'm surprised you haven't figured that out, Alan. This is a standard double agent protocol interrogation. Musgrave thinks you're batting for the other team, and I'm here to test that."

"By giving me psychic tests?" I asked.

"If your target was a female agent and you were required to ... get intimate with her, we'd test just how far your transference had gone, to ascertain your allegiance or if you've been turned."

"And in this case, the transference would be psychic or intuitive?"

Klaus smiled. "Yes, Alan, sharp as ever."

"In your example, just because the guy was boning his target doesn't mean he was turned, nor does my development say the same."

"No, it doesn't. But, it gives us a better sense of your objectivity or its lack," he said.

I nodded my head. This made sense.

"And giving us that little 'Dutch boy' metaphor, or saying in effect that she's not the problem and that we need to adjust neural processors to accommodate earth energy, is rather telling."

"I didn't actually say that," I said.

"No, you didn't, but give us some credit—we can extrapolate."

I closed my eyes to tune in to my inner senses, as it were, and turned them on him to figure out where this was going.

"Psyching me out, Alan? Or is this a projection maneuver?" he asked.

"I'm just trying to get a feel for the larger scope of this ... inquiry."

"And what do you get?"

Interesting response. I had to ask myself—what do I get by giving him my analysis. But I figured that for Emma and me to have any chance of getting out of here alive, I'd have to talk my way out of this standoff. "The psychological schism created by neural processors and some fifty years of their general use, is creating a kind of lash-back cycle where repressed feelings or emotions are short-circuiting the processors, not to mention the rise of earth energy causing further schisms in many, or greater integration in some." I paused. "So you have no choice but to adapt, but *how* is the problem and the whole point of this op."

Klaus' eyes widened. "I don't think I've ever heard a better analysis of the situation." He paused for a moment. "I'm sure my superiors will be impressed, and I think you just bought yourself ... more rope."

"To pull myself out of a hole or further hang myself?" I asked.

"Well, Alan, that's your choice, isn't it."

"And yours is to deny this reality at your own peril."

Klaus gave me another one of his wry smiles. I wished, as the British would say, I could put a sock in it. "Musgrave and others like him see things in black and white—top-down control or nothing," he said.

I nodded my head and wondered if he were listening to orders over his earpiece.

"Others," he continued, "and fortunately those at the highest levels, understand … accommodation. You and maybe Emma— her scores were somewhat interesting—might represent a more … productive model for healing this schism as you call it."

I nodded my head again, but didn't want to be too optimistic. "It sounds workable."

He paused again, as if he were getting more feedback. "So, it comes down to how your neural processor, or its adaptation, has become an integrative force and not a destructive one, as in so many other cases."

I could see where this was heading. "I don't think it genetically adapted itself or was changed. It was just me working with the energy."

"That's one theory, but we need to test that. We would like to remove your processor, check it over, also see how you react without it—if your functionality decreases or even improves."

"Whoa," I said before I could catch myself. "You want to take out my neural processor?" This definitely unnerved me. I had to question their real intent here, and if it indicated something else. "I mean, you'd only have a few hours to examine it before you'd have to replace or reinsert it."

Klaus chuckled. "Ah, 'To die to sleep, to sleep, perchance to Dream; Aye, there's the rub, for in that sleep of death, what dreams may come, when we have shuffled off this mortal coil, must give us pause.'"

"Yeah, no fucking kidding, Shakespeare."

"So you don't want to test your own theory, Alan?" he smirked.

"Seems like with our remote scanning technology, you can get the same results with 3-D neural scans."

"Our brain specialists think otherwise." He was carefully watching my reaction as if I had some inside info. "And besides," he added, "we want to see how you function without a processor."

The door opened and two beefy, military types in scrubs stepped inside. There was no fighting this directive. "Okay, be my guest, but ..." I paused, getting my own sense of things, "Be prepared to be surprised."

Klaus said, "You always surprise me, Alan."

42.

While they didn't have the facility here to remove Jean's neural processor at the time, considering the difficulty her extraction posed, the OR that I was wheeled into had certainly been upgraded since our last visit. The brain doctors were different as well, with Eastern Region accents. I wondered if this was all done in preparation for my processor's extraction, if so this had been planned for some time. I was lifted and placed on the operating table, an intravenous line of anesthetic was fed to me.

The neurosurgeon looked down at me through his digitized glasses, with their electronic feedback, which projected the magnified images on the surrounding vid screens. "Alan, usually with these extractions, we leave the cranial incision open to replace the processor within a short period of time, but with you we're going to close it to see how you ..." I was getting drowsy but could detect a catch in his voice, "... function without it."

I could almost hear him saying to himself, Good luck. I fell off to sleep, when I woke up, I was sitting up in a bed with my hands cuffed to the bed railing. A nurse, who was monitoring my vitals, stepped over. I pulled on my restraints. "We don't want you touching your bandaged head, Mr. Reynard. Please relax."

I closed my eyes and pretended to fall back to sleep, so I wouldn't get pressed for my reactions or interrogated too soon. I felt light—an empty, airy feeling. I tried to focus on what was happening to me, but couldn't call up any recent memories at first. I wondered if I had been in an accident, and if this was trauma amnesia. Then I got a sense of my situation, almost like a visual gestalt, as brief flashes of the last few days came to me as an overview, like viewing an array of pictures on your portable. I understood, without analyzing or mentally picking it apart, what was happening. They, or Klaus and company, had removed my neural processor to gauge the effect on me. I felt my way through this recognition and it made me angry, or I felt angry but instead of that leading to a whole stream of angry thoughts, I just dropped into the feeling and focused on it and it rather quickly dissipated, or the energy spread through my body. This process felt familiar and I recalled, without actually recollecting or accessing memories, making love to … someone … Emma, and feeling the sexual energy running through my body, which felt wonderful.

"Alan, I know you're awake, so just open your eyes." The sound of this man's voice made me really angry, and I had to shift my focus to drop into the feeling. Twenty seconds later the energy dissipated with a major rush that shook my body.

"Nurse, is he having a seizure?" the voice asked.

There was a long pause. "No signs of that, but his brainwave readings got scrambled. I better call the doctor."

"No need. I've seen this before," the voice said, and now I grasped who it was: Dr. Klaus.

Recognizing him, I found myself or something in me, like a wave of energy, flow through him and then quickly withdraw. It didn't like … communing with all this negative and repressed emotion, or so I assumed or felt. I needed visual stimulation to close down this link up, so I opened my eyes.

"Ah, welcome back, Alan," Klaus said, sitting in an elevated chair next to the bed, to bring him eye-level with me.

I squinted to see him, and he turned to the nurse and asked her to lower the light level. She did and I could now bring him into focus better. My body almost cringed at seeing this curmudgeon.

"So, how do you feel?" he asked.

I just stared at him and could sense all of his devious mental maneuvering, past and present.

"Well, not something you'd like to do."

He sneered. "I wouldn't imagine."

The clearer or more conscious I became, the more interesting this ... perception of things became. I mean, my neocortex was still working and without the processor's enhancement, it could function well enough and do its customary analysis, but I didn't want to rely solely on it or so it seemed. I also liked this new way of functioning, how I was intuitively perceiving things, which was way beyond the neural processor's scope. I had to wonder if this was our real human potential, beyond our culture's reductive techno perspective.

Klaus looked at the computer monitor off to my side and out of my line of sight. Apparently it was giving him brain scan readings, or some such thing, because he pursed his lips like someone trying to figure out a problem.

"So, tell me how you're ... operating or perceiving things, since all the doctors here think you should be catatonic."

"You mean like them."

Klaus almost laughed. "If you say so, Alan."

I knew I wasn't going to get out of here, or get my processor reinserted—if that's what I really wanted—without giving them what they seemed to want. I wasn't about to reveal the truth of my being or functioning in this state, but tell them something that would fit into their warped mind scheme. I paused and caught myself; yes, I was back into a thinking mode, but one where I seemed to have a choice as to how I would ... operate.

"Well, I feel upsurges of feeling, some of them ... harsh, would be the word, but they don't seem to overwhelm me."

"And that little spasm dance that you just did?" he asked.

"Don't know exactly, but I felt better afterward."

He nodded his head. "So you're not doing it; it's a bodily reaction?"

"You could say that," I said, which wasn't entirely the case, but that was all I was going to say on the matter for now. "What's happening to Emma? You didn't do this to her, did you?"

He watched my reaction and checked the computer screen for whatever reading it was giving him. "No. It wasn't necessary, or let me say, it won't be if we get what we want from you."

"Which is?"

"How you're functioning and to what extent, without your neural processor."

"More tests?" I asked.

"Yes, on it and you, but at least you can do them in bed."

"Well, let's get started and ..."

"And get it over with?" Klaus asked. "A word of advice, Alan. We've done this before ... extracting processors and gauging functionality, so don't think you can ... fool us."

"Why would I want to do that? We're all on the same team, right?" I asked, trying to keep the sarcasm out of my voice.

Klaus smirked. "I would hope so."

They let me rest for the remainder of the day and sleep without any further intrusion. The next morning after a hearty breakfast, a young Air Force psychologist wheeled in a portable table that bridged my bed from one side to the other, and allowed me to view a testing monitor and give my verbal responses. It was interesting taking an IQ test; I found myself at first trying to "figure" out the answers to the questions and visual puzzles they presented, until I realized I could just "sense" the correct answers. Once I was able to operate from this mode, the testing went quickly and the psychologist, who was scoring my responses as we went along, seemed intrigued by the results. I must have also scored quite high on the intuitive or psychic tests, gauged by the doctor's reaction, but I did "cheat," as it were, to keep the scores lower so as not to reveal my true potential.

After lunch, Klaus returned, finding it hard to hide his Cheshire cat smile. I could also sense a kind of shift in him, and he didn't appear quite as negative—or was it a sense of self-affir-mation? Either way, I had to wonder as to its effect on Emma and me and our fate.

"Well, Alan, you've certainly exceeded all of our expecta-tions, or I should say your test scores indicate a higher function-ality than anybody here ... or in Washington had expected for a non-NP subject. It certainly gives us a model for what could be coming within the borny communities if we ..."

"If you don't stop it," I said. Klaus didn't respond. "And you wouldn't want to adjust neural processors or do upgrades that would allow the general population to function as such?"

"Alan, I would advise you to temper your speculation. It only gives people like Musgrave a reason to burn you."

"Not something you're interested in?" I asked rather genuinely.

"Not really." He paused, then added, "As with many intractable problems, the solutions aren't one-sided, but come from a combination of polarized options. So, we wouldn't want the bornies operating at this advanced intuitive level, but then we'd like our own people, and I don't just mean the upper echelon but people in general, to function better or a little higher in this regard."

But, I asked myself, after years designing processors that suppressed feelings, would they know how to make these adjust-ments? I doubted it. "So, where does that leave us?"

He stood up. "A strategy is being crafted. Be patient. In the meantime, we're going to reinsert your neural processor and get ready to put you back into your life."

My sense was that this wasn't entirely true or was only the superficial side of a much broader and maybe even more insidious maneuver. "Guess that you wouldn't consider just leaving it out?"

"While you may feel comfortable operating as you are now, our scientists tell us that this euphoric phase will pass and you could downgrade fairly quickly."

My sense was that this was possible but just another challenge and that herein lay my true human potential and one that I wanted to explore. But again this development was too problematic for them and I was truly walking on the razor's edge. I would go along with its insertion, knowing full well that "other" doctors could later remove it. "Back to Jerome or New York?"

"Unclear at this point."

I couldn't imagine going back to my old life with Sherry or as a K Industry's analyst, cooped up in our 10th floor surround-screen electronic environment, or for that matter living in a big city, cut off from the energy of the natural world, especially that of the desert. I think Klaus could sense this.

"My guess is that they send you back to Jerome."

"With Emma?"

"I'm not really sure at this point, Alan."

43.

The next morning they replaced my neural processor. I woke up in bed again, but this time I felt rather different. Something wasn't quite right, and not just the fact that the processor was interfering with my previous level of intuitive functioning—this was expected, given its computational bias—but it had a different orientation. The processors facilitate or accelerate the retrieval and processing of information in the neocortex but in this case, it seemed to alter this process to allow for more feelings. It occurred to me that they didn't replace my old processor but inserted an upgrade with some modifications. But, while it seemed to allow more integration of feeling and intuition, it also filtered or modified them in a way that altered my mental perception of things.

What was really encouraging was that at the same time, or

maybe in response to this alteration, some part of me could still objectively watch what was happening—my essence, if you will, didn't reside in my neocortex or its appendage. In other words, I not only sensed but experienced that I wasn't my mind but something totally more expansive—that which connected me to everything else in the universe—our true human potential. I also knew that I had to reside in this self, or I would be overwhelmed by the altered processing of this upgraded neural processor and its rather seductive counter integration of feeling and intuition, or at least until I could get it removed.

Of course, Klaus came in somewhat later to gauge my reaction and test my functioning, or just to view his handiwork and gloat. "So, Alan, how do we feel?"

"Like a headache's coming on," I said.

"That's what commonly happens with these reinsertions."

"Okay. I guess I don't need to be alarmed then."

"Alarmed? You're feeling ... different?" he asked, trying to hide his smirk.

I felt like reaching over and wringing his neck, but decided to play along with him. "Yes, but given my earlier expansive experience, I'm probably just coming down from a high."

"Yes, I would think so."

"Well, has word come down on our new ... strategy?" I asked.

"Yes, we're going to send you back to Jerome ..."

"What about Emma? Is she going back with me to keep my cover intact?"

Klaus was staring at me and gauging my reaction. "Not for now. We'd like you to get ... closer to Maria Fria, become part of her inner group, and your relationship with Emma—since you've become lovers, in spite of a contrary mission protocol—would interfere with that."

I was feeling a strong emotional reaction, a combination of fear for her safety and a kind of rage over their manipulation, but I also could see the test, or at least for me, was not to overreact and let this counter neural programming win out. "Are we still working the double agent protocol?" I asked rather dismissively.

"No, we want you to develop your own healing potential and expand your intuitive powers."

"Okay, to further gauge its effect on my neural processor?"

"Obviously, since we do plan further upgrades, but we also want to better understand how she facilitates energy as a healer, which means making you one."

"And what happens to Emma? She goes back to her civilian life?"

"No. She may be needed later, depending on how this plays out," he said.

Yeah, I thought to myself. She's their hostage, probably why they brought her back to begin with: to form an emotional bond with me, to keep me in line for their end game.

Chapter Fifteen

44.

As I drove through the desert, I felt both a sense of exhilaration having escaped, if only momentarily, from the clutches of Musgrave and Dr. Klaus, but also a sense of desperation at having to leave Emma behind with them. I knew Emma would have told me to leave, sacrifice her if needed, to save Maria and her clan and the hope they represented for the rest of us. But I just couldn't do one without the other, I felt. I watched this feedback as my new neural processor seemingly took my feeling of concern and justified sacrificing her with platitudes like, "the needs of the many outweigh those of the few," which some would call dualistic thinking. I told myself it was a blessing in disguise that forced me to operate from a higher level or plane, but I couldn't do that 24/7 and the more it twisted my feelings, the harder it would be to fight off its counterintuitive influence.

I arrived in Jerome Tuesday afternoon—talk about a hellish four-day weekend—and settled back into my routine, for at least that first day. I told the desk clerk that Emma wouldn't be coming back for now, but to hold her room. He seemed impressed that I was willing to pay double awaiting her return. I really didn't know what came next: did I contact Maria, or wait for her to make a move? I decided to return to the Iguana Café and write again in earnest during the day; maybe my creative juices would give me some inspiration. I also needed to work with this new processor, to better gauge its influence. It did occur to me that Maria, having dealt with other agents with modified processors that couldn't integrate feelings, even though this one was better at it, might have some insight. I also recalled Emma talking about Ling's anti-government scientists and their under-standing of modified processors. Maybe Maria's group was in touch with them or others.

I found that my creative thrust was affected; there was definitely a darker impulse to the writing. I couldn't monitor it and write at the same time, since it came from a subconscious outpouring, but maybe I could alter it on rewrites, not that I was really taking the effort seriously now. Days later, at the cafe, June walked by and passed me a note. I wondered if they had spotted some new people in town, who might be monitoring me or them, or both of us, and were being cautious. The note said that, on the way out, she was going to invite me to dinner at her house and Maria would like me to accept.

I went back to work and twenty minutes later, June did stop at my table, started up a conversation, and invited me to a potluck dinner at her house. I thanked her and accepted. I didn't think I needed to bring anything, or that this was really a gathering. I showed up with some potato salad anyway, from the local vegetarian food market, for appearance purposes. June took the bowl and ushered me into the living room where Maria and Su Ling were waiting for me—Ling dressed in ninja warrior black.

This was a big surprise. "Su Ling," was all I could get out.

"Alan, aren't you glad to see me?" she said with a smirk.

"But, a month ago you were ..."

"Transferred to a minimum-security prison. Thanks to Emma's deal." She paused. "I didn't stay long."

This sounded a little too convenient, and I had to wonder if, besides getting Emma close to me, part of the government play was allowing Ling to escape.

"Too easy? It occurred to me as well, Alan," she added. "Let's see what we can make of it."

June poured me a cup of tea and refilled their half-empty cups. They must've been talking or strategizing before my arrival.

"I didn't know you two knew each other," I said.

"Well, Alan, I'm not part of Ling's anti-government group, if that's what you're thinking," Maria said. "But, given the complexity of the situation, I thought we might need a broader perspective ... and response."

"I see ... and agree."

"Well, this is off to a good start," Su Ling added. "First of all, what happened to Emma?"

"They're holding her at an Air Force base northwest of Phoenix, where we were tested and I was interrogated."

"As a hostage?" Ling asked.

"I would assume."

"Play ball with them, or they do nasty things to your girlfriend."

I nodded my head. "I told her not to come, but she insisted."

"So, you're guilt free," Ling said bitterly.

Maria gave her a penetrating look. "I trust Alan, and you should too."

Ling's reaction indicated that she respected Maria's opinion.

Maria turned to me with the same focus. "Alan, what did they do to you?" she asked.

"Are you sensing something?"

"Better yet, what did you tell them?" Ling spit out.

I said, "Well, I didn't give Maria up, if that's what you're asking. I just insisted that the double agent protocol wouldn't work because she didn't have an agenda. I tried to convince them that the problem wasn't with her and her healers but the psychological schism these processors are causing. But Musgrave just thought I'd been turned."

"And Klaus?" Ling asked.

I stared at her.

"Yes we know about Dr. Klaus, probably more about him than you. His placement at K Industries was an assignment, probably to set you up, Alan. He's an upper echelon Gov mover and shaker."

"That fits with what he said, that an 'accommodation' might be in order, but they still wanted me to get close to Maria, in her inner circle, and they'd let me know."

Maria continued to stare at me. "You didn't answer my question, Alan."

"Well, they took out my neural processor and tested me to see how I would function without it, and got surprising results."

Su Ling nodded her head. "But they didn't put the same processor back in?" she asked.

"No, this one's modified somehow, but at least I'm aware of it, and have been trying to counter its influence."

Maria was alarmed and appeared to be concerned for my welfare.

Ling reached over and touched her hand. "Don't worry, we've dealt with them before. My scientists, if need be, can remove it."

"So you're combining forces?" I asked.

"That's yet to be determined," Ling said. "A lot depends on your cooperation, and just how far you're willing to go."

"So you want to turn me into a double agent for your coalition?" I asked.

Su Ling looked at Maria. "Again, we're not sure about what's needed; there are differing opinions."

"I bet," I said.

Su Ling didn't like my response, but Maria spoke before she could overreact. "Alan, I know you have my best interest at heart, but we need to determine what's best for everyone, as we've spoken about." She now stared down Su Ling. "This doesn't necessarily mean armed conflict or subversion."

"Well, Maria, I don't really think we can expect an alliance with my handlers for the common good."

Su Ling laughed. "You surprise me, Alan. You're like, halfway between our groups in your thinking ..." She turned to Maria. "I see what you mean about him; I think we can all work together. Let me get back to my people." Su Ling stood up, gave Maria a big hug, shook my hand, and left by the back door.

We all just sat there for a moment. June finally said, "Well, let's eat."

I smiled.

"You didn't think we'd let you go without feeding you," she added.

"I hoped not."

Maria took my hand. "We'll talk later."

45.

Besides June and Maria, we were joined at dinner by several other members of her sect, all of them advanced healers I assumed, since the conversation was on critical healing topics but no one got into a head space. Since it was obvious that I was being "sponsored" by Maria, I was just treated as one of the group. After everybody left and June had retired for the evening, I sat in the living room with Maria, sipping after-dinner tea.

"I was thinking, Alan, that the best way to bring you into my 'inner circle' would be to have you enroll in our apprenticeship program."

I nodded my head, then closed my eyes to get a "feel" about this offer. I could sense that feeling drawing its own counter spin, but at least I was aware of this dynamic.

"So, your other half isn't thrilled with the idea?" she asked.

"Let's hope it only stays as an annoying voice of doubt."

"It would be interesting, not only for you but for me, to give you a healing, which is what I do to new apprentices. We can gauge the neural processor's manipulation and see if it can be modified."

"That didn't happen with the other agents with modified processors?" I asked.

"No. As in Brenda's case, it fought the energy and its strategy was flooding the psyche with repressed feelings."

"So it would rather die itself than be ... healed?"

Maria smiled. "Yes, I guess you could say that, but I sense this processor is different somehow and I would like to test its parameters."

"It allows and integrates feelings better but seems to twists their intent."

"Well, since we operate at a non-mental level during the healing process, learning to just 'quiet the voice' could be all that's needed."

"Do you think you can … affect this sort of neural processor?" I asked.

"Since it's still made of brain cells, which are natural, despite their unnatural arrangement and intent, I would think the right feedback would affect it. But, of course, this hasn't yet been put to the test."

"Well, let's do it."

"I'll announce it at our next service and have it posted on our website."

"Hope it doesn't attract a lot of Lewis Hargrove fans here," I said.

"What if we use a pseudonym?"

I thought for a moment. "How about Alan Reynolds, which is my wife's maiden name."

"Which your handlers will recognize, without … ?"

"Blowing my cover," I added. "A pseudonym of a pseudonym, makes perfect sense in this crazy mix."

Maria smiled. "Yes, Alan. It does."

At the next healing service on Thursday, June announced from the podium that they had enlisted a new apprentice in the Institute's healing program, whom everybody knew as Lewis Hargrove, but for privacy concerns would henceforth be known as Alan Reynolds. I was asked to stand up, everybody put their hands up sending me their loving energy. It almost brought tears to my eyes, considering that some of them knew of my tattered history and mission, but all could embrace me or my humanity, given our higher connection. I was scheduled for my "introductory" healing on Tuesday and showed up at the Institute and waited for June to escort me back to Maria's residence. She was standing in her living room ready to greet us.

"Alan, as always, I'm so glad to see you, especially today with the inauguration of your new journey."

June took a seat on my right side, which drew my attention.

Maria added, "June usually sits in on these healing sessions, to take notes and give her impression of the needed adjustments for our apprentices, since she runs the program."

I nodded my head. Maria stood up and walked over to my straight-back chair and stood behind me. "Usually we don't ask the students for their feedback or converse with them during the healing, but you're certainly not only one of our more advance introductory students if most compromised as well. So let's just leave it open and let the process direct itself."

Maria did her healing ritual to call in the energies, then placed her hands above my head. I could immediately feel the energy pervading my cranium and its brain structure. I felt a reaction from my neural processor that was more accepting than I would have figured.

"Did you sense that, Alan?" Maria asked.

"Yes, the processor or appendage seemed to quiver but not shrink away."

Since the energy was conscious, as Maria had told me any number of times, it seemed to do its own dance with the processor, which was different from what it initiated with the last one. The energy seemed to caress it, as a mother might with a recalcitrant child, but did not try to penetrate its inner workings. Interestingly enough, its reaction was to slow down or slightly alter its processing, or so it seemed to me.

"I feel it slowing down and it seems to better accommodate the energy than Brenda's did," Maria said.

"Well, it's been doing that with feelings but twisting the input."

"Okay, and that's probably something you'll have to work on," Maria added.

Maria finished up her healing, then walked to the sofa and sat down. "Alan. You'll need to do what we call, the inside out approach. Or, integrate the feeling before the processor can modify its input and that may affect its programming."

"Well, I've been doing something like that for years, but this might allow me to turn it into a reliable methodology." A feeling now arose as to the manipulative nature of this processor. I felt my way through it until it shifted and its energy spread out through my body, with remnants of this more refined energy getting acquired by the processor which did its programming thing.

Suddenly this peaceful movement or dance was interrupted as my heart went into palpitation. I withdrew my consciousness, and as I did, the palpitations slowed and then stopped. As I sat back and relaxed, Maria asked me to explain what had just happened.

I went through the process from the initiation of the feeling to my shifting it, the heart palpitation, to my withdrawal and I concluded saying, "Seems like, it's programmed to deal with raw feelings or emotions, but my interference somehow short-circuited the process and like an angry child, it lashed out."

"Doubt if it would've actually caused a heart attack, but seems to be programmed to fight back in this manner," Maria said.

"So I stop my processing, or what?" I asked, feeling a little overwhelmed.

Maria closed her eyes. "What I'm getting is that you need to continue to work with the processor incrementally, do partial integrations and let it process the altered feelings and hopefully adapt and allow more in time."

This was brilliant. "Yes, like a gradual detoxifying process, but with energy, not hormones or body chemicals." I had another thought. "It might even evolve it or change its programming."

"Yes, I could see that," Maria added.

June spoke up. "We have an advanced biofeedback machine that might help with this process."

"Yes, June. You're right." Maria turned to me. "I think working with the machine will let you discover the optimum way to interface with the processor and its erroneous programming, and then just do it yourself."

"Okay, I'm open. Can we start today?"

June took out her portable to check their scheduling. "We have an opening at three o'clock. We usually do one hour sessions to start, but could extend them according to your feedback."

"Good. I'll be back." I stood up, gave both of them hugs, and June escorted me back through the building to administration where I set up a payment program for the apprenticeship and biofeedback sessions. I felt great letting the government, who placed this monstrosity in my head, pay for my therapy. I doubted Musgrave would see it that way.

46.

So the work began. At first I just sensed the raw impulses, did a partial feeling/integration process, and the technicians showed me the body/mind before and after reactions. Since this was a lot different from just helping people to lower their blood pressure, we had to work out a protocol, but they were pleased that they could gauge the processor's reaction and help me modify my process to work with it. After I left the Institute, the work continued, since it was really my life in the world that triggered feelings and drew out its programming, and so it was here I would have to deal with it. What was interesting to discover was just how pervasive feelings are, which this process brought to my conscious awareness. Previous processors largely repressed them, but while this new model did try to integrate more of this energy, it was to its own end. I gradually came to see the warped "genius" of their approach: allow more feeling integration while shading its input to suit their design. This had Heir Klaus' input all over it.

It was a long day and so I ate a late lunch at the Iguana Café. As I looked over the menu and felt like choosing healthy items, like a whole-wheat tortilla wrap and organic guacamole, I could feel the initial impulse turning negative. I was getting mental feedback not to choose them. Interesting. The waitress came over and I told her I needed a few more minutes. I closed my eyes and got a sense of this input, quieted my mind, and just felt what was now an emotional reaction for about ten seconds before it dissipated somewhat. I could feel some of the energy getting integrated and the rest processed. I opened my eyes, called the waitress over and ordered the whole-wheat wrap with the organic veggies. When it arrived and I started eating, it tasted great but I got the negative mental feedback that it wasn't as nutritious as the menu claimed. Holy shit, I thought, and I had to laugh at my own reaction. I guessed that "holy shit" would be the result of eating well. Again I did my internal process and the emotional energy was once more somewhat integrated.

I took a walk around town in the late afternoon, and had the impulse to get my UV protective hat, which I did, but my "mind" was telling me I didn't really need it. Back at the hotel, I started to reach for my copy of the Hindu *Upanishads* Maria had given me, but my "mind" was telling to watch the latest video that was all the rage. I made a conscious choice to upload the movie to my portable and view it. It was violent and vile, and while my feelings were repulsed by it, my "mind" was telling me that it put me in touch with my instincts, which was good. Oh, really. The killing of whole populations and subjugating the world, like the hero in this movie, was something to emulate? I quieted my mind, felt how the movie's violence stirred up my emotions, and I did my integrating process with them. It took a while longer to shift this energy, but while it happened, I again felt the heart palpitations and slowly backed off. One step at a time, I told myself.

I was scheduled for another biofeedback appointment the next morning but I cancelled it. June called back, and I told her working with the process in the real world was much more fruitful and that I would get back to her. At the library, a flirtatious younger woman caught my attention, and I could feel my primal impulse to "engage" her and my "mind" telling me to follow up on it, that a little sexual escapade was just what I needed. Fortunately, I shifted the energy/impulse before acting on it. I had read in college about addiction and the "addict's voice," but this really showed how feelings and impulses can be counter-programmed with mental messages. Since I had never been on a so-called spiritual search, never meditated nor did yoga until recently, never tried to "still my mind," this was all a revelation to me. I had to ask myself, who was I? My mind or something else—that stillness I felt when I quieted my "mind" and shifted these base impulses?

I continued the process for the rest of the week, even extending it to my writing, and I was able to get a handle on this darker trend and started integrating these impulses and smoothing out the narrator's voice. The real test came, however, when Musgrave called me near the end of the week. When I saw his caller ID on my remote, I had a split reaction: part of me was fearful, another part defiant—I paused long enough to do a quick integration of the raw feelings and shift myself to a nonreactive mental space.

I picked up the call. "What, were you taking a shower?"

"Who needs to shower in this dry heat?" I replied, without actually answering his question and its implied criticism.

"Give me a progress report," he demanded.

"Well, I enlisted in their apprentice healers' program and became one of the group, not privy yet to their inner workings, but getting there."

"Good. Smart move. I'm sure you can handle the added ... load without freaking out."

"Well, Maria gives new recruits a private healing session to check them out, and sensed something different with me—with my reactions."

"Oh, yeah. Different is good. Might rope her into trying to save you."

It was interesting that he didn't follow up on how my processor reacted, and it dawned on me that he wasn't privy to this aspect of operation. "Okay, I'll play up to that, the wounded healer bit."

Musgrave paused. "Look, I've got an update for you." He paused again.

I nodded my head in anticipation.

"Su Ling escaped from prison, and we want you to keep an eye out. Doubt if she'll show up there, but she could send an agent who might compromise you."

"How did she do that?" I asked.

"You tell me, Alan. She got minimum security due to the deal with your girlfriend."

I didn't react or remind him this was his doing.

"So, things are accelerating. We need you to speed up your timetable, figure out what they're up to."

"Okay. Will do."

Musgrave clicked off without any polite goodbyes. He was really on edge. I wondered if he was still suspicious of me, or was it the pressure being put on him. It also interrupted my own plans. I had been thinking about asking Su Ling if her people could remove my neural processor, but I guess my personal exploration would need to continue along the same lines for now. But, in a crisis situation, when I needed a first-response reaction and didn't have time to integrate the impulse and modify its mental feedback, how would I fare?

Friday afternoon, I received a call from June asking how my biofeedback process was going. I told her just fine; she suggested that I return the next day and have another session with their machine. I told her that I didn't think that would help; she then told me that Maria thought otherwise, and so I scheduled the appointment. I assumed this was a ploy to get me back to the Institute for a covert meeting with them. I showed up the next morning, and June didn't take me to the biofeedback lab but to some sort of "electronic" isolation room converted into a living room setting. Maria and Su Ling were inside, along with a nerdy-looking guy. June and I took a seat on a sofa across from them.

Su Ling couldn't contain her excitement. She looked at Maria, who nodded her head. "Alan, I've got some very exciting news."

I looked at the guy, waiting for an introduction first.

"Oh, sorry. This is Hal Yablonsky, our tech guy."

We exchanged nods. "You were saying."

"Alan, when you visited the Bradbury Institute to interview Dr. Quirk, you met someone there?"

"You're particularly well informed."

"Please, just answer the question," she insisted.

"Sara Irving, in new product development for their neural processors." I stared at Sue Ling smiling from ear to ear. "Don't tell me."

"Yes, she's not so much a plant as a sympathetic party." She paused to let me absorb this info. "Well, she's telling us that the neural processor they put into you is an experimental design engineered to integrate more feelings but also to reprogram the mental feedback."

I looked at Maria and we had the same idea. "Yeah, I figured as much," I added, "and giving a person heart palpitations and maybe even a full-blown heart attack, if you fool with the process."

Both Su Ling and Hal nodded their heads. Hal added, "We can't remove the processor for examination—too many telltale signs—but I have developed an advance kind of biofeedback protocol that would allow me to examine it using feedback, without leaving any traces."

"Okay," I said.

"But, first I need to know what you've been doing to offset its effects."

I gave them a rundown of my feeling/integration process and how I felt it was mitigating the effects of its control functioning.

"Excellent. But, stop the process until I can examine you tomorrow and ascertain the parameters of its programming."

"I will, but let me understand something. Is there some possibility that I can, or we can, reprogram it without their knowledge and have them mass produce neural processors that will aid instead of subvert a higher integration of feelings and intuition?"

Su Ling couldn't help but smile. Hal was less enthusiastic. "Let's see, but there is some possibility of that, but also some serious downside on your part."

I looked at Maria. "Let's do it."

Chapter Sixteen

47.

We waited until Monday to conduct the session with Yablonsky. He placed me in the biofeedback tank and replaced the Institute's machine with one that had a different function. He had me put on headphones and explained that he would be feeding me different sound frequencies through each ear. This was combined with heavy-duty goggles, with lenses for each eye that he could switch to different colors or to clear, with magnification for him to examine the retinas. A portable brain scanner was wheeled in and placed over the top of my head, for live pictures of my brain and its internal functioning. Yablonsky said that he would be giving me instructions and asking for my feedback, almost like an old-time eye examination for glasses. The session began and it was hard for me to figure out from the combination of sounds and colored lights, and my reaction to their intensity or the lack thereof, how he could use it to examine my neural processor. But I went along with him, hoping this would answer some of our questions and give us some direction.

The examination, if I could call it that, took about three hours. Afterward I was exhausted and taken to a room with a bed and soothing lighting and music. I instantly fell asleep and woke up two hours later. June came in and told me that Hal would need another day to process his findings, and that we were scheduled for a get-together Wednesday afternoon and for me just to go back to my normal routine until then. What was interesting was that from the moment I woke up, my neural processor kept feeding me its contrary messages. However, Hal had told me not to integrate the energy but to let it play itself out for now. I was famished and went to the café for lunch and found myself getting conflicting messages about my menu selection; the rice and vegetable dish was nutritious but could I digest it properly?

Of course that was the whole idea for this combination of whole-grains and vegetables—it was easy to digest and assimilate. This continued through the afternoon, again forcing me to remain detached and just watch these reactions and messages. But, without my integration process, it was harder not to get sucked into the dualistic internal debate.

The next day I tried to pick up my routine and write at the cafe, but I wasn't very inspired and just gave up on it after a while. I went back to the Sliding Sands, read for a few hours, took a nap, went out to the pool and swam, and just had a lazy day, which was unusual for me. I assumed the examination was a real strain on my resources at a lot of levels, and that I needed a break in my routine and not more of it. I was anxious to hear Hal's results and showed up for our meeting at the Institute Wednesday afternoon with high expectations. When I sat down, Ling was smiling again and I assumed her colleague had already shared his results with her, but this was encouraging. What made her optimistic should be a plus for all of us, I thought.

"Well, this is definitely a next-generation neural processor, one with both advantageous and detrimental functions." Hal paused and looked around at us. "First of all, as Alan has noted, it allows more integration of feelings and intuitions but prefers, if that's the word, raw or primal input, which it's programmed to alter according to its mental-oriented scheme."

"And the heart palpitations?" I asked.

"Well, when it doesn't get what it's programmed to receive, it treats it like a virus."

I nodded my head.

He added, "But, compared to largely blocking out feelings and intuitions, this is an improvement."

"And that's what's advantageous?" I asked.

Hal smiled. "No, it also has a self-learning function that allows it to adapt, which is why your altered process gets its feeling input through, as it were."

"And the downside?"

"It has very fixed high-end parameters," he said.

"What does that mean, Hal?" Maria asked.

"Well, there seems to be a fixed ceiling on just how much it will adapt."

"Or, it will only allow so much integrated feeling at one time?" I asked. Hal nodded, and Maria seemed to get the picture.

"But again, since this is living brain tissue, I don't see how they can be overly confident of these controls."

"So Alan could start a natural process, like rising Kundalini energy, that could take hold and go beyond what they expected?" Maria asked.

Yablonsky nodded his head. "That's a possibility." He paused. "What I'd like to test, after another period of Alan's 'deprogramming,' is to have Maria do another healing and see what the threshold is at that point, or when the counter movement starts."

"Hal, is this processor more 'accommodating' than earlier models?" I asked.

"I would say … more accommodating than we expected, but then the other processors are breaking down and they need to do something."

"Okay. But, how much longer can you stay?" I asked.

"Not too long," Su Ling said.

"It's Wednesday. How about next Monday?"

Everyone looked to Maria, who turned to June. She pulled up the healer's schedule and nodded. "Whatever works for you," Maria said.

Su Ling said, "Well, what about eleven o'clock? We'll go to Sedona. Easier for us to hide there and come back for the session."

I looked at Hal. "So, by comparing healing sessions and reaction times, you can determine just how much I can affect it?" I asked.

"It'll tell me how fast it's adapting, but in terms of affecting its ceiling, I can't be sure."

Su Ling stood up. "I think this is very positive. Alan, I really appreciate your cooperation. It could be critical for long-term changes in the system."

I wasn't so sure. There had been so much deception on this mission that this seemed too straightforward and the solution too easy—my process evolves the processor to the extent it allows more integration of feelings and intuitions, without the contrary mental feedback. There had to be a catch that we weren't seeing, but I might not be able to figure it until I was back at the base and they were adjusting it.

So, for the next five days, I resumed my partial feeling/ integration process. I also kept a journal for Hal as to how it was progressing: how fast the refined impulses got integrated, which allowed more and more input, also what kinds of impulses were quicker to integrate and which ones harder? This was my main focus during this period, although I kept up my daily writing routine, and it was exhausting and causing my muscles to tighten. I told June, and she set up a schedule of daily massage and yoga practice, which did seem to help. But, as the days went by and I started to review my journal and monitored the process myself, it didn't seem to progress as far or as fast as I had hoped; or maybe I wasn't gauging it right. Since so much seemed to rest on my ability to evolve this and hopefully have them mass-produce a processor that would help the integration process in others, a lot rested on my shoulders, literally.

48.

Monday rolled around and we all arrived at different times, at various entrances but all ended up in Maria's living room. A chair was placed in the center of a circle of chairs, where I sat and Maria began her healing session. I was surprised that Hal didn't want to wire me up, but since he had left his equipment here, he could do that later if need be. Maria did her healing ritual and started to channel the energy down into my cranium. We were both surprised when the neural processor allowed a little energy to penetrate its interior.

"You felt that, didn't you?" Maria asked.

"Yeah, it's moving inside of it," I said.

"Please clarify," Ling said.

"Before, the processor blocked access to its interior but now it's slowly opening to the energy, which my feeling integration process must've initiated."

"This is where it does its programming?" Maria asked.

Hal nodded his head and Maria continued for a few minutes. It allowed this penetration to continue, if only incrementally, and then it reached some kind of saturation point. It began to counter this movement and I could feel the heart palpitations begin again. Maria withdrew her hands and the energy.

Hal asked, "So it reached a point where it reacted and threw what I'm calling its kill switch?"

I opened my eyes. "Yes."

Maria walked around and took a seat in one of the chairs in the circle.

"So, like the input of refined feelings, it allowed a certain amount before reacting?" Maria asked.

"Yes, which is more than it allowed last time, so this is progressive and is what we hoped," Hal said.

Ling looked at Hal. "What's next?"

"Well, I think Alan and Maria need to do this dance together for a while yet, trying to push the absorption time longer and testing if that affects the contrary messaging."

"You mean, does it change its programming?" I asked.

"Exactly."

"Then what?" Maria asked.

"At some point," Hal added, "you need to stop before the alterations become too obvious and allow them to remove and examine it, and hopefully decide to mass-produce it."

"What will happen to Alan at that point, once they've got what they need from him?" Maria asked.

Ling just stared at her for a long moment. "Well, if they don't catch on that we know what they're doing and are countering it, they could just replace it with his old one."

"And if they do 'catch on'?" Maria asked.

Ling didn't want to state the obvious. It seemed like I had to salvage the situation. I added, "It could be that I'm doing exactly what they want me to do, having encouraged me to become a healer and knowing that would expose their processor to this energy, and so I would be rewarded not punished."

"Do you really think that?"

"Well, Klaus readily admitted that while they wouldn't want the general public operating at my level, they did want some higher functionality, but they wouldn't know how to program that."

"Yes, but hopefully more than they expected without them being able to detect it," Hal added.

Maria seemed satisfied with this answer for now, but given her intuitive reach, I suspected that she had tapped into my handlers and knew them for what they were, and this didn't give her an optimistic prospect for my survival.

Ling added. "We could rescue Emma, who might seem like part of our group to them, and grab Alan at the same time."

Maria nodded her head, but wasn't fooled by this offer. The meeting broke up, and Su Ling and Hal gathered up his equipment and headed back to their operational center somewhere in the Midwest. As I got up, Maria motioned for me to stay. After everybody left, she invited me to dinner there at her residence.

It was a great meal. I was surprised that June didn't join us, but I suspected that Maria wanted to talk with me alone. Afterward we stepped out onto a patio and sat in lawn chairs and watched the sunset with its marvelous turquoise colors, while sipping herbal ice tea.

Finally she said, "Alan, I'm concerned about your welfare, and am not particularly happy with how we've left this today."

"I know, but as Klaus put it, they need to make accommodations, and who better to act as a go-between. So why kill the goose who laid the golden egg."

Maria laughed. "Have to remember that at Easter. I'm sure the kids would prefer hunting for golden eggs."

I laughed, but didn't have a comeback. The sun had set and the twilight hush had fallen over the desert below.

Maria just stared into the gathering night. "I think I've mentioned this before, but our etheric body is separate from the mind—be it the neocortex and these neural processors—and is as some call it, the body's natural intelligence. I believe that provided you with your higher understanding, which gave them such remarkable test results when they removed the old processor."

"You mean that's what seems to direct the body's amazing ability to adapt and maintain itself?" I asked.

"Yes, the secular way of looking at it."

I thought about this for a moment. "The night before Emma and I left for Phoenix, we made love and the energy just rode up my spine and exploded in my head; my old neural processor seemed to feed on it and kind of expanded it parameters. All very natural."

"Yes, like I suggested earlier, since the Kundalini energy is the spark that animates organisms and their components, the cells of the body, including those of these processors, would feed on the energy and treat it as ... family, not foe—or not something to change or adapt."

"I wonder if this is another way of approaching this ... challenge."

Maria just nodded her head. I could see where this line of

questioning was leading and it surprised and delighted me.

"Well, I'm willing if you are," I said.

Maria smiled. "You understand that I don't have romantic attachments, nor have I had a ... sexual partner in some time. Most men can't handle my energy, but I feel that if we were to ... make love, the Kundalini energy that would erupt in you from this conjoining, given its more natural base, might greatly affect this experimental processor, in ways that would be harder to detect or account for, or even for us to control."

"Yes," I said, having an epiphany. "Both our sides are trying to 'fix' it according to their limited perspective, so why not let the body do it according to its broader designs."

"Exactly," Maria replied.

I stood up. "Well, shall we?"

"Give me a few minutes to fill the bathtub and turn on the jets, and get ... situated."

"Is there a separate shower?" I asked.

"Yes, of course. In the guest room. Here, let me show you."

Maria walked down the hallway to her bedroom—the guest room was halfway down the hall. I went inside and took a shower. There was a terry-cloth robe in the closet that I put on, and then I walked back to Maria's room. "I'm in here, Alan." I walked into the bathroom, which was dominated by a large floor-level Jacuzzi, where Maria sat amidst the foaming bubbles of the air jets. I removed my robe and slipped into the tub. While her body was largely exposed, I don't think I ever took my eyes off hers, which seemed to glow in the candlelight. We just sat there in the water and soaked while we stared at each other; there was no erotic washing of body parts, kissing or cuddling, but more like a melding of spirits. Her energy was so powerful that I struggled just to stay conscious. At some point I suggested that we better retire to the bedroom before I nodded off. We slipped out of the tub, toweled ourselves off, and walked into the bedroom.

There were candles everywhere. Maria suggested that we just sit across from each other for a moment, gazing into each other's eyes as we had in the tub. It was becoming increasingly difficult for me to remain conscious. At some point I found myself sitting up with Maria's legs wrapped around me, straddling me and gently controlling the flow of our lovemaking. I closed my eyes and could feel the Kundalini energy surging up my spine and exploding in my cranium. A charge much more powerful than any delivered by her hands-on healing or my previous Kundalini rising experiences. However, the processor didn't trigger heart palpitations or any other traumatic reaction, and it seemed not only "comfortable" with the energy, but fed on it like we had suggested and one could only hope—adapted it as well.

At another point, I saw Maria naked and gorgeous, or that was my perception of her despite her aging body. But, mostly I just closed my eyes and melded into the magnificent energy. At some point I must've fallen asleep, because the breeze from the open window woke me and I found myself alone in her bed, the comforter pulled over me. I assumed she had retired to the guest room, and that our conjoining was not about sleeping together, but exchanging energy and exploring the outer reaches of my capacity to activate the body's own natural intelligence. I fell off to sleep again. In the morning I showered and got dressed and walked out to the living room. Maria was sitting at the patio table, sipping tea and eating toast. I sat down next to her as she poured me a cup and we just sat there and stared out into the glorious morning. There was little else to say.

49.

The next day we started to work together without being self-conscious or feeling any need to repeat our previous conjoining. As with anybody you've become "intimate" with, there was another level of affection and concern, but it was all rather transpersonal, as my psychologist would have probably called it. What we discovered from my feeling/integration process and comparing it to the Kundalini awakening, was that the body seemed to have a dual mechanism to accommodate various kinds of energy. Repeated healings, as well as my own feeling/ integration process, showed some progress in terms of evolving the processor, but Maria could sense when my Kundalini energy naturally arose—apparently I had jump-started a process that became ongoing without further "stimulation"—and it did much more. Since Hal was out of reach—we didn't dare try any form of electronic communication—we were pretty much left on our own to explore this phenomenon and draw our own conclusions.

June was kept updated on our progress. A few weeks later, we had lunch together at Maria's residence and talked about what was happening and what came next.

"Well, as you know," June started out, drawing on her classical education, "science has determined that random mutation happens much too slowly to be the driving engine of evolution and that organisms have some kind of feedback loop with their environment. One twentieth-century scientist equated it with how mathematical algorithms operate and called it 'ecorithms.' We call it the etheric body, but we think you've tapped into this 'mechanism' and started a process that may have surprising results … eventually."

I nodded my head and understood what she was saying, but Maria had a little trouble with this explanation. I tried to clarify it, "The Kundalini energy has affected the cells of my neural processor, and since any upgrades would start with these precursor cells, that spark of life would be transferred to them and be self-sustaining long after these neural processors have been installed in other people."

"And your handlers and their scientists won't detect this underlying process?" Maria asked.

I shrugged my shoulders. "I don't think even Hal could say for sure, but it's our best shot at having them replicate a neural processor that may … 'have a mind of its own,' if you'll excuse the extended metaphor."

Maria nodded her head. "So we're finished?"

"Yes, I think we've done what we can do, and now we just need to set up my excuse to have them do the exchange. But, I might add, given your concern for me, that it's not only evolved this processor but my neocortex as well, and I'm operating at a whole another level with it."

Maria nodded her head and then looked to June.

June added, "Well, even though you haven't participated in our healer's apprenticeship, you're probably more advanced than any of them, and we could have you 'treat' a few volunteer patients. The influx of healing energy may trigger your heart palpitations and give you an excuse to get back to them and have the processor taken out."

Maria and I nodded our heads. June added, "Okay, I'll set up appointments for the day after tomorrow."

This sudden end to our work together seemed to affect Maria. June detected it and made her excuses to leave us alone. We remained seated across from each other in her living room and just looked at each other, and let the energy between us circulate. It began to build and I could feel the Kundalini energy start to move up my spine. I closed my eyes as it exploded in my cranium, or what Maria would call my crown chakra. I just rode with the waves of energy but was able this time to stay conscious until it dissipated. I opened my eyes to Maria smiling and I said, "You see. It is self-sustaining."

Maria stared at me for a long moment. "Alan, our time together is rapidly coming to an end, and I'm already feeling the loss and grieving your absence, which is new to me and a little disturbing. We think we've gone beyond such attachments, but I guess what we're seeing here with this experiment of ours, is that these connections really define our humanity, since it's this coupling that initiates the evolutionary energy. It's what most people have instinctively figured out, if not at this level, but we seem to come at it from the top down, instead of the bottom up."

I had to laugh at this analogy. "Well, my bottom-up relationships haven't been as fulfilling."

Maria nodded then took a deep breath and let it out. "Let's gather up June and Brad and go to dinner at the Iguana Café. It's been a while and I guess we have something to celebrate."

It was a marvelous dinner and a great celebration and I don't think I've ever felt more connected with others and with myself than at this stage of our journey together—I guess you could say it that way. It was short-lived, however. My second healing session, a few days later, brought on heart palpitations. I called Musgrave and told him what was happening during my healing sessions at the Institute and that I needed to come in for a checkup. It was set for Friday; I still needed a few days to recover before I could drive back, and a little more time to say my goodbyes. I settled up my bill before I left Friday morning, figuring I wouldn't be coming back or not anytime soon.

Chapter Seventeen

50.

The next morning I drove back to Phoenix and pulled into the Air Force Base late morning. Since this wasn't an emergency NP extraction like Jean's, there was no medical team waiting for me, just another military grunt who walked back to the same conference room. Klaus was patiently awaiting my arrival. I sat down across from him.

"Is Musgrave going to join us?" I asked.

Dr. Klaus gave me a smirky little smile. "Agent Musgrave has returned to Washington, his part of this operation completed."

This was interesting. "So I'm not going back to Jerome, and we're not going to do a double agent insertion?"

"Alan. Please give me more credit than that."

I raised my eyebrows.

"You must be aware by now that this agent protocol was merely a ploy on our part, to get you exposed to Fria's energy, stimulate your development, and gauge both effects on your two neural processors."

I wondered if he could be conceding this scenario or flushing me out. "I figured that there was more to it than Musgrave's infiltration plan."

Klaus nodded his head then glanced down at his computer screen. "So, you enlisted in their healer's apprenticeship, but once you started giving hands-on healing, the energy caused heart palpitations?"

"Well, all apprentices get introductory healings from Fria, and that's when I had my first reaction and got palpitations."

"This didn't occur with your first 'healing' from her back when?"

"No, that was rather benign but … this isn't the same neural processor, is it?" I asked.

Klaus again nodded his head. "When did you first detect any ... difference?"

I thought through my answer. "On the drive back to Jerome. I was getting strange feedback and contrary thoughts from the beginning."

"Contrary?"

"Well, I'd have a feeling and it would integrate pretty well, but sometimes I'd get contrary mental feedback."

"Can you give me an example?" he asked.

"I felt that I was getting too much sun exposure and raised the tinting on my car windows, and then I got to thinking that the sun's rays are actually good for me."

"Excellent."

"Maybe for you, but not for me, if I don't want to get skin cancer," I said angrily without feigning the emotion. "You could have warned me that this was some sort of 'modified' processor."

"But then that would have defeated the whole purpose of not only its insertion, but this whole mission."

"Which was what?"

"Well, Alan, I've said enough until we've taken a close look at your neural processor and how it's functioning now."

"You expect something that different?" I asked.

Klaus stood up. "I expected you to be you, and it to be it, and the dance you did together is what really interests me."

So we were right, I thought to myself. I remained seated, not sure what came next.

"Alan, the MP will take you to the mess for lunch before our flight."

"Flight?"

"We're flying back to New York for your NP extraction, since there's another level of follow-up that needs to take place afterward."

The military grunt stepped into the room. I stood up. "And

what about Emma, what's happening with her?" I asked.

"The FBI has her in custody in New York, so it'll be one happy family reunion."

"I doubt that."

After a quick bite to eat in the base cafeteria, I was introduced to Agent Barclay, a big muscle-bound guy who would be my chaperon and guard. I assumed he was FBI and not DIA, or any other military outfit, since this was looking more and more like a political/civilian operation. We walked out and met Dr. Klaus on the tarmac and boarded a sleek civilian jet, which would probably only take a few hours to cross the country. Klaus sat in the front at a workstation, and I was escorted to the back where Barclay sat down next to me. At least they didn't cuff me to the arm of the seat. The agent picked up a magazine and started to read it. I wasn't interested in any conversation either, but they'd taken away my portable and the entertainment options on the seat video weren't to my liking. So I just closed my eyes and processed the negative feelings that Klaus and his deception routine had recently triggered in me.

"Are you having a fit or something," Barclay asked at some point, after my body did a couple of muscle-spasm shifts, which the integration process caused.

I opened my eyes. "No. It's part of my internal processing."

He shook his head. "If you say so, buddy. But I'll just move over to the next seat and give you some room."

"Don't worry, it's not contagious." I smirked, but he just shook his head. It was all Greek to him.

Just before we landed, Klaus came back and took Barclay's seat. "Alan, I was watching you on the remote camera earlier and heard your exchange with Agent Barclay."

"And?"

"Your internal process?" he asked.

I wasn't feeling in a particularly generous mood. "Something I might share with you, when I get something I want."

"Oh, so we're at the bargaining stage already."

"Since I'm your prisoner and not your collaborator, don't expect my ready cooperation."

"Alan, you're a K Industries agent, who's undertaken a particularly tricky assignment for the federal government. Why would you think you're a prisoner or that our relationship has changed?"

"One is usually honest and aboveboard with collaborators, but you've deceived me from the beginning of this operation, replaced my processor of choice with an experimental device without my knowledge, and I'm being guarded by a federal thug. You tell me."

"By necessity we couldn't read you into the whole program— above your security clearance," he added.

"Yeah, well I don't buy it."

Klaus stared at me for a long moment. "Well, you're certainly no prisoner, but just for curiosity sake, what is it that you want from us?"

I turned in my seat. "I want Emma Knowles release from your custody, her record expunged, full back pay, and her time on this mission properly compensated."

Klaus gave this some thought. "I'll take this up with my superiors." He stood up. "Buckle up. We should be landing shortly."

It was night by now and I could see the jet bypass lit up New York City, with its many airports, and fly along the Long Island coast, and then land at a private airport. A limousine was waiting for us. Klaus sat in the front and Barclay and me in the back. It was a short drive to the Bradbury Institute. I should've known. This was all about their little cash cow, NP fiefdom, and I was the alpha tester for their new neural processor and soon to be their beta tester, no doubt. Well, we'd see about that, I thought.

51.

The next morning they removed my neural processor in a lengthy and delicate operation, that for some reason they wanted me to be awake and witness, if sedated. They had no plan to replace it with another one at this point, not that I would have wanted it, but it was clear that I had no say on the matter. I think they wanted to watch my reaction and gauge my state of mind, before and after the extraction, but I was perfectly fine both ways. I sensed that they had expected more of a reaction from me. I had to remind myself that this was the Mecca of neural processors, and that they had a lot at stake in convincing people they were absolutely necessary, while the bornies operated perfectly well without them, as did I apparently.

After my recovery a couple days later, they ran me through a round of tests. I assumed they didn't believe the earlier results from Phoenix after my last NP extraction or thought the execution was flawed. I could tell from the look in the eyes of my testers that they were not pleased with the results. It must've run contrary to their whole intellectual framework, and I might add, belief system. Fortunately for me, and this was certainly ironic, they weren't my keepers, Dr. Klaus was. The next day he came by to update me.

"Alan, you certainly were able to 'affect' this neural processor and create new neurological pathways, some of which we still can't figure out."

"Well that was the idea, wasn't it? Push me to deal with the dichotomy of feeling and mental feedback and create a process of adaptation before the damn thing killed me?"

"It would've never done that, but it did have its own program that you were able to … alter. For us the next step will be to create a schematic and design an upgrade using your precursor cells, although the people here would call it just another model, insert it in some test subjects and see how they fare."

"So, I'm done with this assignment and ready to get back to my old job," I said facetiously, knowing no such thing was planned for me.

"Well, we would like to understand this process of yours and how it affected the X2, and seems it'd be best not to coerce it out of you but have you cooperate with us." Klaus opened his valise and pulled out a document and passed it to me. "This is a release for Emma Knowles, along the lines you suggested. As you can see, she's already signed it and it's in effect."

"When you give me a brand-new portable, and I call her out in the world to assure me that she's been released, I'll try to show your people what I've been doing."

"Try?" he asked, knitting his brow.

"I can tell you and show you, but your mindset and theirs may not be able to appreciate how integrated functioning actually works. They've designed these processors from the beginning to accelerate mental activity while, if not denying, at least under-valuing the feeling function."

"I see, and rather astute I might add," Klaus said. "But, let's get back to your conditions. Are you that mistrustful of us that you think we'd rig this whole release? I mean, as you can see it's been countersigned by her lawyer."

"Dr. Klaus, despite your pretense to the contrary, I've been consistently lied to and manipulated during this operation, and so yes, I believe I have a right and an obligation to be … mistrustful."

"Okay. I'll see what I can do about that call. In the meantime, the doctors here would like to conduct a neurological exami-nation of your neocortex, since we can't remove it, and see what changes have occurred there."

I almost said—can't remove it yet, but I restrained myself. "Can you tell me how long the beta testing of your next processor will take?"

"You mean the redesign, insertion, and assessment?"

I nodded my head.

"Maybe three months."

I looked surprised.

"Quicker than you thought?" he asked.

"Yeah."

"Well, there's a need, if not yet a crisis, to upgrade and adjust our ... their product line to make it more ... compatible. Or how can I say ... to help bridge this schism that you so like to point out to us."

"I'm all for that."

"Good. So we're on the same page and your cooperation is assured, once you're satisfied that Emma is free as a bird."

I begrudgingly nodded my head. Dr. Klaus stood up, gave me a winning smile, took back Emma's release document and left the room without another word. Now I had to determine just how much I could share with them, or if this would be counterproductive in any way.

The next day I went back into their lab, and the brain scientists ran a number of neurological exams on my neocortex, such as testing the neuron firing-rate, the speed at which it processed new material, etc. Again, from their reactions, I could see that while my neocortex was altered, on its own it could not account for the high test results. What they didn't realize or couldn't compute or understand is that these results weren't strictly a result of a faster neocortex but of my expanded consciousness at this point. Sara Irving, whom I had first met on my trip here to interview Dr. Quirk and who had updated Ling on the new processor, was part of this group. While she maintained her distance, I could see that she was sensing the broader picture of my development, and at unguarded moments a quizzical facial expression seemed to confirm that.

It only took a few experimental sessions to gather up the needed raw data, but Klaus wanted to explore this process of mine and how it had affected their experimental neural processor. So he arranged for me to talk with Emma at her cabin in upper state New York. I examined the new portable and found that it hadn't been tampered with—I would know since as an undercover agent I had rigged more than a few—and they left me alone in an interrogation room, although I figured the conversation was being monitored.

After she showed me shots of herself with the cabin and lake in the background, which I transferred to the wall screen, we had a brief conversation. "So, Mansfield is satisfied that legally you're free and they can't make a further claim on you?"

"Believe me when I say, Paula is even more paranoid than you."

I nodded my head. "Okay, I just wanted to make sure you were all right."

Emma glared at me. "Well, what about you? When are they going to let you go, or are they going to let you go?" she asked.

"I don't see why not. I've cooperated with them, and they seem happy with the results of the mission, which as we guessed was always about the neural processors." I waited for them to interrupt the transmission or garble my response, but they didn't, which was actually hopeful.

"Well, my father was so thankful for your help with my case that he's hired Paula to look into your situation."

"Thank him, but I don't think it's really necessary."

This stopped her, and she stared back at me for a long moment and seemed to get what I was really saying; legal recourse would be a dead end.

"Okay, I'll tell him as much, but he's a pretty feisty old guy, and I can't tell how he'll respond."

Klaus stepped into the room and used a hand gesture to tell me the conversation needed to end. I said my goodbyes, and my hopes that she could get back to the Southwest at some point, since she loved the desert so much. This last statement seemed to annoy Klaus, as if it was some hidden message, and he terminated the connection.

"We've told Knowles that the Southwest was off-limits to her."

I nodded my head. It seemed like they wanted to isolate Maria and her group, or didn't want what was happening in my development to get replicated with Emma, who was already halfway there. This suggested, which alarmed me, that Maria and her healers were still targets.

"So, if you're satisfied, I've set up an open forum with their neural scientists this afternoon, to explore this 'process' of yours."

I stared at him for a long moment. "You've upheld your end of the bargain and I'll uphold mine, but I'm telling you these rationalists just won't get it."

"Well, I understand, but given the framework, we can have you explain it later to others who are ... more attuned to such development."

52.

The session was set up in their mini-amphitheater, that they no doubt used for educational purposes. I sat at a table on the stage, with Dr. Klaus beside me as the monitor. There were also vid screens at the back and on both sides, to enlarge video material sent to their portables. As I sat down and scanned the gathering of about two dozen white-coated doctors and researchers, I spotted Dr. Irving in the back row. I was concerned that she may have a better handle on this process and what was happening to me, and I hoped she wouldn't challenge some of my less-than-forthright answers.

Dr. Klaus started off the session. "We've had a chance now to test the experimental X2 processor that Alan was ... kind enough to alpha test for us in the field. We've determined that he was able to 'effect' changes in its processing by integrating feelings that this ... body-mind schism seems to create." There was some grumbling from the audience, but Klaus ignored it. "While we've yet to test this theory on other subjects but will be able to shortly with the next model, I thought it would be productive to hear how Alan does this process of his." Klaus paused for a moment and surveyed his audience with a lock-eyed stare to preclude any "bad behavior" on their part. I had to remind myself that what I was doing and suggesting was contrary to their whole mindset and was thus threatening on a lot of levels. He turned to me. "Can you give us a brief summation, Alan?"

"Well, if I'm not mistaken, the neural processors accelerate the synapse firing of the neocortex, so what I'm actually doing is working with how the neocortex suppresses feelings at accelerated levels." I figured the best way to deflect blame or criticism away from their precious little NPs was to shift the focus. This drew a few nods from the more accommodating scientists in the audience. I caught Dr. Irving's cryptic smile in the top row.

"It's fairly simple in theory if a little more difficult in application. When a negative feeling arises, with its own angry voice of recrimination or blame, I just focus on the feeling sensation, don't try to figure it out or go mental, and after a while—at first a minute or two and now almost instantaneously—the energy of the angry feeling seems to get integrated and my body experiences a kind of body shift. I've been hooked up to monitoring devices when this happens, and I've been told that you can see the phase shift in the brainwave rhythms."

A hand went up in the audience. I turned to Dr. Klaus, who asked me, "Are you ready to take questions?"

"Yeah, that's basically the process—let's let them fire away." I turned to the scientist in the first row. "You have a question."

"I do indeed." He paused. "Afterward, do you feel euphoric?"

"No, not in a sense of being ... high or wired, just calmer and more settled into my body."

The man frowned. "Do these particular angry thoughts ever

return, or their subject?"

I had to think over this for a moment. "Yes, in another context like, 'she doesn't love me' to 'she doesn't respect me,' but eventually this whole focus dissipates after repeated integrations."

The scientist nodded his head, still a little uncertain. Someone else, an older woman in the second row, said, "It's hard to believe that this process alone is causing the neurological changes we're seeing in the X2."

This drew a round of nods from the others. Sara Irving raised her hand. "Mr. Reynard, at first, when you discovered this ... technique, how many times a day would you do it?"

"Well, I discovered this process back in college. But when I started working in law enforcement and was sent on assignments to borny villages, where erratic feelings run quite high, I'd say twenty or thirty times a day." This drew a few incredulous huffs from the audience.

Klaus wasn't happy with this contrary response and stared down these groups of doctors. Another white-coated scientist from the third row asked, "This was with your old ..." She looked down at her screen, "... R11 model?"

"I'm not sure what the number was, but yes, what I was first fitted with as a teenager and had upgraded later."

"Did you detect any differences with the X2 model that was later implanted?" she asked.

Dr. Klaus turned to me and gave me another one of his cautionary looks.

"Yes, the parameters were ... different, if that's the right word, or at first. It did allow the processing of more feelings but ... had a feedback loop, a mental component."

There were nods of recognition from the audience. "And how did you deal with that?" she asked, as everybody leaned forward.

"I modified my process which seemed to modify the feedback

loop, until it came to some kind of balance." Since this was exactly what they wanted—having me adjust it to a higher if not an ultimate level—they all seemed fairly pleased with this "accommodation."

The woman now looked at her screen and called up something. "And when this healer applied her energy ..."

Dr. Klaus raised his hand. "That's classified ... for now. Please keep your questions ... general."

There was an undercurrent of resentment that passed through the audience; they were all going to need some processing later. After that, I could see that the Institute and the government had its own little schism, and I wondered how they expected to roll out a more adaptable neural processor, if the hands didn't know what the mind was thinking. The questions after this "intervention" were along more pedestrian paths, but they seemed to understand how my process could and did adapt the processor, along the lines they were seeing. I was somewhat relieved that nobody picked up on or asked questions about an alternate approach to affecting the processors. As everybody got up to leave, I had brief eye contact with Sara Irving, who just nodded her head. This went well for our team, if she was actually working with us.

I was informed by Klaus that my services would still be needed, while they ran the beta test on the new X5 processor. I told him that they needed to release me or let Paula Mansfield resolve my hostage situation with the government. I was told that I was still employed by K Industries, that my paycheck was being deposited to my account as always, and that my contract with them allowed them to lend me out to the FBI on assignments. This was part of my assignment, but that they were allotting me an apartment at the Institute. I was to remain on campus and available for further testing of my "development" and the effects on me of living without a neural processor until the next stage of their X5 rollout.

"In other words, I'm your guinea pig for as long as you so desire," I told him at my preliminary wrap-up for this stage of my deployment.

"Alan, as you've said, you work in law enforcement, and while this isn't the type of hands-on, deep-cover assignments you're used to, it is crucial to us maintaining law and order within our society."

I was tempted to dispute the real nature of this operation and its bid for continued government control over their half-asleep flock, but I figured it wouldn't change him or his superiors and would only dig a deeper hole for me.

Chapter Eighteen

53.

I was sure that my little apartment was wired for sound and video, and that they were keeping a close watch on me. Thus, it was important that I didn't have any further Kundalini awakening experiences, or anything remotely transcendent, that might clue them into this alternate process that we had initiated. I suspected that, since they couldn't attribute my higher test scores to changes in my neocortex, while devaluing my own integration process, they were suspicious or maybe even intuited—I mean this faculty was completely atrophied in them—that there was something else happening with me. So I read a lot, took long walks on their campus—I had a subdural tracking device—and used my time out in nature as my meditation and alignment process. I was told that Paula Mansfield had filed a petition with the courts, claiming that I was being forcibly detained by the FBI, and demanded an interview with me. They were forced to comply, but Dr. Klaus warned me in a video feed from his New York offices, that if I wanted to maintain the current "status quo" of my position, I would back her off.

She was escorted to my apartment; I assumed that an interview in one of the Institute's interrogation rooms would only support her contention. I poured us some Chinese green tea and we sat out on the patio of my third-storey place.

"I assume your apartment and even this patio are bugged?" Paula asked.

I smiled. "We do live in a surveillance society."

"Well, I've been briefed about your situation and your voluntary compliance, and I just needed to check that out on my own." I nodded my head. "I've also been told that this 'project' is top secret and that you can't divulge any information about it."

"Yes, and I won't compromise you by violating that agreement."

"What I can't understand is why they have you sequestered out here, and why you can't resume your work at K Industries? I've been assured by your boss, Gene Upshaw, that you still work for them and are on loan to the FBI."

"Yes, it a fairly long debriefing."

Paula stared at me. "Well, according to Emma, it's been more than three months since you've returned from the Southwest."

I let this statement settle for a moment. I could just imagine my handlers listening attentively. "Again, it's all very complicated and involves more than just writing reports or getting interrogated about my last mission."

"Interrogated? Doesn't sound very voluntary to me," she said.

"Well, just a convenient term. I do work in intelligence. But, you and Emma need to know that it is indeed voluntary, and that at some point I will be returned to my regular job at K Industries."

Paula was still unconvinced, but there wasn't much more she could do.

"Okay, Alan," she said while standing up. "I still think there's something … sinister going on here, but without your help I can't get to the bottom of it, and will just have let it go … for now."

I stood up. "Thanks, Paula. Please don't let Emma's father pay for this. Submit a bill for your services, and I'll have the funds transferred."

"It's pro bono, for your help with Su Ling and Emma's cases."

We stepped back inside and I walked her to the door. "Oh, there is one more thing. I contacted your wife, Sherrie, who's just as annoyed with K Industries and their refusal to update her on your whereabouts."

"And?" I asked.

"She's asked me to file a petition on her part to contact you, but Dr. Klaus said he would arrange a visit for her."

"Thanks so much, Paula. Give my ... best regards to Emma." She nodded her head, no doubt confused by the formality of my request. I'm sure Emma filled her in on the nature of our relationship.

Later that afternoon, Sara Irving called and asked me to dinner. She informed me that she had been appointed my liaison because of our earlier contact at the Institute, in regards to Dr. Quirk. I asked how he was doing, and she said that he was serving out his time at a mental hospital in Maine. I agreed to meet with her; she would pick me up and we could walk to the cafeteria. I assumed that I was personally bugged and that even my walks were subject to surveillance, but they couldn't watch eye contact or body language as closely.

When my door detector recognized her presence, I opened the door. She stood back in the hallway, deep enough to be in a shadow blind. She looked at me and shook her head; I nodded; we both understood the limitations of our meet-up. I was ready and closed the door behind me.

"First of all," she said, as we strolled across the campus, "we've rolled out test models of the X5 neural processor, implanted it in test subjects who've been subjected to emotional upsets, and we're pleased with how they've been able to ... adapt."

I wasn't sure how to respond at first, but since I wanted them to succeed and just hoped that this processor would allow higher functionality in some, I decided to be ... collaborative. "That's wonderful. Anything I can do to help? Getting pretty bored with my current routine."

"Well yes, the reason for my invitation."

"So this isn't a 'get to know each other better' dinner?"

She laughed. "I think those were the exact words I used last time. How remarkable."

"For a functional idiot?" I asked.

We walked on for a moment. "Well, you're showing us that the good old neocortex can still surprise us."

"Well, it sure the hell surprised me."

She smiled and brushed up against me on the uneven ground, but I definitely got the message. I was not surprised that a section of the Institute's cafeteria was converted into a restaurant at night, with tables and waiters and a much expanded menu. We ordered some wine and then dinner, and after the waiter poured our glasses, Sara raised hers in a toast.

"To Alan and his most excellent adventure."

I had to laugh at this retro movie reference from the 1990s.

"Yeah, I love quirky old movies," she added.

We just sat there and stared at each other until it became somewhat awkward for her. I imagined like most moderns she didn't feel comfortable with silence.

"You seem a lot more peaceful than at our last encounter."

"With Dr. Quirk?" I asked. She nodded. "Well, I was sent to discredit a man who wanted others to see 'God,' despite his twisted attempt to force-feed it to them, and I wasn't entirely pleased with the assignment."

She smiled. This seemed to play into her agenda—the reason I phrased it that way. "And did you see 'God' on your last assignment with Maria Fria?"

I laughed. "What kind of question is that?"

"Just curious. You seem … different."

"Yeah, well, trying to survive the X2 certainly required an elevated response, that Fria's energy only augmented."

"You didn't really answer my question, Alan?"

"Well, I do feel a connection to the greater whole and realize I'm more than the computing power of my … brain."

She nodded her head. The waiter stepped over and served our dinner. The flounder looked great, even if it was farmed, and we took a few bites of our meals and just let this last exchange settle.

Finally, Sara looked up at me. "Alan, while I'm really inter-ested in your process, from seeing the effects on you, I need to ask you if you'll interview some of our test subjects."

"See if they have this 'unwanted' potential too?" I said with a smirk.

"Well, yes I guess you could say that. No signs of any questionable orientation, but then we might not spot it given our own bias."

I put down my fork. "You expect me to help you quash this impulse in others, or detect if it will arise and if your X5 needs further adjusting?"

Sara looked down; I could sense that she was being pressured and being used to what … seduce me into complying with their request? But, given that I was just as interested, I wondered if I could get what I wanted from the subjects, while not showing my true intent. Interesting challenge.

"Okay, I'll interview them, but don't expect me to help with your little witch hunt."

She squinched her eyes. "It's not, believe me. We just can't account for all the new neural pathways in our upgrade, taken from your X2 cells, so they're concerned."

"Well, my long-term 'orientation' was augmented, not created by my struggles with the X2, so I wouldn't expect the same in others."

"Good. I can take that back to them."

We finished dinner, but this couched request certainly strained the conversation. As we walked back across campus, Sara invited me to her place for an after-dinner drink. I begged off. I had no doubt that they wanted me to engage in sex with her, to see if something interesting was happening in that realm. They must've had consultants who were familiar with Eastern literature and its Tantric practices, and especially after Dr. Quirk's quest, they were suspicious. But it also confirmed that she was no collaborator and had fed Su Ling her information on the X2 as part of Klaus' overall plan. It just showed how much planning had gone into this operation, and made me wonder if my own recruitment by K Industries was part of it.

54.

It was interesting that they were conducting these interviews in the same interrogation room, or living room as it were, as we used with Dr. Quirk. I made a note not to underestimate Klaus and crew, and knew that these interviews would be examined from every angle and a lot of remote electronic monitoring was being conducted. The first beta tester, a Ms. Julie Mays, was shown into the room. She had already gone through a pre-interview, which covered standard questioning and tests, and was curious as what I wanted or needed from her.

"Julie, I'm Alan Reynard, and I have just a few questions for you."

She smiled. "Go ahead. This has been routine so far."

"So, besides handling emotional upsets better, have you noticed any changes in … temperament?"

"Not sure what you mean by that," she said.

I paused. "For instance, have you been more tolerant of others and their quirks," I said and had to smile.

She thought through this question. "You mean like my little brother's weird ideas about everything?"

"Yes, exactly."

"Huh. Now that I think about it, I've only wanted to slap him upside the head a few times this week."

I laughed. "And that's an improvement?"

"You bet. The kid's a major annoyance."

I asked her a few more 'pedestrian' questions, and then excused her. The next tester was more of a challenge—kind of a nervous wreck, and an interesting choice for the program.

"Henry, I see that you're feeling less on edge after this replacement surgery."

"Really, if you say so, Doc."

"So, tell me, what usually sets you off?" I asked.

"People are so fucking greedy and just concerned about their own stuff, and could care less what's happening outside their little world."

"That is annoying," I said. "So has that changed any?"

He stared at me for a long moment. "Them or me?"

"Well, they are interchangeable."

"We've got a real philosopher here." He paused and looked over at the one-way mirror but I didn't react. "Since I don't feel as … emotional about things, I guess it doesn't bother me as much."

"Do you ever catch yourself ready to react, and then hold back?"

He just stared at me. "Yeah, that's the whole idea, isn't it?" he asked. I didn't respond. After a moment, he got nervous. "Yesterday I caught myself catching myself, and that was interesting."

Just what I wanted to hear. The watcher complex. I asked a few more questions and dismissed him before he said too much.

This went on for a dozen more testers, all of whom were handling emotional upsets better and a few seem to be getting an expanded outlook. It was hard to tell within the limits of this format, but it became more evident with George Midas. The beta testers were supposedly picked at random, but I had to wonder if George wasn't slipped in to test someone's theory.

After a few standard questions, I asked if anything unusual had happened since the trials started.

"You could say that," he replied rather cryptically.

"Care to elaborate?"

"You care to tell me what's really going on?" he spit out.

I stared at him for a long moment. He had an asymmetrical face that made reading facial expression difficult, but I sensed that he was having "unusual" experiences.

"Why don't you just tell me what's been happening."

He looked at me and shook his head. "Like you don't know."

I shook my head.

"Okay, the weird dreams started right off, and then I started knowing things."

After a moment I asked, "What kind of things?"

"The phone would ring and I had a pretty good hunch about who was calling, before looking at the caller ID. Things like that."

"This ever happened before?" I asked.

"Yeah, my wife says I'm psychic, not that I give a damn, but what was weird stuff happening every so often, has become pretty regular since the trial started."

"Has this frightened you?"

He stared back at me. "That's the funny thing. It's been annoying as hell but I seem to deal with it better. Hey, maybe I'll hang out a shingle and start giving psychic readings." He laughed.

"Well, don't be surprised if it lets up at some point."

"Oh yeah, you got your own crystal ball or something?" he asked.

"The unconscious mind, as Carl Jung once said, just wants to be acknowledged. I think it's got your attention, and if you don't resist, it should stop 'annoying you.'"

"Okay, professor, if you say so."

At the end of the day, Sara informed me that I had interviewed enough testers and that tomorrow, Dr. Klaus and a few of the brain scientists wanted to get my impressions of how the trial subjects were handling the new X5.

This exchange happened in a corporate boardroom, with a huge oak table and with them sitting across from Klaus and me. To start out Klaus asked me my overall impressions. I had thought about what I would say and had even done some research on the Web, and I felt that I had a good handle on the first stage of this expansion, but would only dole it out to them.

Klaus asked me to make a general statement. "I quoted Carl

Jung yesterday, when trying to explain this phenomenon to Mr. Midas, the would-be psychic." This got everybody's attention. "So I did some research, actually just a reminder from my psyche courses in college. Jung claimed that we apprehend what's happening around us with either our intuition or our physical senses, and for most some combination of the two, and that we process that information either through our feeling or our thinking function."

"Yes, Yes, basic transpersonal theory," one of the scientists replied impatiently.

"Well, I would say with the changeover to neural processors years ago, that a great majority of the population has become sensing/thinking types, which explains the decline in the creative arts over the last fifty years."

"Some would question that," another scientist added.

"Well, by allowing the integration of more feelings, or a slight shift from thinking to feeling processing, you would also see a shift from sensing to more intuition as well."

Dr. Klaus nodded his head. "Brilliant assessment, Alan."

"So you're saying that this adapted X5 isn't causing psychic experiences per se but increasing intuitive leaps?" Sara asked.

"So by adjusting the threshold of how much feeling you allow to be processed, you set a gauge of how much intuition comes into play."

The scientists looked at each other and started nodding their heads. What scared them was a lack of control, or the whole population switching its orientation. But, this gave them a rheostat to control that influx.

"But with Midas it wasn't a quid pro quo, or the amount of feeling integration wasn't proportionate to the … intuitive leaps," a scientist pointed out.

"Well, everybody's makeup is different, and like me he didn't need as much integration, but that's the exception, not the rule here, I would think."

Using this gestalt they seemed to have a better understanding of the interviews and the expansion some of the beta testers were experiencing, or their questions seemed to reflect that view. I also sensed a bit of relief, as they could now convince the political structure that a rollout of the new X5 could correct the social chaos caused by the neural processor breakdowns, without creating a whole new set of problems. I could just hear the advertisements: "Upgrade to the new X5 and get peace of mind." As the meeting broke up, several of the scientists actually stepped forward and shook my hand, as if I were a colleague, which I guess I was in a manner of speaking—if they only knew.

As we were walking out, Klaus said, "You might have righted the ship and saved the day, Alan. We should give you stock options."

Hopefully they would let me go, which was my only concern.

55.

I was informed by Dr. Klaus that, given my overall cooperation, I was being relieved of any further involvement with this FBI mission and that I was being returned to K Industries, to resume my work there.

"So I'm free and clear?" I asked at our last interview.

"Well, you still have another year left on your contract with them, and we would prefer that you honor that commitment."

"Okay, and my subdural tracker?"

"Remains," he said.

"So you can keep tabs on me?"

"You're still suspicious of us, which doesn't bode well for continued government work, but given the sensitive nature of this last assignment and the need for total secrecy, we want to make sure you don't disappear and honor your nondisclosure agreements with us."

"You know, without a neural processor, I won't be as quick or facile as I once was. Is that of any concern, or I should say, have they been informed?"

"No, as far as they or anybody else is concerned, you still have a neural processor. I mean, to them, how else could you possibly function in our society or on your job without one?"

"Otherwise, seeing that I do, would raise questions in people's minds and unwanted speculation and inquiries, which would put my work on this project and its characterization in jeopardy."

Klaus nodded his head. "Sharp as ever as far as I'm concerned."

"Any further … exclusions?" I asked.

"Well, we've placed Maria Fria on the anti-government list and she's gone underground, so you can't have any further contact with her, or any such contact will be considered aiding and abetting an enemy."

"She's no such thing, and you know it."

"You mean from your biased reports of her," he said.

I could see that this line of contention wasn't going to help my case. "Yes, I guess you could say that."

"We've told your wife that you're returning to your job at K Industries. I assume you'll inform her or deal with personal matters on your own."

"That's it?" I asked.

"Well, I've been asked to inquire if you'd be interested in a consultant's position, here at the Bradbury Institute, for considerably more money and stock options that could make you rich one day."

It took considerable restraint on my part not to laugh in his face. "No, this environment's too heady for me. I'd rather go back to catching bad guys." I gave him a searching look, since he was one of them in my opinion.

"Okay, well I think that does it, Alan. I want to thank you for your work on our little project. I hope you don't hold any grudges against how it was conducted. I mean, you'll cross paths with

Musgrave and me in the future, and we'd hate for that to be ... awkward for you."

"I don't see why it would. I mean. We succeeded, and the long-term payoff in terms of social stability has been achieved."

"Well, I'm glad you see it that way, Alan."

After the session I was taken to the legal department, where they had me sign another round of nondisclosure agreements. I went back to my apartment, packed my bags, and a car drove me to the city. I had them drop me at a midtown hotel. I wasn't ready to show up on Sherry's doorstep. It was interesting that I should characterize that way—I mean it was my place as well, but I guess it didn't feel that way to me any longer.

The next day I called Gene at K-Industries. He told me that, since my time at the Bradbury Institute was considered a buffer period, I was to report to work the following Monday. He sounded glad to hear from me, wondering what had happened. I was actually looking forward to the normality of it all. The next weekend I planned to talk with Sherry, tell her I wanted out of our contract, which I was sure would be just fine with her. I mean, given the expansion of my feelings and intuitions, going back to the sterile environment of our marriage just wouldn't work for me. I was sure she'd see that as well after our face-to-face talk.

Sherry had already taken up with somebody else, so our parting was rather amiable and the release quickly signed and notarized. I moved my stuff to a storage facility and stayed on at the midtown hotel for now. They had given me quite a nice bonus for the last assignment, which made all of this possible. Gene and company were glad to have me back. They were increasingly focused on anti-government activity and since these were mostly bornies, my extended experience in their community was considered a big plus.

If they only knew that it was more than just my recognizance time there but the reorientation of my whole psyche, it would surprise them. What surprised me was that my heightened intuition made this kind of intelligence work even easier, while my expansive feelings made the harsher side of people's detainment harder to take. The other downside was that I did have trouble assimilating the vast amounts of information that my neural processor had previously handled without a problem. This was noted, but attributed to my hangover from this last extended assignment.

Emma had not been placed on my no-contact list. I called but could never reach her, so I slipped away one weekend to visit her. However, her cabin was empty, with no signs of any recent habitation. I tried to contact Paula Mansfield, but she had moved with no forwarding address. This was all getting rather suspicious. I wondered what was really going on behind the scenes. I would soon find out. One afternoon a few weeks later, while walking back to the hotel after work, I was picked up on the street by some black ops unit or some such detail, whether national or foreign, and hustled away in a van. I was drugged, but between treatments saw that I was being flown a long distance, probably out of country, to some detention center on a foreign soil, where the amenities wouldn't be as cushy as the Bradbury Institute's.

Chapter Nineteen

56.

Since I had status in our society and legal inquiries had been made of my disposition, the government or Klaus and company couldn't just make me disappear. They would have to insert me back into my life and job, then snatch me and blame it on anti-government forces getting back at me for my undercover work, or even attribute my kidnapping to foreign or black market interests, given that I was largely responsible for the upgrades of the new X5 neural processor. As with computer brands and portables, these processors were sold worldwide and the competition was fierce. I had no doubt that it was the government who snatched me, and this was clearly evident when I reached my destination and was transported by a jeep through the jungle, my hands bound and with a hood over my head, to a black ops detention center in what appeared to be Central American.

While my drivers and guards were mostly local Spanish-speaking hires, this was definitely a US operation, made more evident when we arrived and I was unshackled, my hood removed, and escorted across the common area to an administrative building. After a bathroom break, I was taken to the mess hall where there were lots of military grunts, special ops soldiers and a few scientist types. I was handed over to my handler, who was in his late forties, graying temples, with the sharp eyes of an analyst but also somewhat deadened, by his black ops work I would assume.

He stuck out his hand. "Reynard. Sorry for the rough treatment, but they wanted this handled quickly and seamlessly.

I shook the guy's hand. "And who are they?"

"Call me Clayton."

"And 'they' are?" I asked again.

He smiled and took me over to the buffet counter. "We'll get to that, but it's dinner time and once they close, they're closed."

We stood in line with metal trays and chose from a food selection that was half Mexican and half American. I was hungry and loaded up on the Mexican food. I had got used to this diet in the Southwest, but it was harder to maintain at the Institute. My selection was noted. We walked to the far end of the mess and took a table with a window view of the jungle.

We ate in silence for a while. Finally I stared across the table at him. "Look, Reynard, the less you know about any of this, the easier it will be for you to get out of here and back to some kind of normal life."

"But not my previous life?" I asked.

He shrugged his shoulders; apparently my dispensation was above his pay grade, or so he pretended.

"Well, can you tell me why I'm here?"

"That I can do. The government apparently felt that your previous interrogation was less than … truthful, and since they couldn't use chemical coercion … or other means at the Bradbury Institute, they've sent you to us, since we don't exist."

"And don't follow the Geneva Convention."

"Well, since you're not an enemy combatant, but a US operative of sorts, it doesn't apply, not that we would give a damn."

Since it was obvious that I wasn't going to get any info from this guy, I finished my meal in silence. Afterward Clayton and an armed guard walked me to my cell: a twelve-by-twelve room with a small window, no doubt made of hard plastic and unbreakable, a decent-looking bed, a toilet, and natural spectrum lighting, which was easier on the eyes. I soon realized that the lights stayed on 24/7 for surveillance purposes, explaining the low lighting. This meant no formal meditations, but then I was prepared for that at the Institute, where I learned to conduct my quiet-mind practice disguised as sleep. I had no doubt that they had long-range brain-wave scanners to detect if I was truly sleeping, but I figured I could get around them.

I was exhausted and slept well that first night, despite the lights. In the morning, the door opened and I was passed a tray of food and a change of clothing—army fatigues in my size. The guard told me I could change in the shower room. So I ate, and was taken down the hall, where the guard waited inside while I showered and shaved and put on my fatigues. The whole time I focused on altering my state of awareness or dissociating myself from my mental mechanism, or in my case my neocortex, since I didn't have a neural processor. I figured this was the only way I could lie without detection, to whatever level of electronic monitoring or chemical coercion they would use.

I was taken to an interrogation room which was military standard, unlike the Bradbury Institute's private sector version. I sat down on a metal chair at a square metal table. Clayton came in and sat down across from me, opened up his portable, and read through a few pages before looking up at me.

"Alan, let's do this the easy way. You know we can subject you to chemical coercion, and as an operative you've seen how effective that can be. So, why go there? Why not just truthfully answer my questions, letting us use standard long-range scanners to check their veracity."

"Fine with me."

Clayton nodded his head. He then asked me a series of standard questions about myself, like my name and my mother's name, where I had lived with my ex-wife, Sherry, to establish a level. He rather quickly moved to the gist of the matter. "You did alpha testing on the X2 neural processor?"

"Yes."

"To the best of your knowledge, did your process, which you described to scientists at the Bradbury Institute, alter it in ways indiscernible to their brain scans and neural mapping?"

"No ... but the processing isn't totally under my control."

"How so?" he asked.

"The process involves me sensing and then integrating mostly negative feelings, which relieves a lot of tension, but how it affects neural processors is rather difficult for me to assess."

Clayton nodded his head. "As you know, your whole statement can be subjected to truth analysis and I'm detecting that this was ... generally truthful." He paused and smiled at me. "So, let me rephrase the question. By any means, this process or others, was your neural processor affected in ways that were indiscernible to their brain scientists?"

Since I couldn't close my eyes, I had to shift my consciousness while fully aware of the outside world. "No."

Clayton studied the readout and then looked up at me. "Well, that response is ... more questionable."

"Well, to reiterate, the process isn't totally under my control, but to the best of my knowledge, it wasn't altered in such ways, but could have been."

Clayton stared at his screen. "Okay, I can see that I need a little more background in order to properly conduct this interrogation, which is our fault, not yours." He paused, all the while staring at me. "But, since it appears that you're cooperating, we'll loosen our restrictions and allow you some yard time, as they call it."

I thanked him, and a guard escorted me out to the exercise yard that the soldiers generally used for sports activities, like soccer and baseball. I walked around the field for about an hour and then I was returned to my cell. A vid screen had been installed and some video entertainment options were available. This included an online library, and I was able to call up the Hindu *Upanishads* and read from it. After a while, I pretended to take a nap, but went into an altered state and pulled in energy and had another out-of-body experience. What I detected, as I viewed the compound from above, were a series of unmarked graves in a field to the rear of the overall jungle clearing, and I knew that this was where they would 'dispose' of me, but I sensed, if not totally understood, that there was another option.

57.

The next morning, after my shower and change of clothing, I was taken to the clinic, strapped into a chair, and given a shot of what I assumed was an advance chemical truth serum. Taking this on an empty stomach made it quick reacting. I didn't have much time before it started to affect me and alter my state of mind. I needed to detach my consciousness from my body, so I wouldn't be affected, or less so. I discovered this was much easier not having to 'fiddle' with a neural processor and its programming. By the time I arrived at the interrogation room, my mind and physical reaction time was definitely affected, if not my consciousness.

Clayton was waiting for me this time. I was strapped into a chair across from him. A doctor came in, ran a few physical tests, did a light-in-the-eye examination and told my interrogator that the chemical serum was in effect.

"Sorry, but when we ran yesterday's interrogation by ..." He paused and looked at his portable. "... Dr. Klaus, he said you weren't being truthful and authorized our use of chemical interrogation."

"How nice of him."

My glib response took him aback, and he glanced over his shoulder at the one-way mirror and to his superiors. He turned back to me but apparently didn't receive any further feedback from them.

"Okay, Reynard. Let me ask you again. Was your X2 neural processor affected by any means and in ways that were indiscernible to the Bradbury Institute's brain scientists?"

I stared back at him, my eyes no doubt glazed over, but if not 'clear-minded,' I was definitely 'clear.'

"Would you like me to repeat the question?"

"No."

Clayton glared at me. "'No' to repeating the question or 'no' as your answer?"

"No and no."

He looked down at his screen, then up at me again. "Alan, how old are you?"

"Twenty-eight."

He nodded his head. Apparently, to the best of his knowledge, the truth serum was working.

"Another question. Did you and Maria Fria conspire to undermine your mission objective?"

I realized that they were looking for an excuse to kill me, and I sensed that was part of some larger scheme for me to cooperate and give them what they wanted, and so I did. "No. But, her healing affected me and changed my position in regard to it."

"How."

"I figured that she wasn't the real objective, but that I was being set up to test how her energy affected the R11 and X2 neural processors."

"What was your response to that knowledge?"

"It pissed me off," I said.

"And if you could have reprogrammed it, would you?"

"Yes."

"While you were there, did you come into contact with Su Ling?"

"Yes."

"Under what circumstances?"

"She wanted me to help them free Emma from FBI custody, but I thought it was too dangerous and she might get killed in the escape."

"But otherwise you might have cooperated?"

"Yes."

Clayton now waited for a long moment; he then read his screen and smiled. "Well, Dr. Klaus is satisfied that you've been truthful about the X2, but you've also admitted to treason against your country, punishable by death, the execution to be carried out summarily."

"You know I didn't eat breakfast yet, don't I get one last meal?"

"A real wise guy. I think I'll carry this order out myself."

He had the doctor remove my subdural tracking device. I guess they weren't going to follow me into the afterlife.

Two strong-armed guards stepped into the room, unstrapped me from the chair, and bound my hands behind me. We followed Clayton out of the room, down the hall, and into the exercise yard. There, two grunts were waiting for us with shovels. We crossed the field to the graveyard I had detected last night. I thought I might have some more time, but the grave had already been dug, and they were just there to fill it back up over my dead body.

Clayton pulled out a revolver. "Any last words, traitor?"

It was amazing but I didn't feel any fear. I surrendered to my fate, be it my death at their hands or my more improbable rescue. I was looking him in the eyes as he raised his revolver. I heard a shot ring out and saw blood trickling down from his forehead as he fell over. Two more shots killed the gravediggers and then a rebel guerilla troop stepped out of the forest, put a cloth hood over my head, and pulled me back into the forest. They dragged me for a hundred yards or so, where I was strapped into the backseat of a small jeep-like vehicle. Somebody ran an electronic scanner over my body, to detect any implanted bugs, but I was now clean. We drove off over a rough road at high speed.

I could hear gunshots being fired at us, and I figured we didn't have long before a drone would be sent in our direction and my rescue, if that was what this was, would be all for naught. But then I felt long palm fronds slapping my face, and I figured we were deep in the jungle and the tree coverage was protecting us. What I later learned was that an anti-thermal cover was stretched across the top of the jeep and halfway down its sides, to prevent drones from locking into our thermal signatures.

We had driven for about three hours when we stopped and I was pulled from the jeep. They removed my hood and unfastened my hands and gave me a canteen of water. I gulped it down. The leader, a tough-looking Indian with a scar down his right cheek, told me, "Okay hombre, we walk from here. Don't try escape."

I figured that they were going to ransom me off to the government, or some foreign entity interested in my work on the new X5 processor. Either prospect was not to my liking, but as they say, the alternative was even less appealing. We walked through the jungle for about four hours. It was almost dark when we came to a large compound with high, adobe walls. There was a guard post at each corner. Scarface yelled something to the nearest guard and the huge, metal, swinging door partially opened to allow us to slide through before it was closed shut.

I was bleary-eyed by now, hung over from the drug treatment, and exhausted by the long trek. I saw a woman run down the steps of a large cottage and race toward me. Only when she was within a few feet did I recognize Emma, in her army fatigue pants and white T-shirt, as she jumped into my arms and nearly knocked me over.

"Oh my God, you made it."

After a long embrace and a big kiss, she pulled back, grabbed my arm, and helped me walk over to the cottage. Maria stepped out onto the porch as we walked up the steps. I was really depleted by now, but she motioned me forward and gave me a big hug, and I could just feel her energy coursing through my body and reviving me.

After she released me, I started to say something but she shook her head and the two of them walked me into the cottage and over to a long table set for dinner. I was now restored enough to realize that I needed a shower badly before any social engagement.

"We're informal here, Alan. You can clean up later. Let's eat," Maria said.

I sat down as scarface and his men joined us at the table, while the women, no doubt their wives and daughters, brought out loads of food. I just looked at the spread in amazement.

"Best if you start slow, Alan," Emma said, squeezing my hand.

I followed her advice and slowly added food to my plate and ate it, savoring the delicious vegetable dishes. After a while I was functioning well enough to look across the table at scarface. "Thanks for rescuing me." He nodded his head. "What's your name, if you don't mind me asking?"

He bowed his head and with an elaborate hand gesture said, "Javier Clemente at your service."

"Javier and his wife were students of mine, when I lived here fifteen years ago and they kindly offered me sanctuary when he heard of my ... criminal status," Maria said with a smirk.

"Yes, we always knew she was an ... outlaw," Javier laughed.

I turned and looked at Emma. "Su Ling spirited me away from my cabin in New York. She predicted that once they released you they'd pull this stunt, and that I had to disappear too."

"And Paula Mansfield?"

"She went underground, as a legal consultant of sorts to the anti-government forces."

I let this all sink in for a moment. "But how did you find me?"

Javier said, "Rebel satellite."

I looked askance at him and he laughed.

"We not need old-fashion tech when we got Maria," he said.

Maria turned to me. "Alan, on our last ... healing exchange," she said, slightly blushing, "I planted an energy cord in you that would allow me to track you wherever you are."

"Even noncommercial airliners?" I asked with a smirk.

"Yes, and even through their electronic static."

"Well, thanks everybody. I guess the rest of my questions can wait." Emma squeezed my hand, and we finished our meal.

58.

After the women cleared the table, Maria and Emma took me out to the porch with our after-dinner coffees or cocoa. Someone had lowered the mosquito netting, and we sat there and stared out into the jungle with its amazing bird and monkey caws and its insect chirping and buzzing.

After a while Maria said, "I know you have a lot of questions, Alan, and we'll answer them over the next few days, and I have a few of my own. But you've had quite a shock, and while your consciousness rose to the occasion as I predicted, you're still in recovery and should take it slow."

"Okay, but you need to know, since so much was riding on them not realizing what we've done and rolling out the X5, that I was able to deflect their chemical interrogation on whether I had somehow affected the neural processor."

"We know, Alan," Maria said and turned to Emma. "Show him the news release."

Emma turned on her portable and showed me today's Bradbury Institute's press release on the rollout of the new X5 neural processor, which will 'Give you greater computing power with less emotional interference.'

I had to laugh. "And eventually ..."

Maria put her finger to her lips. "It's better that our little exploit remains within our small circle."

I stared at her, and she almost read my mind. "Javier and crew are engaged in dangerous exploits; any of them could be captured and so the less they know the better for all of us."

I nodded my head. "Are we staying here permanently?"

Maria turned to Emma. "That depends on what the two of you decide."

Emma quickly added. "Alan, I'm not assuming we're a couple, but we do have a similar problem."

I took Emma's hand. "I'm not going to lose you again." She teared up and hugged me with her other arm.

Maria smiled. "Well, you can stay here, where I'm going to remain until the 'climate' in El Norte changes, figuratively speaking. But you may want a more active role, which Su Ling can provide."

I thought about this for a moment and looked at Emma. "I don't want to speak for you, but I've realized the limitations of adversarial opposition and that there are better ways to effect change."

Emma squeezed my hand. "I agree."

Maria seemed delighted. "So we stay here, and if not in this compound, amongst these people who are more in touch with the natural world and the natural state of consciousness."

"How long do you think it will take before the new X5 ... does its job?"

Maria smiled again. "It'll vary person to person, and may even take a generation or two, but we've salvaged their society to seed this eventual change, and must allow it its own timing."

I nodded my head.

Emma stretched. "It's time for bed." She turned to me. "We have limited space, but ..."

"I'm sleeping with you."

Maria stood up. "I'll let the two of you figure this out, and tomorrow we'll work on a plan for the next six months, which may mean getting you up to, if not my level, then a little closer. This way there'll be two of us doing the 'heavy lifting.' But, we'll talk about that later."

Emma and I stood and we each kissed Maria lightly on the mouth, and after she left and while we were still standing, Emma put her arms around me and we kissed, then parted and looked each other in the eyes. The future was indeed unlimited now.

About the Author

John Nelson is the author of novels *Starborn*, *Transformations*, and *Matrix of the Gods*, originally published by Hampton Roads Publishing. He authored the nonfiction book *The Magic Mirror*, which won the 2008 COVR Award as best book of the year and best divination system, and edited the anthology *Solstice Shift*.

John was the editorial director of Bear & Company in the mid-1990s and Inner Ocean Publishing in early 2000. He is the owner of Bookworks Ltd., where he edits fiction and nonfiction books for a variety of authors and publishers. This includes *The Sacred Promise* by Gary Swartz, *The White House Doctor* by Dr. Connie Mariano, *The 12-Step Buddhist*, and *Bright Light* by Dee Wallace.

John has been a yogi and a meditator for over forty years, and brings an expanded consciousness perspective to all that he writes. His fiction is a blend of hard science, science fiction, and psycho-spiritual insights.

COSMIC
EGG
BOOKS

If you prefer to spend your nights with Vampires and
Werewolves rather than the mundane then we publish the books
for you. If your preference is for Dragons and Faeries or Angels
and Demons – we should be your first stop. Perhaps your
perfect partner has artificial skin or comes from another planet –
step right this way. Our curiosity shop contains treasures you
will enjoy unearthing. If your passion is Fantasy (including
magical realism and spiritual fantasy), Horror or Science Fiction
(including Steampunk), Cosmic Egg books will
feed your hunger.